High Praise for
CAROLYN HART
&
APRIL FOOL DEAD

"An honest-to-goodness whodunit, with enough red herrings to fill a pickle barrel . . . The characters all are convincingly drawn, with the formidable, gin-guzzling Emma Clyde standing out as a tour de force."
Columbia State

"The doyenne of American cozies."
Margaret Maron

"If I were teaching a course on how to write a mystery, I'd make Carolyn Hart required reading."
Los Angeles Times

"Carolyn Hart embodies the spirit of Agatha Christie more than any other contemporary writer. With her energy, ingenuity, and sparkling sense of humor, Hart writes stories that Dame Agatha herself would have loved."
Dean James

"Carolyn Hart's craftsmanship makes her mystery's Queen of C's—cozy, clever, and chock-full of charm."
Mary Daheim, author of the Bed-and-Breakfast mysteries

"I'll admit it . . . I'm a sucker for Carolyn Hart's Annie and Max series."
Robert Crais

"The joy in Hart's novels derives from revisiting recurring characters from previous Annie and Max novels—especially Annie's rambunctious mother-in-law, Laurel, and her two cats, Agatha and Dorothy L."
San Diego Union-Tribune

"Hart's strong suit is characterization; the people romping through her pages come vividly alive. And the Darlings are appealing co-protagonists, reminiscent of the fictional 'Mr. and Mrs. North.' "
Cleveland Plain Dealer

"One of the most attractive pairs of sleuths since Dashiell Hammett's Nick and Nora Charles."
Chicago Sun-Times

"The Darling duo is as winning as ever."
Baltimore Sun

Books by Carolyn Hart

Henrie O

DEAD MAN'S ISLAND
SCANDAL IN FAIR HAVEN
DEATH IN LOVERS' LANE
DEATH IN PARADISE
DEATH ON THE RIVER WALK
RESORT TO MURDER
SET SAIL FOR MURDER

Death on Demand

DEATH ON DEMAND
DESIGN FOR MURDER
SOMETHING WICKED
HONEYMOON WITH MURDER
A LITTLE CLASS ON MURDER
DEADLY VALENTINE
THE CHRISTIE CAPER
SOUTHERN GHOST
MINT JULEP MURDER
YANKEE DOODLE DEAD
WHITE ELEPHANT DEAD
SUGARPLUM DEAD
APRIL FOOL DEAD
ENGAGED TO DIE
MURDER WALKS THE PLANK
DEATH OF THE PARTY
DEAD DAYS OF SUMMER

CAROLYN HART

APRIL FOOL DEAD

DEAD

A DEATH ON DEMAND MYSTERY

AVON BOOKS
An Imprint of HarperCollinsPublishers

AVON BOOKS
An Imprint of HarperCollins*Publishers*
10 East 53rd Street
New York, New York 10022-5299

Copyright © 2002 by Carolyn Hart
Excerpt from *Engaged to Die* copyright © 2003 by Carolyn Hart
ISBN: 0-380-80722-X
www.avonmystery.com

First Avon Books paperback printing: March 2003
First William Morrow hardcover printing: April 2002

Avon Trademark Reg. U.S. Pat. Off. and in Other Countries, Marca Registrada, Hecho en U.S.A.
HarperCollins ® is a trademark of HarperCollins Publishers Inc.

Printed in the U.S.A.

10 9 8 7 6 5 4

APRIL FOOL
DEAD

∴ *One* ∾

THE EARLY-MORNING SUN slanted through the pines, throwing huge shadows across the dusty gray road. Bob Tower's face was flushed, his heartbeat elevated. He was suffused with runner's euphoria, his arms swinging easily, his stride long, his shoes thudding rhythmically on the soft dirt. He smiled, at peace with the world. When his run was over, Jessie waited for him, eager and loving. The kids would be off to school. God, what a wonderful—

He was thinking of Jessie, already loving Jessie in his mind, when the Jeep careened around the curve. Suddenly the roar of the motor was upon him, louder and louder and louder, enveloping him. His head jerked. For an instant, he looked into the eyes of the driver. Pain was sudden and absolute, overwhelming, unendurable.

Crumpled in the ditch, too hurt to moan, eyes clouding, throat closing, the last thing Bob heard was the dwindling of sound as the Jeep raced away.

Tulips bloomed in red glory in a circular bed in front of the high school. Teresa Caldwell was chair of the moms' committee that had planted the flowers, kept the weeds pulled. She'd been presented a plaque at the recent Mothers-Daughters Banquet: "To Teresa Caldwell, Who Always Puts Her Family First." Teresa bit her lip. Why had she looked at the damn flowers? She didn't want to think, didn't want . . .

"Mom! Stop. We're here." Lily's voice sullen.

Teresa was accustomed to Lily's exasperated tone when confronted with what she judged to be yet another example of parental stupidity. Teresa had struggled with irritation at being viewed as only marginally competent. But oh, how she wished Lily would say, "Oh, Mom!" and flip her ponytail in mock disgust. Instead Lily, avoiding her mother's quick glance, yanked open the door of the Range Rover and lurched onto the sidewalk, a slightly built girl with frizzy brown hair and uncertain blue eyes, burdened by a backpack big enough to carry provisions for a jaunt to the Himalayas.

Teresa opened her mouth, closed it. Lily wouldn't listen. She wouldn't listen about the weight of the backpack and Teresa could not bear to ask Lily why she was cold and withdrawn.

Without a word of farewell, Lily moved slowly up the sidewalk, tilting to the left from the burden of the pack. Her head was down, her gait plodding.

Teresa stared after her daughter and then, at the sound of an impatient horn, pulled out from the curb. She drove sedately around the curving drive, her lips stretched into a determined smile, nodding, waving. She knew what other mothers saw: a superbly groomed, Lesley Stahl–pretty suburban mother in a bright blue Range Rover with MOMSCAR plates. They couldn't see, would never see, must never know about the fever that raged within, the fever that might yet cost her everything. No one knew, of course. But Lily had looked at her oddly in recent weeks. What if someone had told Lily about the Range Rover parked on that dirt road? What if Lily had overheard one of those late-night calls? Oh, God, would Lily tell anyone? Would Lily tell her father?

Teresa drove automatically, slowing as she reached Sand Dollar Road. All right, she'd turn left. Go home. Clean out the garage. Bake brownies, Ralph's favorite dessert. He was getting in tonight on a flight from New York. He'd had a hard week. When they talked last night, after Lily was in bed, she'd heard the weariness, even a touch of fear, in his voice. The corporate world was always uncertain, and never more so than now. He loved brownies, a nice way to welcome him home. The car eased to a stop. Her hands clenched on the wheel. She heard the rumble of an SUV behind her. She checked the mirror. Cherry Sue Richards. She had to make up her mind. Now. This instant.

If she turned right, if she drove a mile and a half, turned onto a rutted gray road that jolted the car, streaked the gleaming blue paint with so much dust that Ralph kidded her, asked whether she'd been plowing the fields, if she drove as fast as she dared up that narrow road to the cabin nestled among a grove of willows, Paul would be waiting. She knew how he would look—thick, curly black hair, dark eyes, sensuous lips. He'd probably not shaved yet, he'd be bare-chested, his old, paper-thin Levi's hung on slim hips. Paul. Damn him.

As the SUV stopped behind her, Teresa gunned the motor, turned to the right, the fever raging within her.

Frank Saulter moved stiffly in the mornings. He welcomed the late-March sun, a cheerful precursor to spring. Only a few more days and it would be April. In summer the heat from the Low Country sun rolled against his skin hot as oil and just as soothing; yet he loved the crisp sunny days of spring. He smiled. He might be stiff, but arthritis never kept a man from fishing. He had his day planned. The lagoon off Belted Kingfisher Road was full of crappie, bass and bream, and he was just the man to land himself a mess of good eating. He took his time as he walked down the crushed-oyster-shell walk to the mailbox by the side of the road. He didn't expect anything much. Too late in the month for bills. Maybe a note from his daughter, but Sue liked e-mail better than writing letters and every week sent a cheerful message catching him up on the kids: Megan off at school in Australia, if that didn't beat the band; and Tom, who'd decided hang gliding off mountains in Montana had a lot more pizzazz than college. Frank shook his head as he pulled open the mailbox. Kids today . . . He grabbed a handful of magazines—*Sports Illustrated, Ellery Queen Mystery Magazine, Fly Fisherman*—some circulars from the grocery and the Wal-Mart on the mainland, and a letter and a postcard. Oh, hey, the card was from Tom in Butte: "Granddad—Wish you were here. Almost as much fun as our trip on the Amazon. Lots cooler. Love, Tom."

Frank was still grinning when he glanced at the long

gray official-looking envelope with the return address of the warden at the state penitentiary.

Frank's smile froze, slipped away. He no longer felt the springlike warmth of the sun or heard the honk of northward-bound geese or noticed the swarm of no-see-ums swirling around him as he stared at the long gray envelope. He hadn't received official letters of any kind since he'd retired as the island's chief of police. He told all his friends when they met for coffee at Parotti's that he didn't miss the job. He didn't tell them how he had to steel himself not to respond when a siren shrieked or how he sometimes worried about the drugs being unloaded late at night in hidden inlets at the docks of million-dollar houses. He insisted that Pete Garrett, the new young chief, was doing fine. Pete didn't know the people yet, not as Frank knew them: where they worked and how many kids they had and who had cancer and all the other heartbreaks—hidden abuse, kids on drugs, and love dragged and tattered to nothing by troubles heaped on troubles.

Frank pulled his jackknife from his pocket, neatly slit the envelope. The paper was fancy office-proud, crinkly onion sheet. But the message was scrawled by hand:

Dear Frank,

Thought you should know. Jud Hamilton's been paroled. I've got a trustee who keeps his ears open. He says Hamilton's out to get you. Do you remember Hamilton? Back in '90, he . . .

Frank crumpled the letter into a tight, hard ball. His mouth tightened into a thin, straight line. He remembered Jud Hamilton and the flicker of sheer hatred in Jud's eyes when he stared across the courtroom at Frank.

Laura Neville Fleming was halfway down the steps, almost to the cabins for the crew, when she stopped. She would wait until tomorrow, tell Captain Joe she'd changed her mind, tell him to turn *Leisure Moment* around and sail back to the island. After all, *Leisure Moment* was hers to do with as she pleased. But what would Keith say? Did she even care what Keith said?

Laura turned and trudged slowly and carefully up the companionway to the main deck. She shouldn't have had that last drink. It was a little hard to walk and the lights blurred in her eyes. She'd go to the stern, lean over and gulp in fresh air. The dizziness would pass. She was Laura Neville and she never drank too much. That would be unseemly. She gently smoothed the skin on the bridge of her nose with her thumb. She mustn't frown. Nothing made a woman look older than lines on her face.

This whole evening had been odd, uncomfortable. She didn't like the young people from Keith's office. They laughed too loud, and often she didn't understand what they thought was so funny. And she didn't like Keith's booming voice or the way his eyes had followed that girl—what was her name?—oh yes, Cameron—when she walked across the saloon. And that dress—spaghetti straps and a black silk that clung to her. She might as well have been naked.

Laura stumbled. She gave a little exclamation of pain. Who'd left a deck chair here? She would speak to Captain Joe tomorrow. Things were simply not being done correctly. It was so easy, wasn't it, if people only did the right thing?

She reached the stern, leaned against the railing, looked down at the wake from the propellers, the streaks of foam as shiny as satin ribbons in the moonlight. Her head ached. Tears stung her eyes. Why did she have to be so unhappy? But she wasn't going to cry. Nevilles didn't cry. . . .

It all happened so quickly that her scream clogged in her throat: the violent push from behind, the crack of her hip as she banged over the railing and the hideous realization that she was falling into the wash of the propellers. The propellers . . .

Meredith Muir dropped her pink cotton shorty pajamas on the floor. She glanced down in disdain. Stupid pajamas, nothing like the scarlet silk bikini lingerie from Victoria's Secret hidden at the back of the closet in the bedroom of the cabana. She sped past the thought that she hadn't needed to hide the lingerie. No one ever looked at the back of that closet. Nobody cared. . . . Her pleasure seeped away until she glanced at the full-length mirror, at her smooth young body, the breasts high and firm, her hips curved, her legs long and shapely. She remembered the feel of the silk and the even more delicious sensation as the lingerie dropped away. . . .

At first, she didn't hear the ring of the telephone. She stood irresolute for a moment, glancing at the bedside clock. It wasn't the right time for a call. Not the call that mattered. It would probably be somebody who needed a ride to school or wanted to copy her homework. School was stupid. Kids were stupid. She wasn't just a schoolkid anymore. Meredith shivered. Suddenly she felt cold, no longer warmed by her thoughts. She'd better get dressed. The damn phone— the peals continued. Meredith gave an impatient sigh and reached for the receiver.

Her face drawn in a worried frown, Kay Nevis stepped out on the deck, looked at the sun-splashed inlet. She'd planned to get to school early this morning. There was always so much to do, and there was that wonderful new video retracing the Lewis and Clark expedition that should arrive today. But she wanted a moment of peace. The deck had always afforded her peace. She moved slowly across the wooden planks to the railing.

Kay loved the marsh, loved the way it changed by seasons: the cordgrass a rich yellow-green in spring and summer, a soft downy brown in fall; the song of the frogs in the spring, the scampering of the raccoons in winter. Spring was her favorite time of the year. In April the painted buntings arrived, the green-winged teals headed north, sulphurs and painted ladies and monarchs drifted near the plants like pieces of angel wings, their beauty yet another easily seen miracle.

Kay shaded her eyes against the brilliant sunlight. But she wasn't looking at the still, green water or the pelicans skimming low in search of food. She wasn't thinking about the marsh she loved. She felt isolated and disturbed. The perfection of her quiet way of life would not return until she'd met a terrible responsibility. If only she didn't know . . . But she did know and her knowledge imposed a duty. She had to do what was right, no matter how difficult.

Laurel Darling Roethke placed a pink-tipped finger on her cheek, tilted her head and studied the assortment of divining rods. And wasn't that simply the best description of them! She smiled, the beatific smile of a creature overwhelmed by a cornucopia of good fortune. Max's secretary had been so helpful. Laurel took time to wonder if her son truly valued his secretary as he should. When was Secretaries' Day? They must do something special for Barb. Of course, Barb had simply served as Laurel's agent in obtaining the divining rods. The idea had been Laurel's alone. Although she always made every effort to eschew vainglory, wasn't it appropriate to give credit where credit was due? Self-esteem was essential to mental health. Laurel permitted herself to bask. Truly, her idea was simply brilliant. More than that, there was no reason why it wouldn't work. As she had reassured a tearful Rosa on the drive to the airport—Rosa well hidden in the backseat beneath a huge papier-mâché butterfly that Laurel had been intending to get out of the attic for years—it would be no time at all before Rosa could fly home from Mexico; Laurel would see to everything and Rosa was not to worry for a minute.

Laurel smiled, a smile of utter confidence, and walked slowly past the divining rods. Five of them. A tiny frown marred the perfection of the elegant features. Would five be enough? Of course, she also had a pendulum, although a hex nut dangling from a short length of gold chain didn't seem quite as impressive as the divining rods. One rod was rather dark and heavy, fashioned from gnarled cypress. A pink plastic rod, its two arms glittering with paste jewels, was propped against the sofa. The third, made of aluminum, reflected a shaft of early-morning sunlight. Hmm. Quite lightweight, and that would be a plus. The fourth resembled a crimson broomstick that curved into sharp prongs at one end. Long silvery ribbons dangled from each prong. The fifth was majestic, shiny antlers with flashing lights at the tips. Laurel gave a soft coo, envisioning an expanse of snowy tundra glistening in sunlight. One, two, three, four, five—Laurel beamed. Tallyho!

Annie Laurance Darling walked fast on the boardwalk of the Broward's Rock Harbor. She scarcely spared a glance at the dozen or so boats, ranging from the huge yacht *Leisure Moment* to the little fiberglass sailboat *J. P. Vanilla,* and the richly green water slapping gently against the harbor front. Out in the sound, a half-dozen bottle-nosed dolphins arced in an aquatic ballet. Annie heard the unmistakable whoosh of sound from their blowholes and she wanted to stop, but darn it, she didn't have time. There was so much to do. First, of course, she needed to see if Emma's books had arrived. Annie breathed deeply. If they hadn't . . . Not to worry, she reassured herself, as she skirted the thick hose pumping water out of the bottom of a cabin cruiser. That's why she'd ordered the books well in advance. Certainly Annie Laurance Darling, owner of Death on

Demand Mystery Bookstore, was not going to be caught short of books when the island's famous mystery author, Emma Clyde, appeared at Annie's store this coming Sunday to sign *Whodunit,* her latest Marigold Rembrandt adventure.

Annie looked up the boardwalk at the plate-glass windows of her store and felt the old familiar thrill. Her bookstore, the best mystery bookstore east of Atlanta, with the greatest selection of mysteries, everything from Susan Wittig Albert's China Bayles herbal series to Sharon Zukowski's financially savvy P.I. Blaine Stewart titles as well as wonderful adventures from Jeff Abbott's *Do unto Others* to Mark Richard Zubro's *A Simple Suburban Murder.*

Annie picked up speed. Surely, surely, surely Emma's books had arrived. It was always a coup to persuade Emma to do a signing. And it would be a smashing beginning to April. Annie pushed back a prickly worry that Emma was simply playing a huge April-fool joke on Annie with her promise to come to the store. No, surely not. Emma might be flamboyant, but she was dependable and could be counted upon to entrance the customers. Emma was definitely memorable, from her outrageous caftans to her spiky orange (the latest color) hair to the iciest blue eyes shy of a serial killer. Emma was not an author to irritate. Annie, in fact, had managed to tempt Emma to the April 1 signing only by promising a most spectacular promotion, entitled, appropriately, Whodunit.

The promotion was right on schedule. Annie had scattered flyers around the island last weekend, everywhere from the Island Hills Country Club to Parotti's

Bar and Grill. Annie refused to think about the island's stiff litter laws. So, all right, she and Max and anyone else she could cajole were going to have to do major-duty cleanup in a few days. Rachel had promised to get a gang of kids from school to help. Annie frowned, another worry. Rachel hadn't gone to school this morning. A stomachache? Well, sure, it could be true. She'd been fine when she went to her room last night, still bubbling with excitement over her date for the prom. But Rachel's eyes were red-rimmed this morning and she'd hardly had a word to say at breakfast. Annie enjoyed having her new stepsister living with them, but sometimes she felt the awesome responsibility, surrogate mom to a volatile teenager. Annie knew that Rachel was still grieving for her mother. It was too bad Pudge was off island for a while. A smile tugged at her lips. But hey, Annie understood. Her equally newly found dad meant to settle in—and he loved Annie's tree house, her first home on the island—but he had an adventurous spirit and the idea of a trek to Nepal as chief of provisions was not one he could turn down. Oh, well, Rachel would surely be her old self by the weekend. Rachel loved mysteries, especially those by Jerrilyn Farmer and Katherine Hall Page, and she was as excited about Emma's signing as Annie. She'd plastered the school with flyers and said a lot of the kids planned to come.

Annie clung to that thought. She didn't care who came as long as there were lots of bodies with cash or credit cards. Of course there would be a big, big turnout for the signing. If not . . . Annie refused to contemplate the aftermath of a sparsely attended signing for Emma. Would Emma invite Annie to her palatial home and unveil a whirlpool patterned after Poe's Maelstrom? Entice Hannibal Lecter to the island, offering Annie as suitable prey? Whip up puffer-fish sushi especially for Annie?

Okay, okay, it wasn't going to happen. Or, Annie thought confusedly, the Sunday-afternoon signing was certainly going to happen, and the event would be a huge triumph, such a success that even Emma's redoubtable demeanor would soften. Annie tried to envision Emma with a grateful smile, then immediately abandoned that attempt.

Annie paused at the front window of Confidential Commissions. She managed not to gape at the OPEN sign propped in the window. After all, why should she be so surprised? Max had promised to redouble his efforts to be gainfully employed. But for her laid-back, agreeable, easygoing husband to be at his office this early was nothing short of mind-boggling. It wasn't even nine o'clock and he'd had a rooted appearance in his easy chair, intently studying *Baseball Weekly,* when she'd dashed out at eight for the Merchants' Association monthly breakfast. She had presented all the association members with flyers touting Emma's signing and the Whodunit mystery contest that would surely draw even more readers than usual to the store.

Annie blinked at Max's OPEN sign. She would scarcely have been more surprised had Emma Clyde materialized on the boardwalk clad in a sari and crooning Irish lullabies. Annie had smiled at Max's pronouncement last week, considered it a sweet and well-meaning attempt to counter her occasional exhortations for him to become a worker bee, and consigned the promise to the back of her mind along with other high-minded plans, such as cleaning out the drawers in the kitchen, organizing the tax papers for their accountant *before* April 15, or arranging the cans of soups and vegetables in the cabinets in alphabetical order. As for the latter, maybe someday she could hire Jo Dereske's exceptionally precise librarian sleuth, Miss Zukas, to create order in the Darling kitchen.

Annie took a step toward Confidential Commissions, then abruptly marched past. Three doors down was where she must go. She had to get to the store. Now. What if Emma's books weren't there? She'd check with Max later. Dear Max. Perhaps he actually was turning over a new leaf, finding joy in the possibility of work, not heretofore an obsession of his. Well, Annie thought loyally, as she charged toward Death on Demand, Max might not have the work ethic, but he was affable, genial, handsome, sexy as hell, and he loved her. And she loved him.

Annie was grinning when she reached Death on Demand. She paused for an instant to admire the display in the window, surely a prod to all green thumbs to head for the garden to enjoy mulch and murder. Red tulips, bright as splotches of crimson blood, and a bower of red azalea branches framed five gardening mysteries: *The Grub-and-Stakers Move a Mountain,* by Alisa Craig; *The Spider-Orchid,* by Celia Fremlin (definitely a collectible); *The Murder of My Aunt,* by Richard Hull; *Death of a Garden Pest,* by Ann Ripley; and *Suddenly, While Gardening,* by Elizabeth Lemarchand.

That instant's pause kept her on the boardwalk long enough to hear the buzz of a small airplane. The drone of the engine was louder and louder. Annie moved to the edge of the boardwalk and craned to see. A bright yellow Piper Cub swooped down, curved up, then down, then up, leaving behind a trail of silvery smoke.

Annie clapped her hands. Skywriting. What fun. But how unusual over the placid little island of Broward's Rock. This was the kind of display that arced above ball games with thousands of viewers. Who would see the message here?

As she watched the plane's curving flight, she spelled out the letters:

W-H-O-D-U-N-I-

"T!" Annie exclaimed. "WHODUNIT."

The word hung in the sky, the silver smoke clear and distinct against the clear blue sky.

"Fabulous!" Annie exclaimed. "Fantastic!" What a super promotion for Emma's signing and Annie's mystery contest. This was a stroke of advertising genius.

But Annie hadn't ordered the skywriting. As for Emma . . . Annie knew the answer. If Emma ordered skywriting, the smoke would spell:

E-M-M-A C-L-Y-D-E.

There could be only one answer. As the plane droned away, its mission accomplished, Annie moved with glad purpose toward the door of Confidential Commissions.

~: *Two* :~

MAX WAGGLED the putter. Maybe he should order one of those new ones advertised on the golf channel. In the testimonials, cheery golfers claimed to drop putts with more regularity than quarters click into slot machines in the Las Vegas airport. (Get 'em going and coming.) Max pondered the analogy, wondered if it had cosmic significance, thought briefly of his mother, then consciously relaxed his knees, bent his head, addressed the ball, tried to move the club head with both ease and precision—

"Max!" It was an exuberant shout.

He jerked. The ball shot off the indoor putting green, hit the hardwood floor, bounced against a wooden magazine stand and barreled past Annie to skid through the office door into the anteroom.

His secretary, Barb, called out, "Feeling vigorous this morning, are we?"

"Max!" Annie exclaimed again, her face glowing. "You are wonderful."

Max wished he had a camera. Here was Annie as he always pictured her—sun-streaked golden hair, serious gray eyes, kissable lips curved in a joyous smile. Reaching out a slim tanned hand, she beamed at him.

He loved the way she stood, as if captured in mid-stride, ready to move, always in a hurry, always eager and enthusiastic. Apparently he was the object of this moment's enthusiasm. As far as he was concerned, that was a status even more desirable than shooting sixty-seven.

He tossed the putter, didn't care that it clattered on the floor, reached her in two strides, took her hands in his, pulled her close. "All kudos are happily accepted." He loved the feel of her body against his. "Hey"—his voice was eager—"I've got a great idea. Why don't we go home and—"

"Max!" she managed to invest the three letters with appreciative interest, regretful dismissal and the hint of future pleasures, then proceeded to focus on the present. "The skywriting! How did you ever think of it?"

Max had a 5 handicap at golf, was ranked a 4 in tennis and was rather proud of his capacity to relax—the hammock factor, as he fondly deemed it, always an advantage in dealing with people who attacked life like pit bulls run amok. Not, of course, that he included Annie in that category, oh, certainly not. But skywriting?

"Is this on some sort of astral plane?" he inquired gently. Had Annie been communing with his mother? Laurel was rather well known around the island for her enthusiasms. Was skywriting a new one? Had Annie confused him with his mother?

Annie ran her fingers through her flyaway hair and looked at him blankly. She waggled her hand in the general direction of the ceiling. "Skywriting," she repeated. "WHODUNIT. In the sky."

Max was equally blank. "Whodunit? I thought that

was the title of Emma's new book. And the name of your mystery contest."

"Oh." Annie jammed her hands in the pockets of her floral skirt, one Max particularly liked, a bright cherry with silver thingamabobs on the hem. Oh yeah. Annie said it was scalloped. Sounded like a recipe.

Annie grabbed his arm, tugged him toward the anteroom. "Come on."

He was perfectly willing to follow. Who knew? Maybe they might go home for a little while . . .

On the boardwalk, he followed her pointing finger and looked up at indistinguishable blobs of gray in the sky.

". . . a little plane and it skywrote WHODUNIT. It was just gorgeous. I thought you'd ordered it as a surprise."

Max wished like hell he had. "Maybe Emma did it."

"I don't think so." Annie squinted at the now-indecipherable message. "I'll call her and ask. But I really don't think so. Emma"—Annie's lips quirked in a wry grin—"Emma would either do herself or Marigold. Product identification, that's her motto." Annie's voice was suddenly lower, a little raspy, cool as a mountain stream. " 'Annie, my dear, readers read my books because they know my name. Always put the author's name first in any advertisement. In the largest letters, of course. Titles come and go. The author is forever.' "

Max laughed aloud. Annie's rendition of Emma was uncannily close. "Sorry I didn't think of it first. I'll tell you what, I'll find out who did it. I know you have a lot to do—"

Annie clapped her hands to her head. "What am I thinking of? What am I doing? Things to do! Oh, Max, I've got to hurry. The books, have the books come . . ."

The last words were lost as she raced down the boardwalk, yanked open the door to Death on Demand and plunged inside.

Max grinned. Dear, kissable Annie. Oh, well, evening would come. Maybe even afternoon . . . Maybe the books would be there and all the arrangements for the book signing and the contest would fall into place. Afternoon delight . . .

Max ambled back to Confidential Commissions. He paused in the anteroom and his secretary, Barb, looked at him inquiringly. "We have a mystery to solve," he announced grandly. Max wished it were a real challenge, not a matter to be resolved by two or three phone calls at the most. After all, puzzles were the business of Confidential Commissions. His latest newspaper ad, which appeared daily in *The Island Gazette* "Personals" column, said it best:

Troubled, puzzled, curious?
Contact Confidential Commissions.
321-HELP.

Max was always quick to explain he was not a private investigator. To set up shop as a private detective in South Carolina required a license achieved through a good deal of work and experience, much more effort than Max intended to expend. But who could complain about a man eager to counsel those in need of solutions?

It would, in fact, be a most interesting career if only his office phone rang a bit more often. He didn't want to admit how eagerly he had seized upon this small challenge. For an instant, he felt a qualm. Was he becoming imbued with the work ethic? Surely not.

"A mystery?" Barb's eyes lighted in anticipation. Recently she'd been scouring the Internet for information about dowsing. Her usual recourse when bored was to utilize the tiny kitchen at the back of the office and create elegant desserts, everything from confetti corn pudding, in which dots of red and green pepper achieved a striking visual effect, to pineapple-coconut cookies, a taste treat for sweetness freaks. However, with the advent of spring, she was trying to lose weight and had forsworn cooking. Max was reluctant to probe the interest in dowsing, a subject that held no interest for him. As far as he was concerned, water came out of pipes.

Barb's brown eyes gleamed and she already had her hands poised over the keyboard. "What's up?"

"The phantom in the sky. Well, maybe it won't really turn out to be much of a mystery." He described the vaporous appearance of Emma's title. "How many skywriting companies can there be? See what you can find out."

Annie usually took a moment to savor the marvelous (in her estimation) mystery milieu of her bookstore: Edgar, an imposing stuffed raven in honor of Edgar Allan Poe, the founding genius of the mystery; the display case of mystery collectibles, this month focusing on advertising—*Murder Must Advertise* by Dorothy L. Sayers, *Design in Diamonds* by Kathleen Moore Knight, *And Be a Villain* by Rex Stout, *The 31st of February* by Julian Symons, and *Cover-Up Story* by Marian Babson; the coffee-bar mugs emblazoned with the names of famous mysteries and their authors, ranging from Eric Ambler's *Epitaph for a Spy* to Israel Zangwill's *The Big Bow Mystery;* the enclave especially for children with all the Nancy Drew and Hardy Boys books, as well as the newest titles from George Edward Stanley, Bill Crider, Beverly Hastings, Betsy Haynes, Joan Lowery Nixon, Katherine Hall Page, and, of course, J. K. Rowling. However, pride of place always went to the paintings hung at the first of every month to provide a competition for the store's keenest readers. Each painting represented a well-known mystery, and the first person to identify all the paintings correctly by title and author received a free new book and coffee privileges for a month.

As Annie skidded into the main aisle, admiring the fresh shine of the lovely heart-pine floor, she had a fleeting regret about the free coffee. Henny Brawley, island club woman, close friend, the store's best customer, and a mystery reader on a par with mystery author and famed critic H. R. F. Keating, hadn't paid for coffee in months. Annie glanced down the aisle at the watercolors. They looked wonderful.

In the first painting, twin Confederate flags flanked the entrance to the ornate Victorian Gothic mansion distinguished by rose-red brickwork and sand and ivory gingerbread decorations. Four women in smocks unloaded a cleaning cart from the back of a van with the legend: HOUSE MOUSE CLEANING SERVICE. A youngish woman with gray-streaked, curly black hair pointed up the steps to the ornate door. An index card posted next to the painting mysteriously announced: "FYI—11/8/20, brown thrasher."

In the second painting, two huge furniture show-rooms offered startling contrast. In the first, rococo couches, tables and chairs glistened with antique ivory paint and gleaming encrustations of gilt. But the slender young woman in a black jacket and beige slacks hurried toward the display of outdoor furniture. She stared at the man lying facedown on the cushions of a swing, his cowboy boots unmoving. "FYI—13/13, cardinal."

In the third painting, two attractive black women, one young, one middle-aged, stood near a crumbling fireplace in the dilapidated, empty front room of an old house. They stared in shock at the man's body on the floor. Animals had scavenged the body, mutilating it. The older woman, her wise face sad and troubled, had smooth golden-brown skin the color of candied sweet potatoes. "FYI—14/4, Carolina wren."

In the fourth painting, a petite older woman with graying strawberry-blond hair stood by the open door of a car in the parking lot of a Chinese restaurant. A woman stretched on the seat, arched in a convulsion. Among those hurrying to help was another older woman, a six-foot-tall bleached blonde who must have weighed 250 pounds. An index card posted next to the painting mysteriously announced: "FYI—1/7, yellow-hammer."

In the fifth painting, an attractive young redhead in mussed white slacks stood at the foot of some stairs, hold-ing a frayed rope. She stared warily at the woman perched midway up the steps. The woman's nutmeg-bright hair gleamed beneath a fluffy hat. Her Easter-grass-green suit would have looked great on Greer Garson in a World War II movie. "FYI—15/6/2, cardinal."

Maybe this time Henny wouldn't sail to victory so easily. Several of the paintings were not the first in the mystery series. Annie had simply selected a title she had particularly enjoyed which might or might not be the first. She had not, of course, changed her usual procedure simply to make the contest harder. Definitely not. For example, the second watercolor featured the fifth (some might say sixth) book in a series by an author famous in the mystery world. The first title (not counting the prequel) in that particular series was the only book ever to win all of the major mystery awards in a single year. A painting of that winning title would have been a lay-down for most of Death on Demand's sophisticated readers. However, to be fair, Annie had posted beneath each painting an index card with cryptic hints. To Annie, the cards made the identity of each author and locale so easy, Encyclopedia Brown would have solved them in an instant.

A tiny frown wrinkled her forehead. Maybe the hints made it too easy. Maybe she should take down the index cards. After all, the oh-so-Southern centerpiece of Spanish moss and pinecones on the coffee bar was a dead giveaway. Annie took two steps toward the back of the store, then stopped, sighed. Was the compulsion to play fair the result of reading so many mysteries? Or was the hunger for fairness the reason she and her customers loved mysteries? Dammit, she'd leave the cards in place as well as the centerpiece. After all, the month was almost over and no one had solved the contest yet.

Her store, her wonderful store . . . Annie's sense of euphoria evaporated as she heard the clipped words of

Ingrid Webb, standing behind the cash desk, the portable phone clutched in her hand. ". . . must receive those books by Friday . . . Look, I don't care if you have to get some recruits from Parris Island and storm the warehouse; we have to have those books. . . ."

Annie felt a presentiment worthy of any Victoria Holt heroine. She forced herself to remain calm. After all, it was just a signing. Surely Emma—no, Emma would not be reasonable, understanding, or equable. Emma . . . Annie took a deep breath.

Ingrid clicked off the phone, ran a hand through her tight gray curls. "Annie, don't panic. I was talking to the distributor. I told him Dirty Harry would look him up pronto if we didn't get the books." A swift grin lighted her face. "That, combined with the name of the store, got his attention. So I think we'll be okay. He promised the books would be on the afternoon ferry tomorrow."

"Tomorrow . . ." Annie clasped her hands together.

"Take it easy." Ingrid came around the counter. "Come on, let's have coffee. But watch out, Agatha's furious. And something's got Emma's dander up. And what does the light of the moon have to do with dowsing?"

Annie focused on first things first. She moved swiftly down the broad center aisle, taking only a moment to reach down and straighten the Anne Perry titles, which occupied their own shelf. Agatha, the imperious black cat who ruled both the bookstore and its owner, was newly slim from a restricted diet. And always hungry.

Annie reached the coffee bar, where Agatha paced, green eyes glittering, sleek black coat glistening like polished ebony.

"Agatha, you are gorgeous." But Annie slipped gingerly behind the bar, alert for a swift black paw, claws extended. She didn't even think about serving Ingrid and herself first. She opened a cupboard, reached for the dry diet food.

Agatha leaned so far over the edge of the counter, she challenged the law of gravity. Her growl verged on desperate.

"Oh, Agatha. Have you had a hard day, too?" Annie ignored the fact it was just past nine in the morning. Dammit, it had been a hard day. Would the books really come tomorrow? And why should Emma be irritated? And who cared about dowsing or dowsers, whether in daylight or dark? Annie grabbed a Reese's Peanut Butter Cup, ignored Agatha's dry food (after all, fair was fair) and picked up and opened a can of lamb and rice, which might not be the equivalent of a T-bone but Agatha liked it a lot better than the dietary dry food. To be fair, Annie wasn't crazy about rice cakes. Annie filled and put down Agatha's bowl.

A whoosh beside her indicated Ingrid was busy at the cappuccino machine. They carried their mugs to a table with a good view of the front of the store, just in case a customer arrived. Annie clutched the mug like a lifeline. "Ingrid, if I live through Emma's signing on Sunday, I want a gold star, some Godiva chocolate and an afternoon in my hammock to read the new James Lee Burke. Now, what's this about Emma?"

Ingrid pushed her wire-rim glasses higher on a bony nose and frowned. She opened her mouth, closed it.

Annie tensed. She had the same hollow feeling she

always experienced when confronted by Emma, even a genial (oh, rare day) Emma. She pictured Emma, imperious blue eyes sharp as stilettos, spiky hair that should have made her ridiculous but never did, statuesque appearance as daunting as a Sherman tank despite the colorful caftans.

"Oh, God," Annie said simply. "What's wrong?"

Ingrid did not look at Annie and her tone was falsely cheerful. "I'm sure it's nothing. But Emma called a little while ago." Ingrid came to a full stop.

Annie didn't want to know, but ignorance is rarely bliss. "And?" she prompted, then took a reviving gulp of cappuccino.

Ingrid's thin shoulders lifted and fell. "It wasn't what she said. I mean, she didn't say hello or how are you or anything. She snapped, 'Where's Annie?' I said you would be in around nine."

Annie stared at Ingrid, waiting for the guillotine to slice.

There was time for a full turn of the tumbrel wheel before Ingrid concluded, "She hung up."

Annie considered the full import. No salutation. An imperious demand. Abrupt termination. Annie swallowed. "Did she sound . . ." Annie didn't have to finish.

Ingrid studied the carnations in a slender green vase. "Colder than the Greenland ice cap in *Night Without End*."

Annie registered in a far corner of her mind the title of the superb Alistair MacLean suspense novel while a similar icy emptiness spread through her. "So Emma's on the warpath." Annie drank from her mug, still felt cold. "Ingrid, I can't imagine what's wrong." Annie snatched up the top flyer from the stack next to the vase. Similar stacks sat on every table as well as the coffee bar and the cash desk. Flyers were taped to the end of every bookcase. Flyers, in fact, were scattered the length and breadth of the island.

Annie plumped the cerise sheet on the table. "How can Emma be mad?" Annie pointed at the flyer. "This is the cleverest promotion in the history of book-selling!" And the Whodunit contest sponsored by Death on Demand was the sole creation of Annie Laurance Darling, mystery bookseller extraordinaire. "Ingrid, this contest is fantastic!" She looked down at the flyer. Honestly, she would probably never tire of admiring the contents of the flyer, even though she knew every word by heart. For starters, the sheet featured Emma's name in huge letters. Annie smoothed the paper and read her masterpiece aloud:

WHODUNIT???

In whodunits, the detective captures the murderer in the last chapter. Now you have a chance to outdo fictional sleuths. Prove you are a Champion Mystery Reader and you will win:

A SIGNED FIRST EDITION

of

WHODUNIT

A Marigold Rembrandt Mystery

by

EMMA CLYDE

Here's how to win: Identify the AUTHOR (not the villain) and give the title of these famous mysteries from the following clues:

Book 1—A country doctor knows there is more behind the murder of his old friend than anyone else realizes.

Book 2—A messenger dies in a mysterious plane crash, leaving behind a list of ten names.

Book 3—Two strangers travel on a train and talk about murder.

Book 4—A smart-mouth reporter investigates the drug scene on a California beach and meets a man who wants to die.

Book 5—A half-English, half-Egyptian con man, who never quite succeeds at anything, drives a car to Istanbul and finds himself in the middle of a daring robbery.

Book 6—A very conventional English lawyer defends an attractive dark-haired woman and her eccentric mother against a charge of kidnapping.

Book 7—A middle-aged spinster takes a house in the country for the summer, a man is shot to death in the clubroom and her niece and nephew seem to know more than they admit.

Book 8—Three children try to solve a neighborhood murder while their mystery-writer mom races to meet a deadline.

Book 9—Can the new mistress of Manderly ever escape the shadow of her husband's first wife?

NINE FAMOUS MYSTERIES
WHODUNIT???

Be the first to name the authors and the titles and take home your very own signed

WHODUNIT
by
EMMA CLYDE

Annie glowed. So, okay, maybe her pride was over-weening, but who would not admire her brilliance and guile? If Emma didn't appreciate the thought and effort behind the flyers, she was an ungrateful, rude—

The front door of Death on Demand banged open. Heavy steps pounded down the central aisle.

Annie came to her feet.

Emma's spiky orange hair and purple-and-pink caftan were no match for the icy brightness of her blue eyes and the vivid red splotches on her pale white cheeks. She marched up to the table, flung down a crumpled pink flyer. Emma's voice, deep and rough as a rumbling river, always commanded attention. Now the words crashed into the waiting silence with the force and power of icebergs slamming into a ship. "Have you lost your mind?"

༺ *Three* ༻

ANNIE LIFTED her chin, glared at Emma. "Wait a minute, Emma. I've done my best to—"

Emma's rock-crusher voice drowned out Annie's words. "I am appalled. I have lived on this island in peace with my neighbors for almost twenty years. If this is some kind of April-fool joke, I'm definitely not amused."

Knuckles rapped smartly on the tabletop. Ingrid flapped the pink flyer in the air. "Emma, don't be an idiot."

Emma's head jerked back, her orange spikes quivered, her ice-blue eyes blazed.

Ingrid thrust the sheet at Annie, "Annie, take a look. This isn't your contest!" Ingrid threw up her hands. "Emma, how could you possibly believe Annie would do this?"

Annie heard Ingrid's voice, high and sharp as a mockingbird's complaint, and Emma's deep rumble, the tone as stentorian as a Fourth of July tuba, but the words slid past her as she stared at the heavy Gothic printing on the sheet:

WHODUNIT?

The Crimes:
> Hit-and-run
> Adultery
> False imprisonment
> Murder 1
> Murder 2

The Clues:
> Seventeen graves south of the Portwood Mausoleum.
> One-half mile east on Least Tern Lane.

Front page, *The Island Gazette,* September 13, 1990.
Marigold's Pleasure. Ask Emma.
Leisure Moment. Ask Capt. Joe.

WHODUNIT?
FOLLOW THE CLUES TO $1000

Annie's gaze stuck on one startling line: *Marigold's Pleasure.* Ask Emma. Oh, God, were those whispers still around? Some years earlier, Emma's second husband, Ricky (her much younger and philandering second husband), fell to his death from her yacht, *Marigold's Pleasure.* The death was adjudged accidental. Annie avoided looking at Emma. Instead, her face flaming, Annie cried, "I can't believe this. Who *did* this?" She rattled the sheet. "It's outrageous. Somebody's taken my contest and turned it into something hateful. This isn't a joke. This is awful. And why a thousand dollars?"

Emma clapped her arms across her chest, stood motionless for an instant.

Annie stared into brilliant-blue eyes that changed abruptly from blistering anger to thoughtful appraisal to chagrin. Annie blinked. Emma chagrined? That was less likely than James Bond in drag.

Emma cleared her throat. "I'm sorry, Annie. I apologize. I should have known you'd never stoop to this." Her square face was rueful for an instant, then once again hardened into a glower. "But somebody cooked this up. Now who the hell was it?"

Annie wasn't offended. She understood. Emma's book was being used to stir up trouble. And, perhaps even worse, the whispers about her second husband's death would begin again. But Annie was angry, too. The idea for the Whodunit contest—the contest of which she'd been so proud—had been hers. It was Annie who had scattered Whodunit flyers across the island, flyers that on the surface looked so much like the one she held in her hand.

"Dammit, somebody's put these things out"— Annie held up the pink flyer—"and they are obviously patterned after my flyers. People are going to think I did this. Oh, Emma, this is awful."

Emma studied the stack of Annie's flyers on the coffee bar. "When did you put your flyers out? And where?"

"Over the weekend. Monday. Yesterday. Everywhere." Annie had covered the island from the ferryboat dock on the northwest end of the island to the collection of shops on the boardwalk by the marina on the southwest. Those flyers had better visibility than a new John Grisham novel at Christmas. "I wanted to get as much exposure as possible before the signing on Sunday." Sunday, April 1. April Fools' Day. Damn.

Emma pulled out a chair. Her caftan swirled as she sank majestically down.

Annie was irresistibly reminded of the stately progress of *Marigold's Pleasure,* a huge yacht that could just manage the narrow entrance to the Broward's Rock Marina. The only boat to rival it in size was *Leisure Moment.* Who owned *Leisure Moment*? Wait a minute, that was the big boat that belonged to that rich woman from Atlanta. And she'd tumbled off her boat last fall, just like Emma's second husband. Annie forced her thoughts away from *Leisure Moment* and *Marigold's Pleasure.* "Where did you find this? When? Are there many—"

Emma held up a square hand, the blunt fingers ink-stained. "Wait. Let's proceed with order and precision." This was a favorite dictum of Emma's sleuth, Marigold Rembrandt, and was often a remonstrance to dense Detective Inspector Hector Houlihan. "You can take notes."

Annie was tempted to respond that Emma wasn't Marigold and Annie sure as hell wasn't Detective Inspector Hector Houlihan, but one flash of Emma's icy gaze and Annie pulled a pen from her pocket and turned over one of her own flyers to the blank side.

Emma's stubby finger tapped the pink flyer. "I found this in my mailbox this morning. My mail delivery arrives around four in the afternoon. I often don't retrieve the mail until the next morning. The flyer was on top of the letters."

Ingrid scooted her chair closer to the table, peered at the flyer. "Okay." Ingrid was not only the world's best bookstore employee, she was a world-class mystery reader as well. "First." She flipped up her fingers as she spoke. "The imitation flyer must have been placed in Emma's mailbox after four o'clock on Tuesday afternoon, since Emma found it above, not below, the letters. Now, we have to find out whether this flyer was aimed specifically at Emma. Is this the only flyer? If there are other flyers, how widespread is their distribution?"

Annie wrote down: Tuesday afternoon.

Emma's glance at Ingrid was approving. "Good thinking." So might Marigold have said to her young niece, Evangeline, a recurring character who served Marigold as Hastings serves Poirot, and a character whom Annie found supremely sappy.

Annie shook her head, as much to rid her mind of Marigold's damned intrusive presence as to focus on something important, something she knew, something that might—

Annie jumped to her feet. "The skywriting! I'll be right back. Emma, get on the phone to your neighbors. Doesn't General O'Brien live next door to you? Oh, and on the other side it's the Morrison house. Check with Mimi Morrison, see if they got it in the mail. I'll be right back." And she was running up the central aisle. She was a little surprised to realize that Emma had delved into a capacious pocket and was even now punching numbers into her cell phone. For Emma to follow Annie's instructions was startling proof that Emma was shaken by the flyer.

As Annie hurried out the door, she heard the bookstore phone ring. She didn't pause. Ingrid would take care of it. Annie's shoes clicked on the boardwalk. She reached the door to Confidential Commissions and pushed inside.

With a portable phone to her ear, Barb waggled her fingers hello. Her hairdo was as always an amazing bouffant, but Annie wasn't accustomed to the color change from gold to red. Hey, why not?

". . . you didn't check it out at all?"

Annie sped through the anteroom. The door to Max's office was ajar. Knees bent, head down, hands firmly grasping the putter as he started his swing, he chanted, "Drop. Drop. Drop."

Annie skidded to a stop behind him. "Max! The most awful thing's happened!"

The club head jerked, the ball swerved left, clattered from the indoor putting green, caromed from the malachite base of a lamp and scooted across the wooden floor to roll through the open door into the anteroom.

"That one got my foot." Barb's voice was good-humored. "I'm almost off the phone. Be there in a sec."

"Max, listen." Annie described the bogus and vicious flyer. ". . . and I'll bet it's tied up to the skywriting. You didn't order that flight. Or me. And I'm sure it wasn't Emma. So who did? Have you found out anything at all?"

Max reached for another golf ball, tossed it up and down. "Barb's checking out the skywriting outfits. There's one in Beaufort and a couple in Savannah and—"

Barb poked her head in the office. "There's something funny going on about that skywriting. I talked to Gus Harvey. He runs Write It in the Sky and he's the guy who flew over the island this morning." She stepped inside, holding a legal pad.

Annie was afraid she knew the answer, but she had to ask. "Who hired him?"

"That's what's strange. Mr. Harvey doesn't have any idea. He found a letter shoved under his office door Tuesday morning. Harvey worked until after ten Monday night, so somebody left the letter late that night or early Tuesday morning. The message had been typed on a computer. No signature. The envelope contained twenty hundred-dollar bills." Barb glanced down at her pad. "Here's what the letter said: 'As part of a book promotion on Broward's Rock Island'"—she shot a pleased glance at Annie—"'please skywrite WHODUNIT over the island at nine A.M. on Wednesday morning. This is a surprise for a friend.'" Barb stopped.

Max frowned, twirled the ball on his fingers. "And . . ."

"Nada mas," Barb replied. "He had the money. He had his instructions. He did the job."

Max rolled the golf ball in his hand. "Two thousand dollars. Somebody really wanted to get everybody's attention."

"Clever." Annie's tone wasn't admiring. "And we don't have any idea who did it. We don't know anything—"

Emma's deep voice filled the room. "Morning,

Barb, Max. Annie, Ingrid's fielding calls faster than Sammy Sosa's hitting home runs. I suggested she leave the phone off the hook, but she muttered something about customer relations, had to get the word out that the store isn't to blame, but I told her and I'm telling you"—the bright blue eyes didn't blink—"that more is at stake than the store's reputation and my signing. Somebody's broken open a wasps' nest and we're all going to get stung. We've got to find out who did this and tell the world. Now, I checked with my neighbors. They got flyers. And from the number of calls coming in—"

The phone rang in the anteroom. Barb turned and hurried through the door.

"—I'm sure the flyer is all over the island. We have to find out who set us up for this."

Annie shoved a hand through her hair. "Emma, did you see the skywriting this morning?"

Emma's eyes narrowed. "Skywriting?"

Annie explained, concluding, "Somebody anonymously arranged for the skywriting. All we know is that he—or she—left a letter with money in it at the skywriting office."

"To draw even more attention to the damn things." Emma looked thoughtful.

Barb poked her head in the office. "Annie. For you."

Max waved his hand. "Tell any callers that we're in conference."

Annie shook her head, moved to Max's desk, a rather grand desk that had all the dignity of a refectory table in a monastery, and grabbed the portable phone.

Nobody but Ingrid knew she was here and if Ingrid was calling, Annie knew she'd better answer. Annie punched the phone on.

In the background Barb remonstrated: "Annie, wait a minute. I think it's—"

Max said briskly, "We'll canvass the neighborhood. Somebody must have seen something!"

Emma nodded approval. "That's one avenue. But we need to think about the kind of person who would pull a trick like this. Obviously, we have to look for an angry personality, someone in need of attention—jealous, hostile and aggressive. Perhaps the last is most important."

Annie strained to hear. "Annie! I simply don't know what to do." Annie clutched the receiver, understood Barb's warning. The breathless, urgent, well-intentioned voice was all too familiar. If Pamela Potts hadn't invented good works, she'd staked a preeminent claim as the island's super do-gooder. Church suppers? Pamela cooked. Bereaved families? Pamela led the casserole brigade. Island charities? Nobody made more calls, walked farther, donated more time than Pamela. Hospital auxiliary? A staunch member. Annual bird count? Pamela had spotted more purple gallinules than the next five watchers combined. But now was not the moment. Annie didn't have time to bake a casserole or do a walkathon or—

"Annie, you know I always do my best." There was a quaver in Pamela's voice. "However, I find myself in a most difficult . . ."

Max picked up a legal pad from his desk, began to write.

Carrying the portable phone, Annie came up beside him and craned to see:

DISTRIBUTION OF BOGUS FLYERS

1. Do a door-to-door canvass, seeking a description of the person placing the flyers in the mailboxes.
2. Find out if any other means was used to distribute the flyers.
3. Get a story in *Island Gazette,* making it clear the bogus flyers have no connection to Death on Demand.

Annie could have hugged his broad shoulders. Bogus flyers, that was the message they had to get out to everyone on the island. She would never have thought the word "bogus" would become a favorite.

Max continued:

4. Check on last ferry from the mainland Monday night, first ferry Tuesday morning.

The ferry? Why the ferry? Oh, sure. Annie shot an admiring glance at Max. The person who left the anonymous payment for the skywriting had to get on and off the island between those times. Pamela's worried voice droned in Annie's ear: ". . . predicament. I am torn between my utmost loyalty to you and, of course, to Death on Demand, the finest mystery bookstore east of Atlanta, but . . ."

Emma pulled a chair up to Max's desk and grabbed a sheet of paper.

Annie bent to look. Emma printed with a savage swiftness, the letters large and blocky:

LINKS
1. Follow clues, discover identities of suspects.
2. Valid accusations or scurrilous defamations?
3. Explore backgrounds.
4. Determine persons having requisite knowledge of the suspects to create the list of Crimes and Clues.
5. Contrast that list with . . .

". . . I find myself in an untenable position. I want to do everything I can to support Emma's signing—and isn't *Whodunit* a wonderful title, it's one of my favorites, almost as good as *Just Desserts*. You know that's the first in the Mary Daheim series and I wouldn't tell Emma, but I like those books even better than Emma's. They're so funny. Of course, Marigold is amazing and really so different from Emma, not, of course, that Emma isn't wonderful. However, I don't think anyone would call her sweet . . ."

Annie glanced at Emma's corrugated-cement face and at the stubby fingers that held the pen in a death grip. Sweet? Not in this lifetime or any possible lifetime Annie could envision. Sweet, no. Smart, tough, capable, and awesome, oh yes. Annie's eyes returned to point 5:

5. Contrast that list with the identities of passengers on the Monday-night/Tuesday-morning ferries.

Annie felt a trifle let down that the importance of the ferry passengers had occurred immediately to both

Max and Emma and not to her. But hey, it was Annie who had initiated the investigation of the skywriting.

Annie itched to get her hands on Emma's battle plan. What a fascinating insight into the thought processes of America's queen of cozy mysteries. After all of this was over—and please God they would track down the obnoxious creator of the bogus flyer and Annie's own brilliant contest would once again afford canny mystery readers an opportunity to shine—Annie intended to get Emma's handwritten plan. The sheet, especially if Annie persuaded Emma to sign and date it, would be a valuable addition to the store's display of mystery collectibles.

". . . but Emma always champions fair play and that's why I'm so puzzled about the contest. I went to the cemetery and, Annie, it's simply jammed with people. Ben Parotti's set up a stand and he's selling fried catfish and clam fritters with candied sweet potatoes on the side. Of course, I never eat fried food and even so my cholesterol count . . ." A heavy sigh.

Annie was in no mood to swap cholesterol woes. "Pamela, it is so sweet of you to call—" She leaned forward as Max added to his pad:

5. Locate grave at cemetery.
6. Use island map to find residence one half mile east on Least Tern Lane.

Emma shoved back her chair.

Annie followed, covering the phone with her hand. "Emma, where are you going? What are you going to do? Wait a minute . . ."

". . . but I worked my way through the crowds and I was able to get one of the flyers with the new clues and, Annie, I just had to call—"

Annie's head jerked up. Her hand tightened on the portable phone. "New clues. New clues?" No parrot ever screeched with more intensity.

Max pushed back his chair, came to his feet. Emma thudded to a stop, alert as a terrier at a rat hole.

"Annie"—Pamela spoke with weary patience—"I've been trying to tell you. Everybody on the island—well, maybe not everybody, but I had to park a mile from the gate, there were so many cars already here and I've never seen this many people at the cemetery, not even on Flag Day. Apparently there was a stack of new flyers at the grave but they were all gone when I got there. I promised the youngest Brewster boy a collection of Pokémon dolls for his flyer and I really think you should be very careful what you say about people. I mean, the Littlefields have so much money and he's not really very nice even though she's—"

"Pamela, don't go anywhere. Wait there. We're coming."

∻ *Four* ∻

MAX LEANED out the car window and peered up the road. "There's no way. The traffic's stacked like a Braves game during the World Series."

The narrow dirt lane to the cemetery, always dim in the tunnel between live oaks, was bumper-to-bumper with vehicles of all kinds—luxury sedans, SUVs, pick-ups, vans, rattletraps. Annie spotted their plumber's pickup, the silver Mercedes of a local decorator, and the rector's sedate black Taurus. Gray dust roiled in the air.

Behind them, a horn tooted three times.

Annie twisted to look. "Emma's pointing off to the left. She's backing up. Oh, wow, can she possibly make that turn?" The rear of Emma's pink Rolls-Royce veered perilously near the ditch, the wheels churned in the dust, then the big car bucked forward.

Annie leaned out her window and pointed. "Follow that car!" she shouted to Max. Okay, when else would she ever have an opportunity to call out that immortal line?

Max laughed but wrenched the steering wheel, and his small, easily maneuverable Ferrari pivoted and zoomed in pursuit.

Follow that car . . . Yes, she'd had an instant of fun, but the moment of lightheartedness didn't ease the hard, cold knot of anger lodged somewhere in her chest, as real and debilitating as a wound. Someone had taken the good name of her store—and her own good name—and trashed them just as surely as a vandal cracking glass or flinging paint. She'd scarcely had time to absorb the reality of the bogus flyer, but she knew Emma was right. Someone had ripped open a wasps' nest and lots of innocent people were going to suffer, and many of them, so very many, were going to think it was all Annie's fault. Now there was apparently yet another flyer.

"Max"—she spoke through clenched teeth— "Max." She couldn't say another word. Hot tears burned her eyes.

Max reached out, gripped her hand. "Come on, honey. We'll see it through. We'll tell the world it wasn't you. We'll find out who did this and we'll make sure everyone knows."

Annie clung to his hand, blinked away the tears. There was no time to cry. Now was the time to fight. If only she knew who the enemy was . . . Her cell phone rang. She took a deep breath, punched it on and managed to sound almost like herself. "Yes?"

"Follow me." With that brusque command, Emma clicked off.

Annie pointed at the Rolls-Royce. "Our leader has spoken." She was irritated, but, dammit, if she had to be in a foxhole, it was good to have a real soldier in there with her. Even a brusque soldier. Annie managed a smile. "Do you suppose it's too late for Emma to take charm lessons? But what amazes me, Marigold Rembrandt sheds charm faster than Ariadne Oliver scatters apple cores." Annie was a great fan of the charming detective-story author purported to be the good-humored self-portrait of Agatha Christie.

"They say all the characters in a book reflect some facet of the author's personality." Max didn't speak with conviction.

"Emma must be the exception to that rule." Annie leaned forward. "Look, she's turning."

Max slowed. "God, that way?"

The gap between bayberry bushes was almost invisible.

Annie understood. Max hand-waxed his Ferrari and this was a man who limited physical exertion to tennis and golf. And sex, of course.

Max gripped the wheel, turned into the rough road. "I hope she knows where she's going." He winced, his handsome face twisting in misery as the front tires jolted in the uneven ruts.

The live oaks squeezed so close that Spanish moss trailed over the windshield like wisps of fog. A low-hanging branch scraped the roof. Max made a noise between pain and agony.

"Just think"—Annie believed in looking on the bright side—"Emma's car is much bigger and it's going through just fine."

Max hunched over the wheel. "My God, the track's getting narrower. And the cemetery's in the other direction. Where does she think she's taking us? Hey, wait, where did she go?"

One minute the massive pink Rolls-Royce was

dimly visible through the cloud of dust; the next it was gone.

Max picked up speed, slowed immediately. "Annie, did you see that?" He pointed into the dim tangle of shrubs beneath a grove of pines.

Annie hung from her side of the car, looking ahead. "I think Emma turned right. It looks like there's a"— she didn't want to say path or trail or Max might simply back his beloved Ferrari all the way to the cemetery road, which by now had no doubt assumed almost mythical status as a well-traveled byway—"a turnoff. Let's try it."

Max was still peering into the dimness of the forest. "Annie, I saw a cougar. I swear I did."

Annie swiftly rolled up her window. She knew the island was reputed to have several of the big tawny wildcats. That was fine, a nice addition to the tourist literature. She preferred dolphins every time. "Let's catch up with Emma. Try that way."

Max pulled up to the entrance to the track and stopped.

Annie cleared her throat. "If her oversize, lumbering Rolls-Royce can manage to drive that way—"

Max signaled, turned to the right. This tunnel was so dark, they needed the headlights, but after a short stretch, maybe twenty feet, the trail widened into a small clearing with a weathered wooden house on stilts, two sheds and a dingy green tractor. The pink Rolls-Royce was parked by the nearest shed.

Max smiled. "Hey, there's room to turn around." His delight matched Stanley sighting Livingstone.

Emma was striding across the sandy clearing, the sun glinting on her spiky orange hair.

"Come on, Max. Let's see what Emma's up to." Annie hoped Emma remembered that Pamela Potts was awaiting their arrival at the cemetery and that Pamela claimed to have a second sheet of clues.

As their car doors slammed, a white-haired man in worn, dirt-stained coveralls came out on the porch of the old house, a shotgun cradled in his muscular arm.

Annie called out, "Emma, wait. He's got a shotgun."

Emma kept right on going, a careless wave of her hand the only acknowledgment of Annie's warning.

The old man, his wizened face the color of mahogany, looked past Emma at Annie and Max, frowned, gestured with the shotgun. "Private prop'ty."

"They're with me, Daniel." Emma pointed toward a path that angled into the forest. "We need to get to the cemetery and the road's jammed with traffic."

A flush mounted in his face, turning his skin a rusty orange. "People got no right. They're trespassers. Walkin' across the graves like it was picnic land. You hear that?" He nodded his head to his left. There was a dull sound, similar to a faraway roar of a football crowd or the rumble of surf. "I've half a mind to go shoot my gun, tell 'em to leave, but the po-lice . . ."

A siren squalled in the distance.

". . . told me they'd take care of it. I told the po-lice they got to find out who's causing this trouble. Why, they's people so deep around the Tower grave, I couldn't get past on my tractor, and I got to dig a new grave just past there for tomorrow."

"The Tower grave." Max squinted against the sun. "Bob Tower? Insurance agent? Had his own company?"

The old man leaned the shotgun against the porch

railing. The stairs squeaked beneath his weight. "Robert Payne Tower as was buried two years ago this spring."

"That's Bob. He and I used to play tennis. A good guy." Max jammed his hands in his pockets. "Hey, Annie, you remember Bob."

"Oh yes." She remembered Bob Tower's easy grin and the shock of learning he'd been hit by a car and left to die.

Emma was crisp. "They never found out who did it."

The flyer had listed a hit-and-run among the purported crimes. But Annie hadn't realized the victim was someone she'd known. Bob Tower, tall and lanky with curly brown hair and kind brown eyes.

Emma slipped on purple sunglasses with pink rims. "Seventeen graves south of the Portwood Mausoleum?"

"Yep." Daniel rubbed a grizzled cheek. "His wife comes once a week and sometimes the kids are with her. They bring wildflowers—daylilies and coral bean and swamp rose and verbena."

"Did you know Bob?" Max asked.

Daniel hooked his thumbs behind the straps to his coveralls. "Not till he got here. But I know all my people and I don't like what's goin' on now." He jerked his head in the direction of the cemetery.

The siren was louder. It cut off in mid-squall. Over the indistinguishable roar sounded the slam of car doors, an occasional shout, the nervous chitter of birds.

"Neither do we, Daniel. That's why we're here. Oh, Daniel, I want you to meet Annie and Max Darling." Emma nodded at them. "Daniel Parker. He helped me with background when I was writing *The Case of the Gravedigger's Gloves.*"

Daniel rocked back on his heels. "Yes'm." He looked at Annie and Max. "She didn't know graves from nothing. But I set her straight. Listen, Emma, can you figure out what's going on over there?"

"I intend to do just that." She sounded crisp and self-assured. "Tell us what's happened."

He plunged one grimy hand into a side pocket and pulled out a crumpled flyer. This one was mint-green, with oversize black letters. Very legible.

Annie and Emma both reached for it.

Daniel handed the wrinkled sheet to Emma. "They's everywhere. At least they was until all those people come. I don't know if they's any left by now. All those damn fool people stomping around. I'm going to have to get me some helpers to clean the cemetery. There's a burial tomorrow."

Annie craned around Emma's broad shoulder to read the flyer.

WHODUNIT?

Clever of you to get this far. Follow these clues:

> What happened to the Littlefields' red Jeep?
> Who drives a Range Rover?
> Where did the evidence come from?
> When did Emma find out about the girlfriend?
> Have wedding bells rung?

Having Fun?

Keep an eye on the personals in *The Island Gazette*.

WHODUNIT?

"I don't like this." Emma spit out the words like Rosie the Riveter welding a bomber. "It's like trying to catch handfuls of smoke. You grab and there's nothing there." She tapped the crumpled green sheet. "What is the point?"

Annie remembered that Emma had been a battlefield nurse in World War II. She was tough, a survivor, and right now, she was fighting mad. Annie couldn't imagine why the bogus flyers had been created, but if anyone could figure it out, it was Emma. She'd survived the toughest years of the last century and she handled supercomplicated plots with ease. "Okay, Emma, we've got to find out what these new clues mean. We need to split up. You and Max and I can each check out a different—"

"No." The orange spikes quivered.

"No?" Annie repeated.

Max bent forward. "We can't give up, Emma."

Emma's eyes were hidden behind the sunglasses, but the jut of her chin was formidable. "Give up?" She gave a dry laugh. "Never. But the clues don't matter. Oh, I agree that we need to find out who the suspects are." Her lips twisted in a wry smile. "Actually, I have to hand it to the perp, whoever he or she may be. This is a clever way to embroil the island in gossip and intrigue and possibly it may even flush out some criminals. But that"—her voice dropped almost to a whisper—"can't be the point. After all, an anonymous letter to the police chief—if there are any real facts to be found—would make a good deal more sense. No, there's something behind this . . . smoke . . . a smoke screen? . . . smoking gun . . ."

Annie wished she had a tape recorder. Emma's readers would be thrilled beyond measure to hear the stream of consciousness as the plot mistress pondered.

Abruptly, Emma jammed the flyer in a capacious pocket and turned away.

"Emma, wait a minute. Where are you going? What are you going to do?" Annie had a strong sense of déjà vu. Was she doomed to follow the purple-and-pink swirling caftan, imploring Emma to keep to the course?

Emma moved fast for a woman of her size, girth and age. She flung herself into her Rolls. The motor roared.

Annie didn't quite dare to jump in front of the big car. Emma wouldn't run Annie down, of course she wouldn't. But there was no sense in tempting fate. Or Emma. Annie shouted, "Emma, where are you going?"

Emma poked her head out as she backed up. "Nero Wolfe was a wise man, Annie." With that, the big car bolted forward and dust engulfed them.

Annie coughed. "What did she mean by that?"

Max was a special fan of the Rex Stout mysteries. He considered Archie Goodwin a soul mate, especially Archie's consuming interest in the fair sex. "Nero Wolfe didn't career around chasing clues. He sat in his study and thought."

"So?" But Annie understood. Emma intended to think. That was all well and good, but the clues on the flyers had to be figured out and Emma didn't have Archie to run errands for her. Hot on that thought came the cold realization that Emma had a cell phone and Annie's numbers. "Well. Okay. Let her think. Come on, Max, we've got to find Pamela." She looked at Daniel. "Can we get to the cemetery from here?"

The old man rubbed his nose, shrugged. "Why not? Everybody else on the island's there. Come on, I got some words for those po-lice. Emma will see to it that somebody pays the piper, but that don't clean up the cemetery for me."

Despite his age, he moved fast, striding around the smaller shed and ducking onto a trail. Spiny saw palmettos made a dense thicket beneath towering pines. The soft, forlorn cry of mourning doves sounded eerie in the murky half-light beneath the forest canopy. The dusty gray dirt was rutted by tractor tires. The path curved around a shadowy lagoon. Long black plumes cresting a white head, a great blue heron stood immobile near the bank. The smell of pine resin and dank still water mingled with the perfume of magnolia blossoms.

"Watch out for old Charley there." Daniel tilted his head to the left.

An alligator lay half-submerged, his snout resting on the bank, not a half foot from the path.

Annie edged past, trying to remember whether it was alligators or dogs you weren't supposed to look at. "Trust me, Charley," she murmured. "I'm not looking."

The pines thinned. The path led into the oldest part of the cemetery, with graves dating back to the mid-1700s, including some British seamen whose ship sank offshore during the Revolutionary War. More than twenty Confederate dead were buried there. Most of the stones, some broken and tilted, were mossy and the inscriptions difficult to read.

Past a second grove of pines, a hillock overlooked the newer graves. Annie stopped and stared. Normally, the heavily wooded cemetery was a quiet retreat. Today it looked like a combination of movie mob scene and Fourth of July oyster roast. "Max, we'll never find Pamela."

The dull roar had expanded. Women's high chatter was punctuated by deep masculine shouts. An amplified voice echoed tinnily, "Move along now, please move along. The cemetery is closed to the public. Please . . ."

Daniel Parker charged down the path, arms flailing, shouting, "Get out. I ain't gonna have it. Get out of here."

Annie started after Parker, then stopped so quickly, Max bumped into her. Annie stared across the mass of people at an ethereal golden-haired figure moving dreamily on the opposite ridge, seemingly oblivious to the turmoil below.

"Max"—she grabbed his arm—"look! What in the world is Laurel doing?" Annie was rarely surprised by her elegant, fey mother-in-law, whose past enthusiasms had ranged from wedding customs to quoting saints. After observing Laurel in many situations, Annie had, in fact, reached the point where she'd recently told Ingrid, "Nothing Laurel would do could shock me now." Had that pronouncement tempted fate?

Max shaded his eyes, then vigorously waved. "Hi, Ma," he shouted.

Laurel lifted—Annie blinked. Whatever Laurel lifted, Annie didn't recognize it. A pronged walking stick? Annie squinted. Laurel held in both hands something that resembled a crimson broomstick with long silvery fronds poking out on either side of the far end.

"Do you suppose she's here for the clue sheet?" Even as she spoke, Annie shook her head. "But she's nowhere near the crowd and she isn't holding a flyer." Dammit, what was Laurel holding?

"She didn't hear me." Max's grin was good-humored. "We'll ask her later. Come on, Annie, it's getting interesting down there."

The island police force, consisting of Chief Pete Garrett and three officers, was deployed along the main road. Garrett shouted into a bullhorn. "The cemetery is closed to the public. Move along now." The crowd moved slowly toward the front gates but people were jammed shoulder to shoulder on a patch of graves to their left.

Max pointed. "That's where Bob's buried. Come on, Annie, we'll find Pamela there."

Annie shot one more look toward the ridge, but obviously Laurel, whatever she was doing in the cemetery, was not there in search of WHODUNIT flyers. And that was what mattered. Annie started down the slope. Did Pamela still have a flyer? Whether she did or didn't, Max was right. Pamela had come to the cemetery to follow the clues. She would be at the seventeenth grave south of the Portwood Mausoleum come frost, high winds or poltergeists.

As Annie plunged into the crowd, trusting that Max was behind her, she heard calls:

A fellow choir member: "Annie, will you present the thousand dollars to the winner at Emma's signing?"

The peroxided checker at the grocery: "Annie, do you have any idea how many Range Rovers there are on the island?"

A hulking beach bum, tattoos twining on both arms: "Hey, are you the one who put these out?" A sweaty hand grabbed her arm and she shook free. "You should have listed the Carstairs case. Do you remember . . ."

A red-faced matron: "I live on Least Tern Lane and I certainly see this as a basis for a class-action lawsuit. My lawyer will be in touch."

Squeals of recognition followed her. Annie remembered her role in a college production of *South Pacific*. When she made her entrance, her sarong fell to the stage. She might have had a more attentive audience then, but not by much. The shouts and, from deep in the crowd, some boos made it clear that almost everyone here believed that Annie was responsible for this macabre exercise.

"Annie, oh, Annie, you're here!" The call came from above.

Annie looked up. Pamela Potts stood on a thick branch of the magnolia shading the Tower family graves. Pink patches flared in Pamela's pale cheeks. Despite her precarious perch, she maintained her customary dignity—chin up, gaze steadfast. "Annie," she shouted to be heard, "I had no choice but to rise above the melee. The crowd pressure has been intense. I saw no other way to remain as I had promised you." She held up a mint-green flyer. "You would not believe . . ."

A butterfly net swooped through the air, gripped tightly by a burly man wearing a ball cap, sleeveless T-shirt and cutoffs.

Pamela leaned backward, keeping the flyer just out of reach. ". . . the assaults I have withstood. All the flyers are gone and these people"—her voice was plaintive—"have no decorum, no restraint. No manners." The last was a desperate shout as she fended off a poking umbrella with a well-placed kick.

"That's a girl," Annie called. "We're coming."

The burly man in the ball cap shouted, "Hey, how come you're getting the last flyer? You put 'em out, didn't you? Trying to welsh on the deal? Listen, I been back and forth across this island till I got muscle cramps and I damn sure want that flyer."

"Ladies and gentlemen," the bullhorn blared, "the cemetery is closed. Please disperse. The cemetery . . ."

Annie sidestepped Ball Cap and wormed her way to Chief Garrett. He stood atop an overturned trash barrel, his cherubic face glistening with sweat.

Annie stood on tiptoe. "Pete. Pete!"

He broke off, looked down, and glared. "Annie—"

Her name boomed across the cemetery. The crowd surged closer. Annie felt a poke in her back.

Garrett lowered the bullhorn, dropped down beside her. "Annie, listen, you've got to call this off. The whole town's in an uproar."

"It's a hoax," she shouted. "I didn't have anything to do with this. Nothing. Nothing at all." She reached out, grabbed the bullhorn, and swung away, evading his reaching hands.

"People," she shouted. Her voice exploded above the rumble of the crowd. "Listen up. These flyers are bogus. There is no contest with clues to follow. It's a fake. Somebody's played a nasty April-fool joke. On you. On me. On the author. There isn't a thousand-dollar prize. The entire thing is a scam." She felt inspired.

After all, she owed nothing to the dark intelligence that had crafted the vicious exercise. Two could play the game of spurious announcements. The jerk had copied her clever promotion for the bookstore. Well, maybe she had just divined the perfect antidote. "You've been had, people, played for saps. Here's how we know these flyers are fake." She spaced the words with long pauses for emphasis. "Nobody admits printing them!"

"Are you sure, lady?" Ball Cap stood so near she could see the disappointed droop of his mouth and the stubble on his chin.

The word rolled across the crowd: Fake . . . fake . . . fake . . .

"Absolutely." Annie felt triumphant. There were enough people here that soon everyone on the island would hear. Talk about cutting the bad guy off at the pass . . . She stepped to the trash can and clambered up, hoisting the bullhorn. "A rotten trick, right?" Her voice boomed. Hey, she could take to this bullhorn business. "But don't be unhappy. There is a real contest and you can drop by Death on Demand Mystery Bookstore for the real flyers. You'll recognize them because they describe nine famous mysteries and all you have to do is name the authors and their books to win a signed copy of Emma Clyde's latest book, *Whodunit*"—Annie realized she was losing her audience. Glum and sullen, people were turning away, striding across the cemetery, toward the main gates. Good thing Emma wasn't here. America's most popular mystery writer would not be pleased at the lack of interest in her latest book. Annie lifted her voice higher. "And whoever turns in the name of the person who created the fake flyers gets"—was there a momentary pause in the dispersal?—"to drive Emma Clyde's Rolls-Royce for a week."

"Wow . . . Rolls-Royce . . . go to Florida and back . . . dirt track where you can pay fifteen bucks and race . . ." The crowd turned from sullen to eager. A few began to run, then more and more, and gray dust puffed from the road in shimmery clouds.

As Annie dropped to the ground and handed the bullhorn to Pete Garrett, she avoided Max's eyes. So maybe she'd gotten carried away.

Emma's Rolls. Annie jammed her fingers through her hair. "Oh, Lord. What have I done?"

✑ *Five* ✑

CARS INCHED UP the dusty road away from the cemetery. "You'd think somebody would let me in." Max leaned on his horn. "Oh hey, here's a break." He gunned his motor.

A silver Lexus bolted forward, taking up the inviting foot of space.

Max glowered, blue eyes blazing.

Annie pressed a hand against one ear, held her mobile phone to the other. "Nineteen messages on our voice mail!" Lips compressed, she listened. "Oh, I don't have to listen to that." She punched "3" to delete.

The rector's black Taurus, almost unrecognizable with its coating of dust, braked long enough for the Ferrari to edge into the line of traffic. Max waved his thanks.

Abruptly, Annie clicked off the phone.

Max glanced at her. "You've already heard nineteen messages?"

"I heard enough." Her tone was grim. "Not everybody's got the word yet."

He raised an eyebrow.

"About the bogus flyers. That it's all a fake." She

stared straight ahead, her face taut. "Some of the calls . . ." She didn't finish.

Max reached over, patted her hand. "Don't worry, honey. It will be all right. People understand about April fool. But you'll fool everybody and Emma will have a great signing Sunday."

"Don't worry!" Annie took a deep breath. "Oh, Max, it isn't just Emma's signing I'm concerned about. I have to find out who did this. Otherwise, some people will always think it was me. And worse than that, what about the people those awful clues point to? I'm going to find them and tell them I'm a victim just like they are."

"I don't know if that's the smart thing to do." His voice was troubled. The Ferrari picked up speed as he turned onto Sand Dollar Road.

"No." She was decisive. "It won't be pleasant to face them, but I have to make the effort." Annie shoved her hand through her unruly hair. "At least, I will as soon as I know who they are. It's pretty clear about the Littlefields and Emma. We'll have to figure out the rest. And they may be able to help us catch the person behind the thing."

"Help?" A blond eyebrow rose. "How? And why should they?"

Annie clapped her hands together. "Why shouldn't they? After all, think how we would feel if we were on a list that accused us of a crime. You'd think all of them would be wild to catch the creep that's embarrassing them all over the island." She paused, her eyes brightened. "Oh, hey, Max, I've got a great idea . . ."

*　　*　　*

Pamela Potts was the last to arrive at Confidential Commissions.

"Annie, everybody thinks you're simply wonderful, taking charge so masterfully. Well, of course not masterfully, but with such flair!" Pamela stood in the doorway to Max's office, not a strand of her blond hair out of place, soulful blue eyes exuding pride, white suit immaculate except for a magnolia twig snagged near the hem of her skirt. "I was listening as people left the cemetery." Her eyes clouded. "I simply hated to leave with everything in such a mess. I promised Mr. Parker I would round up some volunteers to help with the cleanup. People are so careless. And really, I don't think it was very appropriate for Ben Parotti to set up a food stand right by the cemetery as if it were a ball game or a parade. I actually"—there was modest pride in her clear voice—"told him so and do you know what Ben said? He said nobody there would give a damn, they were either having the best party in the universe or their thoughts were pretty much otherwise occupied. Oh, hello, Max, Henny, Barb. What are you doing?"

Annie pointed to the far end of the table. "Pamela, if you could take the last spot in line. See, there are lots of my flyers there and—"

"An assembly line," Henny called out briskly. Henny had a new hairdo, her dark hair with its glitter of silver shingling in layers. "Come on over, we're going to get the news out to everyone that Annie's flyer has nothing to do with that trash somebody put out. See, we have poster boards." She held up a poster with the message printed in huge bright red letters:

BEWARE OF FAKES

Here's the one-and-only real WHODUNIT contest flyer.

There was a large white space and another sentence at the bottom of the poster:

Death on Demand is offering a reward
for information about the source of the fake flyers.

Henny pointed at a poster with her red marker. "You can paste one of Annie's flyers beneath the message. We'll go all over the island and put up the posters."

Annie was pleased with her brilliant solution. Not only would the posters make it absolutely clear that Death on Demand had no connection to the obnoxious flyers, the posters would also publicize Emma's signing. Talk about win-win. And it wouldn't take long to get a bunch of posters done with Henny and Barb and Pamela helping, especially Henny. Annie smiled fondly at her old friend. Nobody on Broward's Rock could work better or faster than Henny, a retired schoolteacher, two-time Peace Corps volunteer and a veteran of the Women's Army Air Corps in World War II, who had flown a vintage airplane for many years. Annie began to feel relaxed. Everything was going to work out.

Pamela hurried across the room to take her place at the end of the table. She picked up a flyer and began to paste it painstakingly exactly in the center of the white space, then paused. "But why not say the reward is getting to drive Emma's Rolls-Royce for a week?"

Annie carefully began to print on a poster board.

In the odd silence that followed Pamela's question, Henny chuckled. "Annie, did you clear that with Emma?"

Annie's red marker skidded, messing up the W in WHODUNIT. She tossed that poster aside, picked up a fresh sheet, stared grimly down at it.

"Oh my. Oh my, oh my." Henny began to print letters on her poster board. "As Charlie Chan once observed, 'The deer should not play with the tiger.' "

Annie clattered down the back steps of Confidential Commissions. All of the shops on the harbor had rear entrances to a dusty, quiet alley, frequented primarily by delivery trucks. Her red Volvo was parked in the slot behind Death on Demand. Annie felt almost jaunty as she hurried toward the car. It always helped to take action. Her loud announcement at the cemetery was the first step in battling an unseen enemy. Now Max and Henny and Barb and Pamela were spreading out over the island to put up posters in heavily frequented areas and, along the way, ask if anyone had spotted the elusive distributor of the fake flyer. And she, despite Max's concerns, was going to deliver posters to the places she felt they were most needed.

Clutching her stack of posters, she darted around the front of her car, then stopped and stared at the window. Somebody had tossed a brick through the driver's window of her Volvo. A bright green sheet of paper was wrapped around the brick. She didn't have to unfold the flyer to recognize another of the fakes. Fragments of thought raced through her mind: The nearest glass shop was in Bluffton, a ferry ride away. Who was mad at her? One of those accused in the fake flyers who hadn't heard—or didn't believe—that Annie had nothing to do with the scurrilous attacks? Or a disappointed contestant, furious that the thousand-dollar prize wasn't to be had? Or was this the work of the scheming, cruel mind that had created the spurious contest, angry at Annie's denunciation?

Annie was surprised at her sense of outrage that mingled with hurt. How ugly, ugly, ugly . . . But wasn't that to be expected as a result of whatever was happening on the island? All right, no matter what effort it required, she wasn't going to give up her search for the person responsible. It was true that she'd hoped to find out the identity of the trickster to save herself from a difficult moment with Emma. Yes, that mattered. Every time she thought about Emma's Rolls . . . And it mattered that her store, her wonderful mystery bookstore, was unfairly embroiled in what was sure to become an island-wide scandal. But there was much more at stake here. Annie stared at the broken glass, sparkling in the late-March sunshine, and wondered what other violence would be spawned by the flyers.

Leaning her stack of posters against the fender, she unlocked the car. She spotted a box of Kleenex on the backseat, grabbed several sheets. Carefully, she picked up the wrapped brick, deposited it gently on the floor of the passenger side. Fingerprints were unlikely. But she would take care not to destroy possible evidence. She yanked out more tissues, used them to wrap the larger pieces of glass. There was a stack of her own WHO-DUNIT flyers on the passenger seat. She spread out a couple of the flyers on the floor mat and used a handful of tissues to brush the smaller pieces of glass and the hard-to-see splinters onto the floor. As for the jagged remnants in the window, she'd deal with those when she was home and had access to gardening gloves.

She gave a final sweep to the leather seat, tossed the posters, a roll of tape, and a file folder onto the passenger seat, and settled behind the wheel. But she made no move to turn the key in the ignition. Instead, she stared at the folder. Should she start at this end of the island—Emma's house had a superb ocean view, thanks to Marigold—or follow the noxious clues in the fake flyer, or opt for Frank Saulter's familiar face?

Undecided, Annie picked up the folder, flipped it open. It was amazing how much information Barb had garnered while she and Max were at the cemetery. Barb, in her organized fashion, had divided her report into five parts. Annie reread Barb's introduction and her notes:

Background Material
in re Bogus Flyers

Flyers (hereinafter designated F1) patterned after the Death on Demand Whodunit contest have been found throughout the island, including the shops on the boardwalk by the harbor, the local schools, the library, Parotti's Bar and Grill, the hospital, the country club, the largest churches as well as the business district near the ferry dock, including *The Island Gazette* and the police station.

Scrawled in the margin in Barb's flamboyant writing: "Pete Garrett is furious. He took the flyers at the police station as a personal affront."

Annie murmured, "You and me, Pete." She almost skipped past a description of the cemetery gathering, but one sentence caught her eye:

> . . . the second flyer (hereinafter designated F2) has been found only at the cemetery. F2 flyers were bundled next to the grave of Robert Tower.

Only at the cemetery. Annie frowned. She rustled through the folder, found flyers F1 and F2, held them side by side. Odd. It was Clue 1 in F1 that led the curious to the cemetery. There were, however, four more clues in F1. Shouldn't the F2 flyers have been available at all those places as well?

She shook her head impatiently. Dammit, she kept treating the exercise as if it were truly a contest. But the fact that the F2 flyer was found only at the cemetery was surely the clincher that the entire contest was a sham. The point of the fake flyers wasn't to lead people to the secrets or possibly even to crimes hidden in the lives of those targeted. The point was . . . What *was* the point? Malicious mischief? Or a passion for justice, no matter the cost?

Justice.

Annie turned the key, drove slowly toward the end of the alley. Through the broken window, she heard the crunch of the tires on the oyster-shell road. Okay, maybe somebody believed there were guilty persons who needed to be caught. Maybe the point of the flyers wasn't simply to torment innocent victims. Maybe somebody believed crimes had been committed and the flyers might reopen old cases, bring new ones.

Adultery? That was a crime against the heart, a crime against the innocent third in the ages-old triangle, a crime against God, but it certainly was not a crime to be judged in a court of law. But murder, false imprisonment and hit-and-run resulting in death were crimes indeed.

Annie reached the end of the alley, and again she hesitated. Where to start? She glanced down at the open folder. Barb hadn't minced words:

Crime 1

Hit-and-run. Unsolved. Tower was hit by a car while jogging two years ago, April 14. Found unconscious in the ditch on a lonely stretch of Blue Heron Lane shortly after eight-thirty that morning. Died en route to the hospital without regaining consciousness. Survived by his wife, Jessie, and two children, Amy and Cliff. Jessie is now running the Tower Insurance Agency; Amy is a senior in high school, Cliff a sophomore. Fragments of red paint were found on Tower's T-shirt. Island police put out a call for damaged red cars. None were reported.

In the margin, Barb had scrawled: "Probably the car was taken off island for repair before the search began."

Annie remembered the cryptic clue in the second flyer: What happened to the Littlefields' red Jeep? That was as specific as the clue pointing one-half mile east on Least Tern Lane.

Annie returned to the text:

Tower had no known enemies. His wife was driving the children to school. Her car was (and is) a blue

Maxima. F2 asks: What happened to the Littlefields' red Jeep? Either a good question or a matter of geography. Curtis and Lou Anne Littlefield live on Blue Heron Lane a half mile from the site of the hit-and-run. Curtis is a venture capitalist with offices in New York and Los Angeles. Avid golfer. Reputed to improve his lie when nobody's looking. Lou Anne's antique store—My Attic—is second only to Parotti's as the main attraction downtown. They have one daughter, Diane, a so-so student who works part-time at her mother's store after school.

Crime 2

Adultery. Paul Marlow, one sexy dude, lives one-half mile east on Least Tern Lane. He runs The Grass Is Green lawn and garden service. I'm still working on it but so far I've got a list of twenty weekly customers. Don't have a clue who the lady might be, always assuming he likes ladies, but I don't think that's in question. A favorite with the single gals at the Low Places Lounge near the ferry stop on the mainland. He's a bachelor. Scubas down near Cozumel a couple of times a year, has a big black Lab named Hoss.

Crime 3

Here's the lead story from *The Island Gazette*, September 13, 1990:

"A jury convicted islander Jud Hamilton of second-degree murder yesterday in the death of his wife, Colleen, despite Hamilton's claim that he had an alibi at the time of her death.

"According to police testimony, Colleen Hamilton

was found critically injured at the foot of the stairs in their two-story home. A neighbor, Joan Leavitt, testified that Mrs. Hamilton seemed to be afraid of her husband.

"On the witness stand, Edward Miles testified that he had lied when he said he and Hamilton were out fishing on the afternoon in question. Miles testified that he had told the police he was with Hamilton at Hamilton's request. This surprise testimony shocked Hamilton and his attorney, who requested a mistrial. The request was overruled by Judge Larrabee Logan.

"Police Chief Frank Saulter testified that he observed scratches on Hamilton's arms when he interviewed the husband the day after Mrs. Hamilton's death. Chief Saulter also testified that Mrs. Hamilton was conscious when he reached the scene and that when he asked her what happened, she said, 'Jud pushed me.'

"Hamilton took the stand in his own defense and vigorously denied harming his wife and claimed they were happily married. The prosecution then called to the stand a series of witnesses who confirmed that Mrs. Hamilton was often observed to be suffering from injuries such as bruises on her face and arms and twice was treated at the hospital emergency room for a broken arm.

"Hamilton was employed as a trust officer at the Seminole Bank and Trust. Judge Logan said the sentence will be pronounced next week."

Barb's scrawl in the margin was deeply indented: "Jud's a scary, scary man. Colleen was terrified of him. She was a teacher at the high school, one of the best my son ever had. A sweet woman. Jud got twenty years, but a story last week said he's been paroled. Have you ever noticed how wives convicted of their husbands' deaths stay in jail forever? And how a guy can get busted for robbery and get a big sentence but rape will net a couple of years? But don't get me started."

Annie looked at the clue list in F2: Where did the evidence come from? It was like taking a step on a familiar stair and suddenly finding yourself falling. The evidence, the evidence that very likely convicted Jud Hamilton, came from then Police Chief Frank Saulter, a man Annie knew well. The first flyer claimed there was a case of false imprisonment. Frank? Annie pictured his worn, bony face and serious brown eyes— okay, she'd thought him totally humorless when they first met—but he was simply an intense man who cared about his island and the people who lived on it. He wasn't impressed by the rich folks who lived in condos and the gated community, and he'd put Annie at the top of his suspect list when a writer was murdered at Death on Demand shortly after she took over running her late uncle's bookstore. Frank was dogged and tireless, and he always got his man. Or woman. Annie thought about Frank's brown eyes, determined, intelligent and sometimes bleak.

Annie felt cold despite the soft warmth of the April sun. She would talk to Frank, that was for sure. She glanced at the next heading in Barb's report:

Crime 4

Ricky Morales, Emma's second husband, fell off *Marigold's Pleasure* fifteen months after Emma and

Ricky moved to Broward's Rock. According to the Coast Guard report, Morales's fall was adjudged an accident. He was a non-swimmer. The body was found the next day. Emma's bio attached.

Barb had scrawled in the margin: "Ask Emma? I don't think so!"

Annie didn't need to ask Emma. She knew more about the island's most famous writer than was contained in the many voluminous biographical essays by mystery critics. Annie and Emma went way back. Oh, not as far back as Emma and her second husband, but Emma had been a member of the mystery writers' group that met at Death on Demand when Annie inherited the bookstore from her uncle Ambrose. Annie was quite sure that Emma had then been paying blackmail to another member of that select circle and the payoff money was to hide information about Ricky Morales's death. The investigation had been officially closed all these years, but there is, of course, no statute of limitations on murder. However, nothing came of the suspicion of murder at that time and nothing would come of it now. No one but Emma would ever know the truth of that night. All Emma had to do was keep quiet, and Annie had no doubt that Emma would do precisely that. It didn't matter now whether or when Ricky Morales had had a girlfriend. That would suggest a motive, but it gave no evidence about what happened on Ricky's final night aboard *Marigold's Pleasure.*

"Nope." Annie said it aloud. There might always be a suspicion in the mind of some about the drowning, but putting Emma on the list of possible crimes was puzzling. No matter who looked or how hard they looked, no one was going to come up with evidence to change the ruling of accidental death. So why include Emma?

Annie concentrated. There was something here, something important. . . . But she wasn't sure what. She shook her head, read the final heading:

Crime 5

Poor little rich girl, that was sure true about Laura Neville Fleming. Inherited millions, but she was plain as a bowl of oatmeal and had about as much zip. Oh, she wore designer clothes and did everything expected of her, all the charity dos, that kind of thing. Husband quite handsome. Keith Fleming was a poor boy who had worked his way up in Papa Neville's fancy furniture store in Atlanta—all the best from High Point—and married the boss's daughter. Happy ending? Not really. No kids. Lots of social events. The only passion in her life was the family yacht, *Leisure Moment*. They say she sometimes drank a bit too much and that's what happened the night she fell off the yacht and drowned.

Annie rubbed her nose. Two drownings? Was this a coincidence, or was this simply an easy way to expand the list of possible crimes for the flyers? Annie sat very still because that glimmer in her mind was brighter. Expand the list . . . Somebody could always be pushed from a boat. Oh, wait a minute, wait a minute. Was this the truth she needed to ferret out? What if the flyers really were meant to expose one particular crime and the others were included to keep the spotlight away from those who would care, and care passionately, about one particular event? That would explain Emma's name on the list. She was camouflage, a smoke screen. . . .

Annie reached for her cell phone, punched a private number that she knew by heart. When the answering machine message sounded, Annie came on strong. "Come on, Emma. I know you're there. I'll keep calling. Automatic, every fifteen seconds. You went home to think. Listen, I've got to talk to—"

"Annie." The cool gravelly voice was remote.

"Emma, you went away muttering about a smoke screen, a smoking gun. What did you mean?" Annie glanced at Barb's report. Five crimes. Was there only one that mattered?

There was a whisper of what might have been laughter if it hadn't been a snort of disdain. "Even Detective Inspector Hector Houlihan would have tumbled before now."

Annie wanted to snap that Emma better be damn glad at this particular moment she wasn't standing at the stern of *Marigold's Pleasure* with Annie behind her or there might be another drowning. Annie blurted, "Of course you can probably swim," and knew she was in trouble. When, oh when, would she ever learn to control her quick temper? She could hear Max's oft-repeated suggestion: Breathe deeply, Annie. That's right. One breath, two . . .

But Emma was never predictable. Following a thoughtful silence, there was an unmistakable deep chuckle. "I swim quite well, my dear. Is that why you called?"

Annie refused to be diverted. "Smoke screen, Emma. Come on, what did you mean?"

"As Marigold often reminds Houlihan, 'Gnats distract. Get the big picture.' " With a sharp click, the connection ended.

"Emma . . ." But there was no one to hear Annie's outraged bleat. Gnats distract . . . Oh, damn. Did Emma think she was Charlie Chan? As far as pithy statements went, Emma's had far to go. And Annie wasn't getting anywhere. But she still had the glimmer, a deep rich glow in her mind. What if the whole point of the fake flyers was to stir up investigation into one particular crime and the others were mentioned simply to keep anyone from wondering who might care enough to set these events in motion?

Annie turned out of the alley. The Volvo picked up speed. As Charlie Chan might have said, had it occurred to him: To start, you must begin. And she, by damn, was going to begin.

～ *Six* ～

FIVE POSTERS TUCKED beneath one arm, Max pushed in the heavy wooden front door of Parotti's Bar and Grill. He stepped inside and waited for his eyes to adjust to the dimness. Although it wasn't quite noon yet, the foyer was full of people waiting for a table, a tribute to the excellence of the food. The menu included smothered pork chops, chicken wings, steamed oysters, gumbo, she-crab soup, catfish stew, fried okra, barbecued pigs' feet and, Annie's favorite, the fried-oyster sandwich.

Max sniffed the smells beloved to islanders, though newcomers sometimes found the combination of hot cooking oil, barbecue sauce, beer, sawdust and fishy aromas from the bait coolers a touch too tangy. Saying hello to friends, he worked his way through the crowd, heading for a spot at the bar against the far wall.

Parotti's was a much more genteel establishment from when Max first came to the island. Ben's marriage to the cook, a well-traveled lady from Tallahassee with tea-shop tastes, had transformed Ben from a scruffy leprechaun in an armless union suit and baggy coveralls to a natty leprechaun who often sported a gold-buttoned blue blazer and Tom Wolfe white trousers. Ben had agreed to the addition of quiche and fruit teas to the menu and wildflower bouquets in slender vases on the initial-scarred wooden tables, but he drew a line in the sawdust. Sawdust there had always been, sawdust there would always be, even if purchasers of bait no longer carried out their wiggly, smelly shrimp or minnows and the occasional eel in leaky cartons. Mrs. Ben insisted on plastic-covered buckets but gracefully yielded to Ben about the sawdust.

The jukebox belted out Little Richard, the doors from the kitchen clattered as waitresses hurried out with laden trays, the old-fashioned cash register pinged, and the roar of conversation kept every conversation private.

Max was halfway across the sawdust-strewn floor when a familiar voice called out, "Max, hey, Max!" Tall, lanky redheaded Vince Ellis, owner and editor of *The Island Gazette,* pushed up from a nearby table, still clutching an oyster knife. "I've been calling you and Annie."

Max wasn't surprised. Vince was a hardworking editor who never missed any excitement on the island.

Vince reached Max in two strides. "What's all this about Annie's flyers?" He looked sharply at the posters under Max's arm.

Max slipped one free, handed it to the editor. "Annie's gone on the offensive."

Vince scanned the poster. "Good idea. I figured Annie had been set up. Can I have this? We'll run a picture of it. I got some quotes from Ingrid. We'll have a story in tomorrow's paper about Annie's Whodunit contest. We quote Ingrid saying there are some spurious flyers out there that have nothing to do with the store. Ingrid said Annie's investigating. You got a handle on who's behind the fake contest?"

"Not yet. Do you have any ideas?" Little happened on the island that escaped either Vince or the columns of his newspaper.

"Nope. I've got Marian working on it." Frazzled, fast-talking, frenetic Marian Kenyan charged every story like Mike Hammer ogling a blonde. "She's set up a phone brigade. If anybody saw the person who put out those flyers, Marian'll come up with it. I'll let you know."

Max wasn't hopeful, but he asked anyway. "How about the cemetery flyer asking people to keep an eye on the personals in *The Island Gazette*?"

Vince raised a sandy eyebrow. "That has to be phony, Max. No ad goes in the paper unless submitted with a verifiable name and address. We do carry personals that don't have a name listed, but we know who placed the ad."

"But if anything comes in—"

Vince clapped him on the arm. "You'll be the first to know." He started to turn away, then said quickly, "Keep us informed, Max." Vince rubbed a freckled cheek. "The other stuff—it's pretty damned nasty. I'd keep a close eye on Annie."

Max stood very still. "On Annie?"

"It could be that somebody doesn't like her very much." Vince shrugged. "Or it may be that her contest gave somebody a way to poke at tigers from a safe distance. Be in touch."

Max watched the energetic editor stride away, taking with him Max's sense of well-being. *Keep a close eye on Annie*. . . . Damn, it would be easier to herd cats. But surely Annie was all right. . . .

"Yo, Max."

Max felt a tug on his arm and looked down. Today Ben's sport coat was Masters-golf-green and his slacks a pale yellow, but his inquisitive, combative, and eager face was as raffish as ever.

"The missus with you?" Ben craned to peer toward the ladies' room.

"Not today, Ben." Max held up the posters for Ben to see. "Can I put these up? And I've got some flyers to put out on the bar."

Ben grabbed a poster, peered at it. "Oh yeah, this is what Annie was talking about this morning. I wish she'd waited a while before she got on her high horse. Hell, I was selling catfish and hush puppies faster than a cotton rat hustling greens." His snort of laughter drowned the music. " 'Course, I ain't got quite the hurry of a cotton rat." He looked philosophical. "Has to eat all the time, and when it ain't eatin', it's making babies. Busy all the time. Anyway, no hard feelings. If the missus was here, I'd fix her an extra-thick fried-oyster sandwich. Sure, you can put up the posters and I'll put the flyers around." He took the stack from Max.

"Listen, Ben, I need to talk to you—"

Ben pointed toward the big mahogany bar at the far end of the big room. "Gotta get back to work, Max."

"I'm going to have lunch, Ben. I just have a couple of things I need to find out." Scuffing sawdust, Max followed Ben. Max slipped onto one of the tall red leatherette stools.

Ben darted behind the bar. "The usual?"

Max nodded.

Ben checked on a half-dozen customers as he scooted up and down behind the bar and brought Max a Bud Light.

Over the croon of the Ink Spots, Max said quickly, "Ben, I need to know who took the late ferry back to the island on Monday night or the first ferry back on Tuesday morning."

Ben tufted his grizzled eyebrows. "Late ferry Monday night, first ferry Tuesday morning," he muttered. He turned to the window into the kitchen, barked out an order. When he brought a steaming bowl of okra, crab and shrimp gumbo, he rubbed his nose and looked speculatively at Max. "I ain't no priest and I suppose I don't owe my riders no immunity. But I never made it a practice to talk about who goes on or off island and when."

Max shook some pepper on his gumbo and added an extra dash of Tabasco. "You don't like sneaks, do you, Ben?"

Ben folded his arms and leaned against the bar, waiting.

Max put down his spoon. "Somebody's sneaking around causing a lot of trouble and that's why I'm asking about the ferry."

Ben's eyes narrowed. "Yeah, those flyers are causing a mess of trouble. I heard Bud Harris punched his wife. They live on Least Tern Lane but not a half mile from Sand Dollar. She's gone to stay with her folks in

Greenville. Bud's always been a jealous man, though
my missus says it's all in his head, that Rhonda is a
good woman."

Max stirred the gumbo. "All because somebody
snuck around and put out those fake flyers, Ben. And
we know that whoever did it had to get to Beaufort either Monday night or Tuesday morning to leave money
at a skywriting—"

Ben held up his hand, swung away to get another
order from the window, plunked it three places down
and scooted back to Max. "You mean Annie didn't
order that WHODUNIT in the sky? I thought for sure
that was Annie."

"Not Annie. There was no name left with the order,
so we're pretty sure it was made by the same person
who put out the bogus flyers. If you could tell me who
was on the ferry, it would be a big help."

Ben folded his arms across his chest, shook his
head.

Max was shocked. "But, Ben, why not?"

"Max, I guess you forgot where you live." Ben's
look was a mixture of pity and embarrassment. "Now,
if you was going to sneak about and do somethin'
wrong, would you prance right onto the ferry? Where
me and God and everybody would see you? Why, Max,
how many people are there on this island who can't
handle a sailboat or a motorboat? You can bet whoever
took that money to Beaufort popped a bike in the back
of a boat and slipped across the Sound quieter than a
Carolina cougar coming up behind a deer." Ben picked
up a rag, polished the shiny wood. "So it don't matter
who was on the ferry and I don't s'pose it's harmin'

nybody for me to speak out. Monday night there was
3ridget Jones, who'd been into Savannah to shop, and
Matt Hosey, who runs the Buccaneer Inn. Only had
hree passengers Tuesday morning and none was is-
and people—two vacation families and a salesman
vho lives in Columbia, nice fellow named Jefferson."
3en punched Max on the shoulder. "No, sir, you be
ookin' for somebody with a boat."

As Annie slowed to make the turn into Least Tern
Lane, a sleek yellow convertible spurted around her,
.orn blaring. Her mother-in-law, golden hair attrac-
ively (of course) tousled by the wind, gestured ener-
;etically, always graceful fingers fluttering.

Annie hesitated, clicked off her right-turn signal,
.nd followed the convertible and the swooping hand
hat continued to make encouraging waves. Obviously
Laurel wanted to see her. Annie knew from long expe-
ience that had she ignored the summons, Laurel
vould simply have turned her car and pursued Annie to
he end of the island. And beyond, if necessary.

The convertible's signal blinker came on and Laurel
werved into the Forest Preserve. Annie swerved, too,
.nd stopped behind the convertible in the clearing by
he paths that snaked into the preserve.

Before Annie could open her door, Laurel was mov-
ng quickly toward her. As always, Laurel was expen-
ively and beautifully dressed, although Annie thought
he crimson blouse and black slacks and short black
>oots a trifle odd on such a springlike day. But it was
he two lengths of polished copper, one in each hand,
hat truly puzzled her.

Laurel flung her arms wide, the copper flashing i
the sunlight. "Annie, your window!"

Annie dismissed the shards of glass sticking fror
the well. "It got broken. Uh, hey, Laurel, what ar
those things?"

"Darling, I've been looking for you everywhere." /
husky laugh. "Of course, had I employed these"—he
glance at the copper rods verged on adoring—"
should no doubt have found you sooner. However, a
times I forget the possibilities and I was focused solel
on aiding you in your efforts. And so I made inquirie
of that dear man, Daniel Parker."

Laurel had the capacity to enchant males of ever
age, from toddlers to septuagenarians. Annie had n
doubt Daniel was quite eager to be of service to Lau
rel. "He didn't point the shotgun at you?"

"Shotgun? Oh, my dear. Actually, I was delaye
there for a while because he was simply fascinate
with my divining rods and I had to help him find a
appropriate tree so that he might make his own in th
old-fashioned way from a nice forked piece of wooc
Hazel, apple, beech and alder are quite traditional bu
not here on the island. I suggested oak or perhaps hick
ory. What do you think?" She stared into Annie's eye
as if the forthcoming words might just be the most im
portant ever uttered on the subject.

Annie had that old familiar sense of bewildermen
overlaid by irritation, with just a soupçon of suspicion
feelings often engendered by contact with Laurel. And
dammit, she didn't have time for a Looney Tunes ex
ercise. She had to find the jerk who was trying to rui
both her reputation and the cleverest book promotio

n the history of Death on Demand. And she needed to
check on Rachel, see how she was feeling. Was she truly
sick, or was something wrong at school? And she had to
get ready for the Sunday-afternoon signing. Her stom-
ach lurched. Was Ingrid still checking on the order?
Would Emma's books arrive on the ferry in time?

Annie forced a smile. "Laurel, I'm sure whatever
wood you and Daniel pick will be just fine. And now,
if you'll excuse me—"

Laurel eased the two copper rods over the broken
points of glass, jiggling them a little impatiently until
Annie took them. The rods were L-shaped, the short
length obviously intended to be gripped and, in fact,
still warm from Laurel's hands.

Laurel's exquisitely lovely face, the patrician features smooth and ageless, managed to exude commis-
eration without engendering a single wrinkle. "I know,
Dear Child. I understand. You Have a Mission. I didn't
realize the problem until you spoke out at the cemetery.
It was simply serendipity—or do I mean synchronicity?
Do you know, I always confuse the two . . ."

Annie felt that confusion was the least of Laurel's
difficulties.

". . . because I was there solely as a result of the
map. Although truly"—a deprecating smile—"I will
admit I didn't use my pendulum over the map."

Pendulum? Annie briefly closed her eyes, but when
she opened them Laurel was still speaking.

"I found reference to a map in an old history of the
sea islands. Of course, it wasn't a treasure map or I
should certainly have opted for the pendulum. I—"

"Laurel." Annie paused, made an effort to leach the

desperation from her tone. "Please, what are we talk
ing about?"

"Dear Child." Laurel's fjord-blue eyes widened i
concern. "Truly You Are in Need. Now, it will eas
your efforts to find the culprit"—she paused, nodde
firmly—"oh yes, I know all about the flyers, yours an
the others. I admire your determination to root out th
person responsible for what is truly an outrage agains
our community. That's why I was looking for you, al
though I do try to commit myself to a schedule, tw
hours in the morning, two in the afternoon and, o
course, those marvelous witching hours near mid
night"—the enormity of her dedication lifted he
voice—"but I felt that your search, as it were, for
modern-day miscreant as opposed to my quite thrillin
but less socially necessary attempt to find the fruits o
long-ago crimes—"

"Laurel."

Her mother-in-law clapped her hands together
"Yes, of course, let us cut to the chase. Isn't it wonder
ful how the world of film has added to our language?
Her trill of laughter was gentle. "Although Morgan—
you never knew him, dear. He was my husband wh
loved oil—always insisted the phrase had nothing t
do with skipping the preliminaries before the conclud
ing chase scene in a movie. Morgan said it was a tern
used by those who drill for oil in the great Southwes
and their attempts to reach the Chase formation." He
coiffed head nodded, presumably in the direction o
the great Southwest or perhaps the Chase formation
"Now I always thought it had to do with foxhunting
but no matter, it speaks to us. Yes. Dowsing, Annie."

Annie looked from the copper rods to Laurel. Dowsing.

A decided nod. "Take the rods, hold them like pistols—wasn't dueling a great though dangerous tradition—"

Annie opened her mouth.

Laurel broke off, continued rapidly: "Hold them straight out waist-high like pistols and"—she leaned forward, blue eyes mesmerizing—"determine with great precision your question. That is at the heart of success or failure. It won't do simply to muddle about and think, Well, why did someone put out the posters?, or to wonder whether the clues have merit. No, you must be precise. March up to the suspect in question, hold up the rods and think"—a worried shake of that smooth golden head—"I know that can be a challenge, Annie, but you must simply do your best. March up to the suspect, point the rods and think, Who put you on that list? And voilà, if the rods cross or perhaps even dip or simply wiggle, you will be close to ending your search."

The copper rods, next to the clumps of glass and the brick, rattled on the floor of the passenger side as Annie's Volvo jolted onto Least Tern Lane. Gray dust roiled as the wheels churned in the deep ruts of the narrow road. Annie added another black mark against the vandal who'd smashed her window. She tried to concentrate on her objective, but she kept glancing at the shiny metal rods. Cut to the chase. . . . Okay, it was spooky that Laurel had in her own bizarre way suggested a new method of attack. Oh, not the dowsing rods. And what did Laurel mean by saying that she was seeking the fruits of past crimes? Oh, well, wandering about the island with dowsing rods certainly seemed to be a harmless pursuit. But Laurel had, unwittingly, given Annie a good lead. The fake flyers listed five possible crimes. The clues led to suspects in those crimes. The question to pose to each person implicated was simple indeed: Who put you on that list?

Henny Brawley loved mysteries and enjoyed emulating the great detectives, everyone from the insouciant Saint, derring-do hero of the Leslie Charteris adventures, to tart-tongued Julia Tyler, Louisa Revell's indomitable Southern gentlewoman. As Henny parked in the lengthening shade of the pines behind the library, she wondered how to approach the present problem. She had a title in mind: *The Case of the Counterfeit Flyers*. She, of course, planned to star as chief investigator. No way would Emma solve this first, not if Henny could help it. Just because Emma wrote mysteries she fancied herself as best equipped to uncover the truth. Pfui! as Nero Wolfe might exclaim. After all, the mystery author knows whodunit before it even happens, so where was the skill in that? No, Henny was determined to demonstrate deductive powers far beyond those possessed by Emma.

Grabbing a stack of flyers and several posters, Henny slammed the car door shut. She didn't bother to lock it, one of the advantages of living on an island and driving an old black Dodge everyone recognized. As she hurried up the back steps, she considered possibilities. Should she hope for the insightfulness of Georges Simenon's Inspector Maigret? Or perhaps this was the moment for Miss Marple's clever parallels. Or maybe she should opt for a tougher modern-day investigator such as B. J. Oliphant's Shirley McClintock.

Henny paused in the narrow corridor. The names of the detectives all began with *M*. Was this an omen? She grinned. She'd never thought of life in terms of omens, karma or presentiments until she met Max's mother. Perhaps Annie was right. Perhaps time spent around Laurel was dangerous to mental health. Anyway, the answer seemed clear. Maigret all the way. Too bad she didn't have a handy raincoat or a pipe. But the externals didn't matter. Maigret was a man who made himself one with the milieu. When he understood the people, he understood the crime. That would be her task. The people—who mattered most, the author of the flyers or the victims of the flyers?

Henny paused in the back corridor, eyes narrowed. It was essential to understand the psychology, as Poirot always pointed out. What kind of person would create the flyers? Clearly that depended upon the reason for their existence. Emma was in her lair, presumably thinking. Annie was doggedly seeking out the victims. Perhaps they were missing the forest for the trees. Why not take the flyers at face value? After all, they had certainly set in motion a scramble for facts about the alleged crimes. Police Chief Pete Garrett had to be engaged in digging up every fact available about the incidents because he would have had a series of messages from worried members of the city council, Henny was sure of that. Pete would be busy looking for evidence. Except, of course, for the charge of adultery.

Adultery—Henny would have clapped her hands together if she hadn't been carrying posters and Annie's flyers. Wait a minute. Who would consider adultery a crime to be publicly announced, shades of *The Scarlet Letter*? Talk about psychology! All right, she needed to think, figure out who on the island combined the sensibilities of a vigilante with a rigid code of morality and more than a dash of self-righteousness.

With a clear sense of mission, Henny hurried up the corridor. She reached the main foyer, the heart-pine floors glowing from sunlight streaming through tall, clear-paned windows. The library was housed in a three-story Greek Revival mansion bequeathed to the city by an ardent library lover and it had a thick scent of mold as well as the acrid undertone of electronic equipment and the familiar beloved scent of books, books, books. Henny took a deep satisfying breath and waved a poster at the librarian behind the information desk. "Edith, can I put these posters up? There's been—"

Edith Cummings always moved fast. The SECTION CLOSED sign was scarcely atop the information desk before she was through the swinging half door and planted squarely in front of Henny. Jamming a hand through her thick dark curls, Edith bristled. "I know what they're for. Everybody on the island knows by now. Somebody put out fake flyers imitating Annie's contest for Emma's book and you are putting up posters disclaiming any responsibility. I know what you are doing. Do you know what I've been doing? Have you ever worked until your tongue hung low enough to lick your shoe tops? Was the library jammed this morning? Did I have more people here than attended the last mud-wrestling contest at the Low

Places Bar near the ferry dock? Did we almost have mortal combat between a blue-haired woman whom I shall not identify—and yes, she's a member of the Altar Guild as well as the Rose Painting Society—and the portly, pugnacious pastor of a local church whom I also shall not identify over who should be first to use the library's computer to access the Internet? And would anybody, would a single one of the motley horde that descended upon the computer bank as soon as we opened, would even one of these greed-driven, salacious-minded creatures let me look at a flyer? Oh yes, there were apparently oodles of flyers on the library's front steps this morning, but I was late, caught in a traffic jam trying to get here, and all of those flyers were snatched up. And I've been chained to the library because the director is on vacation and everybody else called in sick and I'll bet they're all out there with flyers. And I can't tell you how delighted I am"—her smile was wolfish—"that the whole damn thing's a sham and nobody's going to get an easy thousand bucks, but, dammit, I want to see those flyers."

As Edith sputtered, Henny had efficiently taped a poster to the front of the information desk. She stepped back to judge the effect and opened her purse, pulling out a couple of folded flyers. She thrust them toward Edith.

The paper crackled as Edith scanned the sheets.

Henny hung a second poster by the stairs and stepped out on the front porch to hang another.

"Henny, hey, Henny!" Edith charged onto the porch, the flyers held high. "Now I know why we had a ghost here Monday night!"

∴ *Seven* ∾

THE SIGN, scrawled in huge red letters, was taped next to the doorbell:

DON'T RING
DON'T KNOCK
THIS MEANS YOU

Annie poked her finger toward the doorbell, hesitated. This house on Least Tern Lane was precisely one-half mile east of Sand Dollar Road. The house belonged to Paul Marlow, owner of The Grass Is Green lawn and garden service. And, according to Barb, one sexy dude. A deep-throated bark sounded beyond the closed front door.

The house was built on sturdy wooden pilings, savvy Low Country architecture in anticipation of hurricane storm surges. The wooden front porch had been recently whitewashed. The shutters were painted a bright red, emphasizing the soft gray of the weathered wood. Two wicker chairs with yellow cushions sat near a wicker table. The house presented a smiling, contented face, a place where leisure and quiet were ap-

preciated. The landscaping was sheer beauty, the blaze
of crimson azaleas, the purity of shining white azaleas,
the sweetness of pittosporum and honeysuckle and
gardenia.

Annie's finger hovered near the bell. She looked
away from the sign, stuck her fingertip against the button, heard the shrill buzz.

A clatter sounded to her right.

She looked through a clean windowpane at a darkly
handsome face twisted in a scowl. One hand gripped
the pull cord of wooden blinds. Abruptly, the blinds
fell.

Annie pushed harder on the button.

The front door banged open. He shoved the screen
door, stalked outside to glare at her. He was a little over
medium height, lean, muscular and definitely a hunk.
His blue work shirt was neatly pressed, his jeans un-
belted and worn low on slim hips. Dark eyes glared at
her. "You can't read, lady?"

Annie wished she were anywhere other than where
she stood—on a freighter steaming into Malta, an expedition up Mount Everest, a hog farm, anywhere.
She'd known this was going to be hard, but she'd not
realized how hard. "Mr. Marlow, I'm Annie Darling."
She thrust a poster at him. "I own the mystery bookstore and I did not put out the flyer listing your house."
And, she thought as she looked into burning eyes, accusing you of adultery. "I want you to know that I had
nothing to do with those flyers."

Marlow jammed his hands into the jeans pockets.
"I've seen the flyers from your store. They look the
same as the ones that . . ." He didn't finish.

She didn't look away from his angry stare. "Some-body took my idea and used it. So we're both victims." She held up her poster with its urgent warning against fakes.

He pulled his hands free, took a deep breath. He stepped toward her, standing so near she could see the slight tic in the muscle of one cheek, smell fresh dirt and grass. He looked deep into her eyes. Gradually, the tightness eased out of his body. He pointed at her poster. "If you didn't do it, who did?"

"That's what I want to find out." Annie tucked the poster under her arm. "I'm hoping you will help me."

"If I find out"—he stared at Annie, his face bleak and cold—"I'll kill him." The words hung in the soft spring air, ugly words on a lovely day. He took a step toward her. "I've got to find out. Do you know what this has done to—" He stopped, pressed his lips tightly together. "Listen, the flyers are like yours. You must have some idea who could have done it. Somebody in your store, maybe?"

For an instant, Annie felt a tingle of shock. No, it wasn't anyone in her store. But perhaps she should ad-dress the question she intended to ask him. She lis-tened to her own words with an odd intensity. "No, the fake flyers weren't intended to damage me." Oh no, surely they weren't! "But someone wants to cause trouble for the people on the list. Do you have an enemy? Why are you on that list?" It was just another way of asking Laurel's pointed question: Who put you on that list? Who knows enough about you—and your lover's Range Rover—to mark a big black X one-half mile east on Least Tern Lane?

"An enemy . . ." He slowly shook his head. "Why? It doesn't make any sense. And those other people, I don't even know most of them. I did some landscaping for the Littlefields. Yeah, their kid has a red Jeep. But I didn't know the Tower guy. Somebody hates all of us? It doesn't figure. But if I find out . . ." He was turning, yanking open the front door.

Annie took a step after him. "Will you call me if—"

The door slammed, cutting off her words.

"It was exciting while it lasted." Edith flashed a gamine grin. "Ever since Monday night, the intern has refused to stay after dark. My take is she can think of more fun ways to spend an evening." Edith's sardonic gaze mimicked innocence. " 'Mrs. Cummings, I'd just love to be on the evening shift, but it gets so dark out here and I'm on my bike and what would I do if the ghost came back?' "

"Ghost? You mean the boy killed at Secessionville?" Henny knew the old and sad Civil War story about the dark-haired young daughter of the house who hurried late at night to the end of the avenue of live oaks, certain she'd heard hoofbeats and that her lover waited there.

"Not that ghost. Our very own ghost here at the library on Monday night. Flashing lights. An open window on the second floor." Edith snapped for air like a beached fish. "Damn, ever since I quit smoking . . ." She plunged her hand into the pocket of her denim skirt, fished out a handful of bubble gum. As she unwrapped two, popping them in her mouth, she offered a third to Henny.

Henny smiled. "No, thanks. What happened Monday night?"

Gesturing for Henny to follow, Edith sped toward the stairs. On the second floor, she pointed down the hall. "See those windows? They open onto the rear balcony. The second one was wide open Tuesday morning. Nobody admitted leaving it open. Cordelia Whipple . . ." Henny nodded. As a past president of the library board, she and the library's director, Ned Fisher, had dealt several times with Cordelia, who lived in a cabin just past the parking area. Cordelia had strong views about parking, noise and after-hours activity at the library. ". . . called Ned Tuesday morning to say she'd seen lights in the library around eleven o'clock and she'd been promised there would be no night events except for those included in the annual calendar. And Cordelia said further—"

Henny held up her hand. "I've heard it all before."

"Anyway, Ned soothed Cordelia and nobody thought anything about it until we found the window open. We started looking around. Now"—Edith threw open the third door from the stairs—"I can't swear to it, but I thought I left the cover over my monitor. It was tossed on the worktable. Hey"—Edith fluffed her hair until she looked like an excited cockatoo—"wait a minute, wait a minute!"

She dashed to the computer station, flung herself into her chair. Her fingers flew over the keyboard. "Oh, God, if we only had DSL. How long is it going to take this time?" The mutter rose, cut off abruptly. "Okay, okay, here we are. Let me check." She clicked on a window, scrolled down. "Oh." Her tone was awed.

Henny peered over Edith's shoulder at a listing of web sites.

The cursor highlighted www.IslandGazette.com. "This is my computer. I haven't called up the *Gazette* in a couple of months."

Henny understood. "That means somebody else used your computer to go to the *Gazette* site."

"There it is, fourth from the top. And I didn't go to the web site." Edith tapped her fingers near the mouse. "No one on the staff would use my computer without asking. There'd be no point to it anyway. Everyone has a computer. So, not the staff. This room"—she waved her hand—"is off-limits to patrons. Whom does that leave?"

"Monday night's ghost. But Edith, I don't understand why anyone would go to the trouble to sneak into the library just to look up something on the paper's web site."

Edith folded her arms, her bright dark eyes serious and thoughtful. "Oh, I get it, Henny." She pointed at the computer. "That's where all the information came from that was used in the flyers." She pulled the flyers from her pocket, spread them out on the worktable. "Look at this." Edith pointed at the list of clues on the first flyer. "There are stories in the *Gazette* files about the hit-and-run and Jud Hamilton's manslaughter conviction and the deaths of Emma's husband and Laura Fleming, lots of information in lots of stories. But you know what scares me?" She swung toward the computer monitor, her dark eyes intent.

"Getting information from *The Island Gazette* web site?" Henny looked puzzled.

"No. What scares me is, Why did the ghost go to the trouble and effort to come here? After all, Cordelia could have called the police." Edith tugged at a sprig of hair, wrinkled her face in thought. "You see, the person who did this must be really computer-savvy, smart enough to know that the computer used would always contain the information on its hard drive that it had been linked to *The Island Gazette* site. Now this person, our Monday-night ghost, obviously knows computers, probably has one both at home and at work. What scares me is, Why was it so important not to have that information on his or her computer?" Edith swept up the flyers from the worktable. "What's going to happen next, Henny?"

My Attic occupied a beautiful brick Georgian house with a glorious view of the harbor. A pleasure boat moved slowly out into the Sound on calm water that glistened in the April sun like polished jade. A flock of royal terns rode high in the sky. Annie breathed deeply, enjoying the mingling of creosote, salt and fish smells.

Carrying two posters, she climbed the creaking wooden steps of the antique shop. An old Flying Red Horse MOBIL sign leaned against a barrel with faded letters: MILLER'S FLOUR, SOUTH CAROLINA'S BEST. Tattered books overflowed a wooden trunk. A sign read: YOUR PICK $1. Annie took a step toward the trunk, forced herself to march to the screen door. She opened it, stepped into dust, must and dimness.

As her eyes adjusted, she had the overpowering feeling of sadness that always swept over her in antique stores. Bits and pieces of long-ago lives jostled each other in disconnected chaos. On a scarred Federal-style table, a toy soldier in Napoleonic uniform, the musket broken off, stared blindly at a little French clock studded with semiprecious stones—garnets and lapis lazuli and carnelian. Some child once played with the toy soldier. Some drawing room was once proud host to the little clock. Some gentleman's study held a shining mahogany table. But the human eyes and hands and hearts that cared for these pieces, as well as all the other relics—tables and chairs and mirrors and clocks and tapestries and china and silver—had long since turned to dust. Now the mute pieces awaited new owners, who in turn would yield their prized possessions to time and death.

The spacious entryway was filled with antiques, and more could be glimpsed in the matching rooms to either side. Near the staircase, a slender teenager in a red-and-white-striped blouse and red capri slacks lounged on a beanbag, oblivious to the opening door. The scarlet-tipped fingers of one hand tapped on a knee.

Annie grinned. The headphones added a nice, young, modern note. As she crossed the foyer, Annie heard the faint *whump-whump-whump* of drums. Hard rock? Hip-hop?

Annie's shadow fell across the heart-pine floor. The girl glanced up. Bronze hair emphasized a milky-white complexion. Slowly she focused on Annie. She pulled off the headphones, pushed up with a fluid grace. The music ended in mid-whump. She had a nice face, although her blue eyes looked uncertain and there was a touch of petulance—perhaps unhappiness?—in the droop of her mouth.

"Hello." Annie spoke normally, but it seemed over-loud in the sudden silence.

"Cut glass and silver are on the second floor. Furniture, toys and china on this floor." A brief, disinterested smile scarcely touched her face. She lifted the headphones.

"Please." Annie turned a poster toward her. "I have a poster I'd like to give you."

"We don't permit solicitations of any sort. Thank you." She didn't even glance at the message and started to turn away.

"Wait a minute." Annie was crisp, holding on to her always volatile temper. All right, maybe the girl wasn't trying to be rude. Maybe she simply didn't give a damn about her job. "Is Mrs. Littlefield here? I need to talk to her."

The girl tossed her hair, gorgeous coppery hair that glistened in a shaft of light through the window. "Mother's not here."

"You're Diane?" Annie stepped closer. "Look, I know your mother will want the posters. Somebody probably picked your family because you live on the road where Bob Tower was killed and they knew you had a red Jeep—"

Diane Littlefield stiffened. Her blue eyes widened. Her face sagged. "Jeep?" Her whisper was so low, Annie barely heard it. Step by step, she backed away. Whirling, she ran to the end of the hall, yanked open a door, slammed it behind her.

Annie followed. But when she turned the handle to the door, it was locked. "Diane?" Annie called out. "Please, I need to talk to you."

There was no answer.

Annie frowned, then propped a poster against the beanbag chair. Outside, a car motor roared. Annie ran to the front door. She stepped onto the porch in time to see a red Jeep careen out of the dusty drive.

Laurel Darling Roethke glanced at her reflection in the windowpane of Confidential Commissions. The blood-red of her crimson blouse was rather startling and, of course, the black slacks fit quite well. She was well aware that the dark colors would attract notice and quite likely evoke head shakes of surprise at such a costume when it was almost April. Laurel smoothed a golden curl. Costume! She must simply remember that her attire reflected her present enthusiasm and in no way betrayed a lack of fashion sense. Not, of course, that it was important to her to be regarded as fashion-able. In a moment of rare self-appraisal, Laurel smiled at her reflection. All right. She genuinely abhorred ap-pearing publicly in unseasonable colors. She must simply lift her chin—her reflection moved in the win-dow—and remember that the ultimate goal was worthy of sacrifice. She took a step toward the door to Max's office, resisted the temptation. Dear Max. No doubt he was striding about the island, purposefully assisting Annie. Wasn't that sweet? Max would be most ap-palled if he knew what his mother was doing. But what Max didn't know . . .

Beaming, Laurel saluted herself in the windowpane and moved gracefully up the boardwalk, sunlight glint-ing on the forked dowsing rod that trailed skull-and-crossbones flags from each tip. Nordic blue eyes staring straight ahead, chiseled features aglow with eagerness, she held out the dowsing rod, calling out, "Billy Bones, where is your treasure?"

Out of the corner of her eye, she noted that she had an audience. She passed several stores, including Death on Demand and the fairly new gift shop, Smuggler's Rest. Laurel lifted her voice, repeating the chant in a husky singsong. What fun!

Henny Brawley hefted the grocery sack onto her hip as she climbed the steep steps to her high porch. Her weathered gray house sat on stilts at the end of a dusty gray road overlooking a magnificent marsh. She had no near neighbors and treasured her splendid solitude. She quietly observed and enjoyed her surroundings, feeling at one with a magical, beautiful and fragile world where a keen ear could hear the crackle of fiddler crabs racing to avoid the incoming tide and a keen eye could spot a marsh hawk plunging down to capture an unwary rabbit.

At the top of the steps, she paused to catch her breath and look over the greening cordgrass sprouting from the dead winter hay. She took a deep breath of the brackish, briny, sulfur-laden air and smiled. As soon as she put up the groceries, she'd fix a glass of iced tea and come out to her porch and emulate Maigret. Although she usually preferred the approach of vigorous detectives—red-haired private eye Desmond Shannon or ever-energetic Perry Mason came to mind—this surely was a good time for reflection.

Her eyes glinted with wry humor. To tell the truth, she didn't at the moment have a plan that called for action of any sort. Annie was talking to those accused in the flyers. Emma was no doubt employing her little gray cells to advantage. But she, Henny, might ace them all. She was rather taken with her idea of emulating Maigret. . . .

Inside the house, the phone rang.

Henny set the sack beside the door and fumbled with her keys. She opened the door and hurried the length of the window-bright room, admiring the sweep of the marsh, the gurgle of the tide as it rolled in. But the phone was silent when she reached the desk. She glanced at the caller ID. Kay Nevis.

Henny put up the groceries, giving Kay time to leave a message if she chose. If not, Henny would give her a ring. Henny fixed the tea, pouring it into a tall tumbler full of ice. She carried the glass with her when she dialed her voice-mail number. There were two messages:

MESSAGE 1: Henny, this is Margaret Maguire. Long time no see. I'm flying my plane down to a show in Florida, stopping over in Savannah tonight. If you can, come in for dinner. I'll be at the hotel from five on. Give me a call at . . .

Smiling, Henny wrote down the number. Maggie Maguire. A redheaded wisp of a girl in 1943, just barely tall enough to qualify for flight training. Still flying, after all these years. Of course Henny would go into Savannah for dinner. Oh dear, tonight was her bridge night. She lifted her shoulders, let them fall. She'd have to call and cancel. They'd simply have to understand and, hopefully, forgive her.

MESSAGE 2: Henny, this is Kay. I can't play bridge tonight. I've already spoken to Dolly and Jane. Sorry.

Henny raised a quizzical brow. Vintage Kay. Brusque. Unapologetic. Oh, well, it cleared the way for Henny to see her old friend. She glanced at her watch. She'd catch the four o'clock ferry, call Maggie on her cell phone.

Henny carried her iced tea onto the porch, settled in a chair, sat very still when she spotted a four-foot-tall wood ibis, its snowy-white plumage made even brighter by its black vulturelike head. The events of the day rippled in her mind—the flyers with their accusations, Annie's efforts to absolve Death on Demand of responsibility, Edith Cummings and her description of an unauthorized intrusion into the library. To use a computer secretly? Edith thought so and she was probably right. It seemed too great a coincidence for the library to be entered and *The Island Gazette* called up on Edith's computer just before the spurious flyers made their appearance. Henny was always suspicious of coincidence. Yes, Edith was quite likely right and her judgment that the intruder was computer-literate made sense.

Computer-literate? So who wasn't these days? Almost everyone Henny knew had a computer, used it to a greater or lesser extent, checking out flight schedules, buying books, doing research. But that information led precisely nowhere.

Henny shook her head. No, what they had to do was focus on the reason for the flyers. Why were they created? When they knew that, they would know every-thing.

Henny ticked off possible reasons on her fingers:

1. To seek justice.
2. To cause trouble for those suspected of crimes of one sort or another.
3. To embarrass Annie.

"Justice." She spoke the word aloud in a musing tone. What kind of person would seek this means of re-opening inquiry into past events?

A very private person. Someone convinced of the righteousness of that course. A person undeterred by the possible ramifications of a scattershot approach.

Henny finished her tea. She shivered, uncertain whether her sudden chill came from the icy drink or from the sun slipping behind a cloud or from a sense of grim purpose not yet achieved.

Annie stepped inside Parotti's and realized she was starving. She glanced at her watch. Almost two. She'd forgotten all about lunch. There were only a few cus-tomers. She walked into the main area, eyes squinting in the dimness.

Ben strode from behind the bar, red face glistening. "You missed him, Annie."

"Captain Joe?" Annie frowned. She'd called *Leisure Moment* and there was no answer and no voice mail. But Barb could always be depended upon. It hadn't taken her more than a quarter hour—Annie had waited with her cell phone on the pier, welcoming the brisk onshore breeze and watching silvery-brown pelicans skim the choppy water—to discover that Captain Joe Wilkins played cards every afternoon at Parotti's Bar and Grill.

"Joe? He's back that way." Ben pointed at an enclave near the bait coolers. "I meant Max. He was here for lunch." At Annie's quick frown, Ben added, "You hungry? I'll bring you a double-decker fried-oyster sandwich."

As he turned away, Annie called after him. "Pack it to go, please, Ben. And lemonade." Some people might take time for luncheon interludes, but others hewed to the course. Clutching her poster, she skirted tourists watching in wide-eyed quiet (verging on horror) as a sunburned fisherman eased a live eel into a bucket. As she passed them, Annie pointed at the departing bucket of eel. "Sharks love 'em." That would give the visitors something to chew on.

The card players were hunched in solemn silence at the farthest table. Annie scanned three intent faces: one long and angular with a droopy silvered mustache; the second wind- and sun-reddened with plump cheeks and a big chin; the third scholarly and severe with watery-blue eyes and a small mouth. Annie noted the white cap at the second place and walked briskly to his side. "Captain Wilkins, I'm—"

A massive hand rose, palm up. He turned over a card. "Blackjack." His florid face exuding satisfaction, he flicked an easy glance at his companions.

"Damn," said Droopy Mustache. He scratched his nose, sighed heavily. "All right. You win. Again." He scrambled to his feet with a frown.

"Regrettable," observed Small Mouth as he picked up a box from the floor.

Captain Wilkins plucked an empty pipe from his pocket, sucked on it contentedly as he gathered up his winnings. Small Mouth clicked the cards into a pile with a practiced hand. Droopy Mustache lowered his head and stalked away.

Annie smiled and held out a poster. "Captain Wilkins—"

Again that broad hand was raised.

Annie gritted her teeth, but tried to maintain her smile.

"Thirty-six bucks. Not bad." He heaved his six-foot-five, two-hundred-and-fifty-pound frame out of the chair. Pale green eyes reminiscent of pond algae focused on her. "What can I do for you, little lady?"

Small Mouth licked a spot of salt from his one-third-full margarita glass and settled back to watch.

"Did you call Mrs. Fleming 'little lady'?" Annie snapped.

His thick lips moved in a cold smile. "She owned the boat. You don't own a damn thing that matters to me." Wilkins took the poster. "As for those flyers, I'll tell you what I told all the people who came to the marina this morning. I don't talk about my employer. Past or present. If you have any questions, check with Mr. Fleming."

Annie stepped close. "But you're the captain of the boat. Mrs. Fleming's safety was your responsibility."

Something moved in those murky green eyes. A glint of anger? "Mrs. Fleming"—his voice grated— "had an accident." He spoke loudly. To convince himself?

Annie asked quietly, "Are you sure?"

He tossed the poster on the table and swung away.

Annie stepped in the big man's path. "All right, I'll talk to Mr. Fleming. I'll tell him you aren't interested in finding out who put out the flyers saying Mrs. Fleming was murdered."

He massaged his florid jaw. "You know who's behind those flyers?"

"Not yet. But I intend to find out. And you can help. And so can Mr. Fleming. Why was *Leisure Moment* listed? Why did somebody think you might know something?"

Wilkins folded his big arms across his chest. "I'll tell you straight, little lady, same thing I told the Coast Guard. Mrs. Fleming liked the bottle a little too much. Sherry." His nose wrinkled. "And no, there wasn't any hard feelings between her and her husband, not that I knew about. That night was like any night." Those murky eyes narrowed. "Pretty heavy swells. A storm was passing by to the east of us. She must have lost her balance. If she cried out, nobody heard her. Mr. Fleming had a group of guests on board. They were dancing in the saloon. He'd said good night to Mrs. Fleming about ten. We didn't know she was gone until he got to their cabin about midnight and she wasn't there. He looked all over for her, and when he didn't find her he came and got me." He lifted his big heavy shoulders, let them fall. "That's all we know. All anyone will ever know." He tilted his head, stared at the poster, reached down and picked it up. "I'll put this by the gangplank. When Mr. Fleming gets back, I'll tell him you tried to help out."

"Gets back?" Annie fell into step with him.

Wilkins was a moment in answering. His murky green eyes were unreadable. "In Bali. He and the new Mrs. Fleming."

Ben came through the swinging door from the kitchen with a carry-out sack.

Annie looked up at the captain's expressionless red face. "The new Mrs. Fleming—was she on *Leisure Moment* the night Laura Fleming fell overboard?"

Wilkins rubbed one cheek. "I believe she was." He stared down at the floor for a moment, then strode away, his heavy steps loud on the wooden floor.

Annie stared after him. He pushed through the front door, taking with him knowledge that he would never share, leaving behind tantalizing questions about the night Laura Fleming died.

Ben passed the jukebox, gave it a whack and "Slow Boat to China" played again. "Here you go, Annie." He handed her the sack.

Annie could feel the warmth of the sandwich through the brown paper. "Thanks, Ben. Put it on our charge." She walked slowly toward the door with food for thought as well as sustenance.

Max leaned against a rough gray piling, cell phone to his ear. The onshore breeze was whipping the Sound into a series of whitecaps. The sun was hidden behind scudding gray clouds. There was a 30 percent chance of afternoon showers in the forecast. Max took a deep breath. He didn't need a forecast to know rain was coming. He could smell it. He listened to message number 36. Annie would be pleased to know the tenor of the calls had changed since morning. Word had spread across the island that the accusatory flyers had no connection to Annie's Whodunit contest. She would especially like one caller's pronouncement: "Listen, Annie, if I find out who put this tripe all over the island, you'll be the first to know. My cousin's uncle's shrimp boat took on water Monday night and barely made it back to the harbor and he saw somebody on a bike tossing stuff around but couldn't see well enough to make out the rider. Somebody in a dark outfit, that was all." Max punched "save." Annie might want to talk to this guy. Now for message 37: "Max, it's me. I've got my cell phone on. Call me when you get this. I'm parked in front of Frank's house."

∿ *Eight* ∿

THE VOLVO WAS parked behind a pine tree, out of sight of the small weathered gray house tucked between the grove of pines and a small lagoon. Annie reached to open the car door, let her hand fall. She stared at the cell phone in her lap, willed it to ring. When it did, she was so startled, it took a moment to grab the phone. "Hello."

"Annie." Max's voice had that special tone that was for her alone, a richness of timbre deeper than music, warmer than sunlight.

She felt such a surge of comfort that all the worry and uneasiness and, yes, looking at the sharp slivers of glass poking up from the car window, tendrils of fear were banished, rolled up in an awkward and ugly ball and thrown into a dark recess of her mind, a mind now flooded by light and peace.

"Oh, Max."

"Love you, too."

She wanted to cling to this moment, but it was as ephemeral as sea foam, as impossible to grasp and hold. She could only say, and she knew he would understand, "I'm glad you called."

"I always will."

Always. Yes, she and Max were for always, whatever the span of time that would be theirs. She knew, no one knew better than she, how precious love was, how hard to find, how terribly difficult to retain. She thought of her father, who had loved her mother well but not wisely enough for their love to last. Now Pudge was having a great adventure in Tibet, but there was no one for him to call and speak to as Max had spoken to her. She and Max shared a love story that should never have happened—the rich indolent good-humored dilettante and the serious quick-tempered striving young bookseller. They'd met in New York, where Max was dabbling in off-Broadway shows and Annie was discovering that her acting talent was that, simply talent. They'd glimpsed each other across a smoky, crowded room, a tall fellow with crinkly blond hair and laughing blue eyes and a slender tanned eager young woman with steady gray eyes and an energy that was evident even when she stood still. They met and both knew that moment marked an end and a beginning. Certain their lives were too disparate—he was rich, she was poor; he played, she worked; he saw life as a joke, she saw life as a quest—Annie had run away, fled from New York to the lovely sea island of Broward's Rock. Max followed and, as he loved to point out whenever possible, he had arrived just in time to save Annie from the toils of the law. Annie was always quick to retort that it was she, with a well-aimed golf ball, who rescued Max from a killer's gun. Their countering claims always ended with fond smiles. And love. Max's love helped Annie open her heart when the father she'd never known came unexpectedly to the island. Max's love gave her strength and purpose every day. And it was his support at this moment that she needed. "I want Frank to know I had nothing to do with the flyers."

The offer was quick. "Want me to come?"

She did want Max with her. But she had to handle her own problems and the ersatz flyers were definitely her problem, one she had almost discharged. She had dealt with everyone accused except Frank. And Emma, of course. "No, it's okay. I'll handle it. Max, will you go home and check on Rachel?" Annie looked at her watch. Almost three. "I've called a half-dozen times and either the line's busy or nobody answers. I've called her cell phone, too." Annie's hand tightened on her own cell phone. Could Rachel truly be sick? Did she need them?

"Don't worry, Annie. She's probably just ignoring the phone or out on the lagoon. It's still a pretty day, though it looks like rain. Will you come home after you talk to Frank?"

"Yes. I shouldn't be long." She pushed away the thought of how bleak Frank's face could be.

"I'll go home and see if Rachel wants to help me whip up a pineapple upside-down cake. We'll have fun." There was utter confidence in his voice. Max believed in fun.

When Annie clicked off the phone and dropped it in her purse, she picked up the poster and slipped out of the car with a happy picture of Max and Rachel in the kitchen, Max with a precise array of ingredients, heated oven, utensils and bowls at the ready, Rachel perched on a kitchen stool, dark eyes eager and adoring. Max was the big brother Rachel had never had, just as Annie had become the sister Rachel had dreamed about.

Thunder rumbled. A big drop splatted on Annie's nose. She broke into a run on the crushed-oyster-shell walk that led to Frank's back door. She hurried around the side of the house to the front, where a covered porch overlooked the lagoon. She clattered up the steps as rain dropped in a silvery curtain over the live oaks and pines, pocked the surface of the dark water. Annie buzzed the front bell, peered at the windows. The blinds were closed tight. She waited a moment, knocked firmly. Damn. Nobody home. She should have known. Frank was a fishing fool. Where were some of his favorite haunts? An engine rumbled. She turned, saw the twin beams of headlights shining dimly through the rain. The garage was a separate structure about twenty yards from the house, but the pickup—she recognized Frank's battered old Ford— stopped near the edge of the walk to the porch. Despite the rain, the driver's window slid down.

"Frank. Frank!" She shouted to be heard above the motor. She could just glimpse his slicker-clad figure behind the wheel. For a long moment, he remained there, his head slowly turning in every direction.

Annie frowned. What was Frank looking for? Not that anyone could see any distance in the rain. And still he sat behind the wheel. Suddenly, a flashlight beam, big and thick and bright, danced toward the shadowy porch, played over her, dropped to the shrubs in front of the porch, returned to blaze on her. Abruptly, the light clicked off, the door slammed. Frank strode the few feet, came up the steps, a canvas creel over one shoulder.

"Annie." His voice sounded familiar and unfamiliar, the soft drawl she'd come to know so well over the years, but with a cool reserve.

"Frank, I didn't put out those flyers." She held up a poster, spotted with raindrops. "I'm going around to see everyone who was mentioned . . ." Her voice trailed off as Frank moved past her to the front door.

He glanced her way. "Over there, Annie." His tone was brusque, an order, not a request. "By the swing."

Annie took two uncertain steps, stopped by the old-fashioned wooden swing and watched, eyes wide.

Frank unlocked the front door, kicked it open, moved swiftly inside in a crouch but not before Annie saw the heavy black revolver in his hand.

It wasn't long before he returned. He no longer carried the creel. She glanced at his right hand, saw it was empty. He still wore the slicker. One pocket bulged. His bony face was unreadable. He carried a man's golf umbrella. "I saw your Volvo out by the pines. I'll walk you to it."

"I want to talk to you, Frank." She held out the poster. "I want you to know—"

"I got some bait at Parotti's. It's okay, Annie. I never thought you put out those other flyers. So come on"—he squinted at the rain, now more of a fine mist—"it's easing up. I'll walk you to your car." Once again, his eyes raked the yard, checked the shrubbery and the pines.

"If you're not mad at me"—she rolled up the poster, slipped it under her arm—"why don't you want me to come inside?"

" 'Cause I'm not mad at you, honey." The distant tone was gone. He was Frank, her uncle Ambrose's best friend, her friend and Max's, a fine and good and decent man. "Come on, we'll talk out there." His voice was low and weary.

He walked a little in front of Annie and she knew he was checking the line of pines. Once he stopped, wheeled, his hand deep in the bulging pocket. A raccoon loped from behind a yaupon holly, stopped, looked quizzically at them, dark eyes curious in his elegant masked face, then turned and plunged into the shrubbery. At the road, Frank looked both ways, then guided Annie to the Volvo. He stared at the broken window. "What's this?"

Annie shrugged, opened the door, resented the glisten of rain on the leather seat. "I've made a lot of people mad today, including the jerk who put out those flyers. Or maybe somebody tossed the brick because I said the other flyers were fakes. Frank"—she reached up and caught his hand—"who put you on that list? Jud Hamilton? A friend of his? Someone in his family?"

Frank's mouth twisted in a tight smile. "I thought about that when I found the flyer in my mailbox. Somebody sure wanted me to see it. And it's a damn funny coincidence."

She slid behind the wheel. "What is?" She wished the light were better, wished she could see Frank's face in the shadow of the brim of his slicker.

"This game somebody's playing, using your contest to hide behind, riling everybody up, setting them on the trail of . . ." He rubbed his nose. "But it's damn odd that Jud Hamilton just got out on parole."

"Frank"—she was eager—"maybe he's the one be-hind this!" Annie realized abruptly that she wished desperately to know the identity of the shadowy figure who had turned her world askew. It would be a huge relief to focus her anger and, even better, to have everyone on the island know without any doubt that Annie wasn't responsible.

The brief shower ended as quickly as it had begun. Frank furled the umbrella and pushed back the hood of his slicker. "No. Jud wouldn't give a damn about those other people. Jud's only interested in me."

There was an undertone to his voice that frightened Annie. She looked at his sagging pocket. "Interested?"

The deeply grooved lines in Frank's face hardened. "Let him come."

She scarcely managed the words. "You know he's coming?"

Frank's eyes made a final survey of the road and the thick tangle of growth beneath the pines. "Yep."

Annie stared into bleak brown eyes. "Jud Hamil-ton's out of prison and he's coming here? Is that why you have the gun? Frank, you've got to call Pete." The police chief would protect Frank.

"You get along home, Annie. I'll tend to my busi-ness." He spoke almost casually, but she heard the anger. And the determination.

"I read the story in *The Island Gazette* about the trial." She tried to hold his gaze. "Jud said he had an alibi when his wife fell down the stairs."

Frank looked away, looked far beyond the road and the pines. "That's what he said." Frank's hand tight-ened on the knob of the umbrella. "He was lying. I found her at the foot of the stairs. Poor little girl, her face all bruised and bloody. He'd knocked out a couple of teeth. Poor little Colleen." Poor little Colleen. It was a lament.

There had been a picture of Colleen Hamilton in *The Island Gazette*, probably a yearbook photograph, a smiling face with big eyes and a delicate chin and laughing lips. Annie had a sudden vision of bruises and blood and broken teeth. It was as if she and Frank were no longer alone. "How did you know her?" She didn't ask whether he'd known Colleen. Annie was already certain of that answer.

"Colleen and my Sue. Happy little girls, playing jacks on the porch after school, practicing for the cheerleading squad. Oh, they didn't get elected, but they had fun. One summer they did so many roundoffs I thought they'd forget how to walk. They were best friends all the way through school, working at Parotti's to save money to go into Savannah and shop. One summer they were lifeguards over to Hilton Head and Colleen's mama worried she'd get too much sun. Too much sun." His voice faded away. His lips folded into a tight line. But it wasn't too much sun that damaged the little girl Frank remembered so well.

"You found her." Annie tried not to think about that moment.

"Somebody in the next house heard her screaming. Called nine-one-one." His hand dropped to the bulging pocket. "I knew what had happened the minute I saw her. Well, I got the sorry bastard. Thought he was smart, fixing up an alibi."

Annie looked into an implacable face. She didn't

bother to ask whether Colleen had accused her husband with her dying breath. She knew the answer as surely as Jud Hamilton, who knew he left a dead woman behind. "How did you break Jud's alibi?"

There might have been a glint of amusement in his cold brown eyes. "Turned out there was some cocaine in Edward Miles's car. But sometimes these things can be worked out."

A fake charge to bust a fake alibi? "Frank—" But she couldn't ask him, couldn't put it into words.

"Go home, Annie. What happens here has nothing to do with you." His voice was tired but firm.

"Frank, I'm going to tell Pete." Surely the police could do something.

"You do what you need to do. I'll do what I need to do." He turned away, then looked over his shoulder. "She was a sweet girl, Annie. Just like you."

Emma Clyde poured gin into a frosted glass, added ice cubes and tonic. She carried the glass to her study, settled in a comfortable chintz chair. She sniffed the drink, smiled, took a sip. She'd spent a productive afternoon. Trying to trace the elusive creator of the fake flyers was almost as much fun as maneuvering Marigold Rembrandt into the right place at the right time in the current manuscript. Emma took an instant to be pleased with both her progress on the new book and the tentative title: *Case of the Curious Catbird*. The telling clue, of course, was the resemblance of the catbird's cry to the mewing of a feline. There was always a telling clue in an Emma Clyde mystery. It was a point of pride to provide that clue. But the structure of the books was no accident, reflecting her conviction that events in life overlap and interlock to an astonishing degree. And by God—her eyes glinted—that overlapping was going to lead to the truth behind the flyers. Emma sipped her drink and smiled. It was a grim, satisfied, confident smile. The creator of the flyers felt secure, hidden in anonymity. Emma had called up and scanned every news story about Bob Tower's hit-and-run, the death of Colleen Hamilton and her husband's conviction, Ricky's accident and Laura Neville Fleming's fall from her yacht. Her efforts made it clear to her that the shadowy figure behind the flyers had indeed revealed himself—or herself—by the choice of information used in the clues. Emma had recorded the most important points. She picked up the legal pad from the side table:

MODUS OPERANDI

1. Quite probably obtained the information for the accusations concerning the deaths of Ricky Morales and Laura Neville Fleming from news reports.
2. Is almost certainly computer-literate. The files of *The Island Gazette* would only be available on the Internet or on computers at the library or at *The Island Gazette* offices.
3. Has lived on Broward's Rock at least sixteen years. [Ricky had fallen—she took pleasure in the verb—from *Marigold's Pleasure* sixteen years ago this coming July 15.]
4. Knows that the Littlefields own a red Jeep.
5. Knows that Paul Marlow is having an affair with a married woman.

6. Knows more than was reported in *The Island Gazette* about the conviction of Jud Hamilton. There has never been public mention of suspicion of wrongdoing regarding Hamilton's conviction.

7. Knows that Ricky had a girlfriend. . . .

Emma stared at the pad, scratched through number 7. No, that could be a guess. She quirked an eyebrow. Actually, it was a very good guess, but that was neither here nor there. Just as what happened the night Ricky died didn't matter because no discussion of his death would ever change the Coast Guard ruling of accidental death. Not without specific evidence, and as no one knew better than she, that evidence did not exist. The same was true in suggesting Laura Fleming's widower might have remarried. That took no special knowledge.

Emma tapped the pad with her pen. All right. There were no links then between herself and Laura Fleming and the author of the flyers. Emma sipped the gin and tonic. It was like drawing a picture by following the numbers. It was impossible to know what the result would be until the picture was complete. The shadowy form was taking shape—computer-literate, islander for many years, and, most important of all, most revealing, someone who knew the Littlefields, Paul Marlow or his lover, and Jud Hamilton, his dead wife or former police chief Frank Saulter.

Emma pushed up from her chair, purple-and-pink caftan swirling. Her face was meditative as she crossed to the wet bar, lifted the decanter and poured gin into her glass. Now, the most important question had yet to be answered: What was the point of the flyers?

*　　*　　*

Annie made up her mind at the last minute and yanked hard on the wheel to turn right into Main Street, the two-block-long area that served as the Broward's Rock business district. Her tires squealed and a piece of glass tinkled and collapsed into the window. She jolted to a stop behind a school bus and waited until the last disembarking passenger had safely crossed and the bus rumbled away, belching smoke. She waved at Betsy Michaelson, a tall, thin girl who liked to spend Saturdays at the Darlings' pool, plaintively telling Rachel how hard the SAT was and how they wouldn't be able to make scores good enough for college, and had Rachel ever thought about picking bananas in Ecuador? Betsy's sentences had a tendency to fade into the ether. She would wave a limp hand. "Or we could march against feeding the porpoises." A forlorn sniff. "I don't think anybody pays for that." A sigh. "Whatever . . ."

The bus turned right and Annie picked up speed. She pulled into a parking space in front of the low-slung cinder-block police station, which sat on a slight rise overlooking the Sound. Out on the green water, a motorboat bucketed past, slapping against the white-caps. A buoy rolled, its mournful bell warning of the freighter that had gone down in a hurricane and the rusted hull a few feet below the surface that posed a hazard to passing ships.

Inside the police station, Annie looked first at the main counter, then down the hall at the door marked CHIEF.

Mavis Cameron, whom Annie had known a lot longer than the new young police chief, looked up from her computer. "Hi, Annie. What can I do for you?" Mavis had a young-old face with sweet eyes that still held remnants of sadness. She'd come to Broward's Rock, an abused wife, seeking safety for her little boy. It was on the island that she met Billy Cameron, the big young policeman who'd welcomed her and her son into his heart. Mavis pushed back her chair, crossed to the counter. "The chief's out right now . . ."

Annie almost asked if Mavis could catch him on his cell phone, but she hesitated. Frank Saulter wasn't going to be pleased by Annie's interference, but Annie couldn't forget that chilling moment when Frank kicked open his own front door and moved in a swift crouch, gun in hand. Annie knew she would never forgive herself if she remained quiet and something happened to Frank. Something? Why not put it into words? Jud Hamilton was out to get Frank. Frank needed protection.

". . . but Billy's here. Could he help?"

Annie felt like hugging Mavis. Of course Billy could help. He'd been one of Frank Saulter's officers when Annie first came to the island. "Yes, please." Dear Billy, six feet three, sandy hair with an unmanageable cowlick, loyal, brave and decent. He wouldn't have a clue what *pukka sahib* meant, but he would be any leader's choice to meet an enemy charge.

Mavis lifted the movable portion of the counter. "I'll get him. He's out in back checking the crime van."

Annie knew where the force kept its two patrol cars, one unmarked sedan and the lone crime van. "That's okay. I'll find him."

"The gate's locked. I'll buzz you out the back door."

Mavis pointed down a long corridor. "Straight down the hall."

The onshore breeze tugged at her skirt as Annie stepped out the back door. The black van was parked in the shade of a live oak by the back fence. The side door of the van was open.

Annie hurried down the steps. "Billy. Billy!"

Billy poked his head out. His huge shoulders dwarfed the opening. He jumped to the ground. "Hi, Annie. You need something?"

She'd known Billy for a long time. When she reached him and stood with her hands in her pockets, the onshore breeze riffling her hair, tugging at her skirt, the words spilled out in a rush. "Billy, I've been at Frank's. You saw that stuff in those flyers about Jud Hamilton and Frank, didn't you? I went to tell Frank I didn't have anything to do with those flyers. And it was scary, Billy. Frank thinks Jud Hamilton is coming after him and Frank's got a gun. I saw it. Billy, you and Pete have to do something."

Billy lifted a big hand, slid the door panel shut. His face closed, too. "Thanks, Annie. We know all about Jud Hamilton." He turned and walked toward the door.

Annie hurried to keep up with his long stride. "What are you going to do?"

He stopped and looked down, his nice face creased in a sad frown. "We'll keep an eye out for Jud. We'll do what we can do."

She was impatient. "Can't you watch Frank? Put a guard at his house?"

Billy kneaded his cheek with a big fist. "Frank didn't ask for help." He looked away from Annie, out at the shining green water, as if seeking an answer that he didn't have.

"Frank has a gun." She didn't try to keep the worry and fear from her voice.

"He has a license." Billy moved toward the steps, opened the back door, held it for her.

"Billy . . ." It was a plea.

"Annie, Jud started down this road a long time ago." Billy's eyes were bleak.

She held her car keys so tight, her hand hurt. "Frank was the chief."

Billy's pleasant face hardened. "He was a good chief. He did his best for everybody all the time. But he's a man, too. He knew Colleen Hamilton. He knew Jud Hamilton hurt his wife and then he killed her. Jud should have gone to jail for life. But they couldn't prove premeditation. And now Jud's out of prison and he's coming after Frank. But you know something, Annie? Frank's mad as a hornet. He's been mad for a long time."

Henny stepped out of her car, moved toward the railing, where she could watch the waves. The ferry pulled away from the dock, leaving the island behind. She wouldn't admit it to anyone, but she felt stymied in her search to solve the mystery of the unauthorized flyers. Maybe her evening in Savannah would give her subconscious time to mull the facts she'd gleaned. Henny was a firm believer in giving the subconscious free rein. Perhaps in the morning she would awake and exclaim, "Voilà!" For now, she was ready for an evening of good company.

She leaned against the railing. Long slow swells rocked *The Miss Jolene* as she hove toward the mainland, now a green smudge on the horizon. *The Miss Jolene,* Ben's new wife. What a lovely tribute. Love and marriage . . . Memories swirled like confetti fluttering after a wedding. Henny remembered Jonathan Wentworth, who had lived and died with gallantry. She had watched his plane crash into the Sound. Dear Jonathan. And she remembered from—oh, so long ago—her husband, Bill, who had not come home from World War II. Just for an instant she was at an officers' club, she and Bill, dancing cheek to cheek to the slow sad strains of "As Time Goes By." Henny smiled. She would talk about Bill tonight in Savannah, almost sixty years after his bomber crashed in a raid over Berlin. He always lived in her mind, slim and young and eager, eyes bright and glowing with love, but it would be a pleasure to say his name. "Bill." She spoke softly. Tonight she would speak of Bill many times. Maggie had known Bill, too, when she and Henny won their wings at Avenger Field in 1943. Henny was glad Maggie had called. They would have a cheerful dinner, talking about old times and new. And it was such good luck that Kay had canceled their bridge game tonight. A tiny frown drew Henny's dark brows together. Kay's absence was certain to irritate the other players, since her message was simply a brusque announcement. Was something wrong? Perhaps she should give Kay a ring tomorrow. Kay, however, would likely tell Henny to count her own sheep or something to that effect. Kay was blunt, direct, strongwilled, uncompromising and a cherished friend.

Henny lifted her face, welcoming the sweep of the wind and the smell of the water, looking forward to dinner with Maggie, dismissing her sense of unease about Kay.

∹ *Nine* ∾

ANNIE LOVED coming home. The dusky lane meandered among live oaks festooned with Spanish moss. She always took pleasure in her first sight of their multilevel sand-toned wooden house, which shimmered with expanses of glass. She punched the automatic opener and drove into the garage and felt complete, for Max's car was there. When she stepped into the utility room, she smelled brown sugar and butter and pineapple. "Max? Rachel?" She hurried into the kitchen and dropped her purse and three posters on a countertop.

Max eased the last pineapple ring into the pan. He wiped his hands on a dishcloth, then stepped toward her, his arms open. "You get caught in the rain?"

"Just a little. Frank walked me to my car." Annie came into his embrace, kissed his cheek that smelled oh-so-nice, and dusted a smudge of flour from his chin. There was so much she wanted to tell him. Most of all, she wanted to share the relief that buoyed her like a giant inner tube on a turbulent river. She'd done what she'd promised to do, made certain that everyone mentioned in those ghastly imitation flyers knew the attacks had not come from her, had no connection to

126

her bookstore. Concern over Frank still nagged like a tooth with an intermittent pain, even though she'd done what she could there, too. But for right now, her personal landscape was sunny again. Except . . . She glanced around the kitchen. "Where's Rachel?"

Max's brows drew into a worried line. "She's upstairs. When I got home, I called for her and there wasn't any answer. I went upstairs and knocked. She wouldn't open her door. And her voice was kind of funny."

Annie took the mixing spoon, dipped into the batter. "Funny?"

Max caught her hand. "Raw eggs."

"Oh, Max." She sighed. "When I was a kid that was the best part of making cookies and cakes."

"Chickens were healthier then. Or something," he added vaguely.

She reluctantly poked the spoon back into the batter. "What did Rachel say?"

"Not much. I asked her to help me make the cake and she said she wasn't hungry." His eyebrows arched. Rachel was little and thin and had the appetite of a longshoreman. "She said she had a headache."

"I'll go see." She hurried across the kitchen, paused in the doorway. "Everything's okay about the flyers. Except—well, I'll tell you later."

Max picked up the mixing bowl, began to pour the rich yellow batter into the pan.

Annie reached the stairs. Sun poured through a floor-to-ceiling window on the stair landing. That was the loveliest aspect of their house—windows that let the sunshine in. Even on a gray, rainy day, the house reached out to the sky.

Annie hurried up the steps and down the hall to Rachel's room. How nice to think of it as Rachel's room. It had simply been the pink guest room until Rachel came to live with them this past Christmas. Rachel moved in after her mother's death, and so had Pudge, Rachel's stepfather and Annie's late-come-but-now-cherished father. Annie smiled contentedly. Rachel and Pudge had enriched this house and her life and Max's. She and Max had urged Pudge to stay with them, but Pudge had grinned his insouciant lilting smile, and said, "You know me. Here a while, then gone. I'd better have my own place. But I'll always come back." His look at Annie was sweet and serious. "I promise." Pudge had moved into Annie's old tree house when the tenant moved out last month. It had been fun for Annie and Rachel to help Pudge redecorate and to hear his pleased exclamations: "Honest to God, it's a tree house! All I have to do is step out the door onto the deck and I'm up in a tree." An island developer had built perhaps a dozen of the sylvan aeries before the town council amended the building code to prohibit construction that encroached on trees. The existing houses, however, were exempt from the new regulation. Rachel adored Pudge's new home and begged for a thick hawser to be attached to a jutting limb so that she could sweep to the ground, à la Jane of the Jungle. Pudge had grinned and said, "We'll see." Rachel suggested twining ivy for new kitchen wallpaper, but Annie pointed out that the sun glancing through leaves already made a lovely shadowy pattern on the cream-colored walls.

Annie was smiling when she knocked on Rachel's

door. "Rachel, it's me." She turned the knob. The door was locked. Annie's smile slipped away. "Rachel?"

"I'm resting." The words wavered.

Annie lifted her hand, touched the ceramic tile they'd put in place at Christmas: RACHEL'S ROOM. Annie's fingertip traced the raised letters. What to do? Should she try to persuade Rachel to let her in? Or should she leave Rachel in peace? Everyone needed an inviolate place. Sometimes it is too painful to share unhappiness with someone who cares, but sometimes a word of love could banish sadness as easily as sun spilling into a dark room transforms gloom to brightness.

Across a span of years Annie suddenly remembered a day when she'd huddled in her room after coming home from school to find the letter turning down her application to the college she'd wanted above all others and her mother's light steps in the hall and the twisting of the locked knob, a pause and her mother calling out in her direct way, "Annie, I need your advice." Annie had opened the door, and after they'd dealt with her mother's problem, Annie handed her the rejection letter. Her mother had read it without expression, then said briskly, "Obviously, it is their loss." It was said with such conviction, such passion, such utter devotion that Annie had laughed in the midst of her tears. Her mother hugged her tightly. "Always remember, honey, when God closes one door, He opens another."

Annie bent closer to Rachel's door. "Rachel, I need your help. Do you know Diane Littlefield?" She'd not planned to say this, heard herself with surprise.

Slow footsteps crossed the room. A click and Rachel opened the door. Her dark curly hair was glossy and pretty, but her face was pale, her eyes huge and forlorn. And curious. An extra large blue T-shirt sagged almost to her knees, exposing only a few inches of white capris. She was barefoot. Her toenails glistened a vivid scarlet. The scent of fingernail polish and the pungency of polish remover mingled with a heavy overlay of a musky perfume.

Annie managed not to wrinkle her nose. Okay, even though Rachel was in the midst of the crisis du jour, she had enough spirit to experiment with beauty aids. All was not lost.

"Diane Littlefield's so freaking boring." Rachel whirled, the big T-shirt flapping. She marched across the room, flung herself onto a wicker couch, looked up at Annie and began to cry.

"Rachel, honey." Annie was into the room and holding the slender girl in her arms.

Rachel's muffled voice ached with pain. "They're all mad at me. Diane's never liked me. I'm not pretty enough and I haven't been here long enough. And she's one of the senior girls. I can't ever go back to school." Rachel pulled away from Annie, sat up straight and still. "Nobody'll have anything to do with me."

"They?" Annie smoothed back a tangle of dark hair.

Rachel lifted her head, peered at Annie out of eyes brimming with tears. "The senior girls. They're mad because of Ben." She sniffed. "You know. I told you Ben asked me to the prom . . ."

Oh yes. Rachel had burst into the house Monday afternoon, her dark eyes glowing. And amazed and proud. She'd grabbed Annie's hand, pulled her into a dance around the kitchen, caroling, "I have a date to the prom and oh, Annie, it's with Ben Bradford!" Now she massaged her temple. ". . . but last night, Christy called . . ."

Annie dredged for a face. Was Christy the tall, sinuous brunette who wore too much lipstick or the tiny bouncy blonde with hair as wiry as a terrier's?

". . . and Christy said the senior girls were passing the word that I was totally nowhere and nobody was going to even speak to me because who did I think I was, getting a date to the big dance with Ben Bradford. I mean, I guess they all think if he isn't going with Meredith, he should take one of them. I mean"—and Rachel's thin face was earnest—"I know the date doesn't mean anything. Ben's the best-looking guy in school. He's president of the senior class and editor of the newspaper." There was awe in her tone. "I got to know him working on the *Blade* . . ."

It was only last month that Rachel had proudly shown Annie and Max her byline on a feature story on the third page of the weekly high school newspaper.

". . . and I guess he asked me because"—she sat up straight, snuggled her knees beneath her chin, looked directly at Annie—"I know about being sad. Because of Mom."

Annie took Rachel's hand, gripped it tightly. Rachel's mom had been brutally killed, and for a while the police had suspected both Rachel and Pudge. That frightful time was past and done, but the loss would never be done. Annie wished she could erase the droop to Rachel's mouth, but no one could restore her mother's life. Annie understood. Her own mother had died when Annie was not much older than Rachel. She knew sadness would always be with Rachel. But along with sadness came kinship with others in trouble.

Annie gave Rachel's hand a squeeze, let loose her grip. "Why is Ben sad?"

"It was last week. I opened the door to the editor's office. I didn't know he was there and I was going to put my story in the in-basket. We still do that," she explained earnestly, "though I e-mailed the file to him, but he likes to see the copy printed out, too. Anyway, I opened the door and I just stood there for a minute. I could tell he was sad. He was looking out the window, but he wasn't really looking. He was resting his head against the glass. I went up and took his hand and held it. He turned around in a minute and his eyes were bright and he said, 'Thanks.' That's all he said and I put my story in the basket and went out. And this week he asked me to the dance." Rachel clasped a throw pillow, rested her chin on the end. "You see, Meredith's dumped him. Meredith Muir. And he's crazy about her. Maybe he's really in love." There was wistfulness and uncertainty in her voice. "And they always seemed so perfect for each other." Rachel popped to her feet, darted to a bookcase. "Look, I'll show you." She flung herself down beside Annie, riffled through the pages of last year's red yearbook. "See." Her finger pointed at one of the informal photos on an activity page, a shot in the gym at an assembly. A boy in a letter jacket stood next to a laughing girl in a cheerleader's uniform. Each held a big trophy. "That was the awards assembly and they got the Outstanding Junior Girl and Outstanding Junior Boy Awards." Ben was tall and husky with a broad open face. The girl was strikingly lovely, long hair and an oval face with wide-spaced eyes. "Why, everybody knew they were in love. See how he's looking at her, not at the trophy?"

Annie almost told her that they all were so far from love, from understanding love, from sharing love. "Rachel . . ." Annie stopped, remembering for an instant what it was like to be that age, when emotions ran fast and hard and deep and how much everything mattered—the hope for love, the pain of slights, the hope for attention, the pain of not belonging. Most of all the pain of not belonging.

"Anyway"—Rachel brushed her dark curls back from her face—"Meredith's not even going to the dance. She told Ben she didn't care about kid stuff. And I was so happy when he asked me because I can't take Mike. You can only go with somebody who's in school now. I mean, they won't let me bring Mike, even though he just graduated a year ago. I hadn't told Mike yet. I think it will be okay with him. But now everything's ruined. If nobody'll speak to me . . ." Her lips trembled.

Annie wished she could wave a magic wand, tell Rachel not to worry. But she knew better than that. This was the kind of episode that could grow like a pus-filled blister, and even if lanced, leave an ugly scar. But Rachel was looking at her with such hope, such confidence.

Maybe, just maybe, there was a means of diversion. "Rachel, the best thing to do is get busy telling every-

body—get on the phone tonight, ask Christy to help—
that Ben's like a big brother to you and he asked you because he knew you couldn't bring Mike." That might
deflect some of the older girls' spleen. "Also you and
Christy need to call a meeting for after school tomorrow."

Rachel looked shocked.

Annie grinned. "No, this isn't about you. But let's
see if you can get everybody at school interested in
finding out—" She stopped, shocked by the realization
that Rachel knew nothing of Annie's day. "Oh, Rachel.
You don't know! Listen, I'm sure if you'd gone to
school, there would have been some of these." Annie
pulled the ever-more-crumpled flyers from her pocket
and handed them to Rachel.

"These look like our flyers." As Rachel scanned the
sheets, her narrow face drew into a tight frown. "Oh
hey, Lily Caldwell's mom drives a Range Rover, a big
blue one. But that doesn't mean she's the one. Gee, this
is terrible."

"Isn't it, though! Of course, it's lots worse for the
people who end up being suspected of one thing or another, but it's bad for me, too. It's obvious the flyers
were deliberately made to look like mine. Somebody
wanted everyone to think these were part of our contest." Annie jammed her fingers through her hair. "Or
maybe not. Maybe my contest just gave the person
who did the flyers the idea and the fact that people
would get mad at me didn't matter. Anyway"—Annie
paced up and down—"this morning"—Annie started
with the skywriting—"there were huge letters spelling
out WHODUNIT"—and recounted Emma's angry arrival at Death on Demand and Pamela Potts's frantic

call from the cemetery and Annie and Max and Emma's foray there—"I grabbed the bullhorn from Chief Garrett and told everybody they were being scammed, that it was all an ugly April-fool joke"—and ended with her determination to visit every person accused in the fake flyers. "So that's where we are."

Rachel rattled the pink flyer. "Diane Littlefield. That's why you asked about Diane. Oh, Annie, she does have a red Jeep."

"I know. I saw her in the Jeep this afternoon." Annie frowned. "She was working at her mother's antique store. Why wasn't she in school?"

"She goes to school half days and works in the afternoons. Lots of kids do that and she doesn't care about school, not really. I mean, she doesn't make good grades, just barely passes. Everybody treats her like she's a big deal because she's"—Rachel carefully folded the flyers—"different. But not"—and her honesty was painful—"different like me. I mean, I'm too skinny and I don't talk like the other girls and I've only lived here a couple of years. It's like Diane's special because she goes to Europe all the time and she's thin like a model and her clothes are always perfect. She's better than everybody. She doesn't have to make good grades. She's going to go to some school in France after she graduates and all the guys are hot for her. Except Ben, and he's been in love with Meredith since they were in fourth grade. That's what Christy told me. Anyway, Diane's special." Rachel flipped open the second flyer, pointed to the cryptic sentence: What happened to the Littlefields' red Jeep? "Is that what you want Christy and me to do, call a meeting and ask

everybody about Diane's Jeep? I don't think Christy
will help me. She won't want to be left out of everything." Rachel's eyes were huge and forlorn. "But I can
do it. I'm not going to have any friends anyway."

"No, no, no." Annie understood in a flash. Rachel
was in despair because she saw her life at school tum-
bling into the misery of ostracism, and yet to help
Annie she was willing to brave the very girls she
feared. "Oh, Rachel, absolutely not." Annie's eyes
shone with love and admiration. "That wouldn't be fair
to Diane. Everything in these flyers may be a lie.
That's not what I have in mind at all. In fact, you can
say you want to help Diane by finding out who's behind the awful flyers. Here's what I'd like for you to
do . . ."

Annie loved the sounds of night, the *who-oo-oo* of
barred owls hunting for unwary cotton rats, the contin-
ual call of the chuck-will's-widow flying low to devour
roaches and moths, the rustle of magnolia leaves. Max
gave a shove and the wooden swing creaked. Annie
rested her head against the curve of his arm and looked
up at the star-spangled sky. The shadows of the palmettos on the deck of the pool were squat and chunky
in the moonlight. The charcoal embers still glowed in
the grill. Annie gave a contented sigh.

Max gave her a squeeze. "Feeling better?"

"Yes." How could she not feel better? Max's outrage
at the smashed window made her feel cherished. Moreover, through her own efforts—and it hadn't been easy
or pleasant to make that circuit of those accused in the
fake flyers—she'd wrested vindication from, at the

least, and perhaps made a good start on vanquishment of, her nemesis, whoever that might be. Annie gave a little chuckle and pointed toward the unshaded window on the second floor that blazed with light. "I checked on Rachel a few minutes ago and she'd only eaten half her hamburger—oh, Max, that was a great hamburger . . ."

Max gave a modest shrug, but he did consider himself to be a world-class hamburger chef, his ground-chuck patties studded with diced Vidalia onions and mild green chilis.

". . . anyway, she was too busy talking on one phone and taking calls on her cell phone and printing out leaflets offering a hundred-dollar reward for the identification of the person who left the fake flyers all over town. Christy told Rachel there were a couple of hundred flyers at the school this morning. And Christy's telling everybody Rachel skipped school today to help me investigate. Rachel said everybody's calling and asking all about it—including the senior girls. And a couple of them are helping organize the meeting tomorrow after school and it's turned into a 'Defend Diane' rally, which is also a plus for Rachel with the senior girls. So—"

"So all's well that ends well." Max bent closer to nuzzle her cheek. His lips were soft and seeking.

"Oh, Max, I hope so." A cloud slid across the moon and it was suddenly darker. An owl hooted. A rustle sounded in the tangle of growth beneath the towering pines. Perhaps a raccoon, smelling the hamburgers, knowing there might be tasty remnants in the garbage. Or perhaps a fox or a cougar. Annie stared into the shadowy night and felt uneasy, but Max's lips were warm and suddenly the world beyond them mattered not at all.

Henny was smiling as she unlocked her front door. A wonderful evening. Old friends were best friends. And Bill had been there with her and Maggie, a part of their memories of the heat and dust and wind in Sweetwater, Texas, the roar of the planes, the fatigue and the fear and the fun, the jukebox with the hits by Glenn Miller and Lena Horne and Rudy Vallee, especially Rudy Vallee's "As Time Goes By." Odd in a way that she still felt like the Henny of so long ago and yet, should she glance in the mirror as she opened the front door, she would see an old woman past eighty, dark hair streaked with silver, lined face, a woman who had lived almost sixty years longer than her young husband. She wasn't the same and yet in a way she would always be the same. Would Bill still love her?

Yes.

Had she spoken aloud or was the swift answer simply in her heart? She closed the door, dropped her purse and keys on the small table beneath the mirror. In the daytime, the mirror reflected the world of the marsh through the bank of windows that ran the length of the long room. Now there was the blink of a tiny red light.

Henny crossed to the kitchen, separated from the living area by a serving counter, and looked at the caller ID. Kay Nevis. Henny stepped out of her low-slung pumps, massaged an instep sore from a long though leisurely after-dinner walk on the Savannah waterfront. Odd. Why would Kay have called again?

Henny picked up the receiver, dialed her voice-mail number, punched in her ID, then 1:

"Henny, this is Kay . . ." The troubled voice trailed off, as if undecided whether to continue.

Henny stepped out of her other shoe, padded to the refrigerator and plunked ice into a tall tumbler. She opened the door, found the apple juice, poured it over the ice.

". . . I can't decide exactly what to do. I've made a stand." A sigh. "It would have been so much easier had I ignored the situation. But I can't do that. And I won't back down. It can be handled without anyone knowing, but if I must make my knowledge public, I will do so. Some actions cannot be countenanced." A deep gong sounded the half hour. "Oh, well, it's getting late. Never mind my call. I'll take care of it. I wish I didn't have to do this. But right is right." A click signaled the end of the connection.

Henny listened to the message again. The call was very unlike Kay, who always knew her own mind and never hesitated to share her convictions, whether or not others agreed. Kay had sounded troubled and worried.

Henny glanced at the clock. Almost eleven. It was too late to call. Whatever it was, it would have to wait until morning.

Laurel picked up her knapsack, which bulged uncomfortably when slung over her shoulders. It contained a 35-mm video camera equipped with the Night Quest 6010 Ultra pocket scope, a versatile, lightweight camera night-lens system that was very efficient in recording nighttime activity in extremely low-light conditions.

Fortunately, there was sufficient moonlight that she should be able to obtain excellent footage when the action began. So far, her evening excursions had been unremarkable except for the startled raccoon near the country-club trash cans and an even more startled amorous couple on a (they thought) deserted beach. She'd been a trifle disappointed that she'd not encountered more people. However, last night she'd driven her motorboat slowly past Gull's Point. She'd worn her miner's hat with the light on—she tucked a strand of golden hair beneath the rim—so she had been clearly visible. When she'd smelled tobacco smoke—it was rather astonishing how many people still smoked, both so bad for them and definitely so apparent and wouldn't one think those engaged in nefarious activities would try hard not to be noticed!—she'd edged the boat next to a rather large hummock and stood in the bow, her outstretched arms holding her rhinestone-studded pink plastic dowsing rods, and called loudly, "I seek treasure stolen from Blackbeard." She'd continued her request—and truly sound carried so beautifully over water, surely not one word was missed by the listener—until the smell of the cigarette was gone and so, very likely, was the smoker.

Laurel glanced at the clock, gave a small yawn. These late-night forays were a bit tiring, but she wouldn't have to do them much longer. Tomorrow night—if Rosa had heard correctly—was the important night. Once that was past, it would be essential to continue the thrice-daily performances with the divining rods for at least a week or two. Then she would announce to the world at large that the divining rods sim-

ply refused to focus on ill-gotten gains, so they were of
no use to Laurel in her search for the booty looted from
Blackbeard by a rather daring associate. On no account
must anyone connect Laurel to the incident she intended to record tomorrow night. That would lead
straight to Rosa. But if all went well, no one—especially not the young and very rich Crawfords, who
lived near Gull's Point on their profits from cocaine—
would ever have any idea that their downfall had anything to do with Laurel and the maid who had worked
at both their house and Laurel's.

Another yawn. Laurel patted her lips with pink-
tipped fingers. Coffee? No, that would keep her awake
upon her return. Oh, well, once she was in her boat and
out on the water, she'd wake up. And, after all, something interesting might occur as she putt-putted around
the island.

Frank Saulter lay quietly on the air mattress across the
room from his bed. In the wash of moonlight, the pillows beneath the sheet looked very much like a sleeping form. Frank was not sleeping. His Smith & Wesson
stainless-steel pistol rested inches from his hand. His
other arm was crooked behind his head. He watched
the shifting shadows as the breeze rustled the magnolia outside the bedroom window. He knew the noises
of the night. He had no doubt he would hear a step on
the porch, the squeak of an opening window or the
smash of glass. Would Jud Hamilton pad as quietly as
a prowling fox? Or would he bull through a window,
glorying in attack?

That Jud would come, Frank was coldly certain. If

not tonight, the next night or the next. Frank touched the hard steel of the gun and looked at the dusky images on the wall. He was justified in defending himself. The images on the wall melded into memories in his mind: Sue in her pink bridesmaid's dress at Colleen's wedding; Colleen dead at the foot of the stairs; Annie's eyes when she said, "But you were the chief of police."

∿ *Ten* ∿

THE MOTORBOAT ROSE and fell in the deep swells. Laurel was far enough offshore to avoid the hummocks, near enough to keep the dark shore in view. The light in the miner's hat cascaded down, bathing her in a gentle glow. She was confident she looked simply fetching in her white middy blouse and black slacks with scarlet piping on the pockets. Her black tennis shoes sported red laces. Surely Blackbeard would have approved. She hummed a sea chantey as she neared Gull's Point. The three-story house that belonged to the Crawfords was quite modern, with an interesting assortment of electronic aerials and dishes. Tonight no lights shone. The Crawfords often entertained, lavish parties with a band from Savannah and catering by the country club. There would be no party tomorrow night, but Laurel was willing to wager—though she was not a betting woman—that there would be a huge party Friday night. How better to distribute bricks of cocaine than an evening of merriment with many off-island guests? Who would note as the band played and guests danced that men moved quietly in the darkness shifting containers into unlocked trunks of cars parked in a shadowy lane?

Laurel idled the motor. She reached inside the backpack in the next seat, pulled out the video cam with its attached nightscope. She looked through the viewfinder and was astonished as always at the clarity of the picture. She frowned. Was that a boat without running lights? How odd. The last vestige of sleepiness fled. She was alert and wary. But it was an outboard, not a cabin cruiser. The boat coming to the Crawfords tomorrow night would be a cabin cruiser that had made the run from Colombia. If this boat had shown running lights, she would never have given it a thought. She pressed the record button and the film whirred.

A thick bright beam from a flashlight blazed, pinning her in a harsh circle of light.

Laurel lowered the video cam, shoved it into the backpack. She held up a hand, squinted against the piercing shaft of light.

The outboard bucketed toward her. A gunshot exploded.

Laurel registered the fact of the gunshot (she'd been a skeet champion at one time) and the dark boat bucketing toward her. Quickly, she clicked off the light on the miner's hat, bent low over the wheel, gunned her motor and sped out into the Sound.

The phone rang. Max flailed upright. He peered at the clock. Three A.M. Three A.M.! Had to be a wrong number. That, or big-time trouble. He fumbled with the receiver.

Annie rolled over on her side, turned on the bedside lamp.

"H'lo." His voice was thick with sleep.

Annie checked the time. "Max, who is it?"

Max held up his hand, blinked as he listened. "Dear boy. I'm so sorry to wake you, but I felt I should. Being shot at, of course, was rather startling."

"Shot at?" Max swung his feet to the floor. "Ma, who's shooting at you?"

"My dear"—there was a hint of impatience—"if I knew, I should be much better equipped to deal with the situation. However, I'm afraid I was clearly visible, so I rather think my house may have been broken into. Possibly not, but if my demise is definitely intended that would surely follow, wouldn't it? I know it's rather late to call, but I wanted to get in touch with you before the police called. In case they should. But that does seem rather likely. At least, to me."

"The police? Are the police after you? Ma, did you shoot somebody?" Max struggled to his feet, began to unbutton his pajama top.

Annie rolled out of bed on his side, stood on tiptoe next to him, trying to hear.

Max held the receiver between them and Laurel's voice flowed into the room. ". . . Dear boy, do listen. I have not shot anyone. Someone shot at me." There was puzzled speculation in her tone.

Max was not reassured. "Where are you?" His voice was grim.

"Oh, here and there. But not at home, of course. That's why I called. Should the police get in touch with you, simply tell them I've gone shopping in Atlanta and will return"—a thoughtful pause—"actually I'm not sure. I have a matter I must see to and it is most unfortunate that this has occurred. Rather a problem, to be honest."

"Ma, wait a minute. Why did somebody shoot at you?" He jammed his hand through his uncombed hair.

"No running lights." Her husky voice hung in the air. "Hmm. That scarcely seems reason enough to shoot an observer. However, I can't worry about that now. In any event, be assured I am fine. Energized, in fact. I must, however, impress upon you"—she was suddenly quite firm and serious—"that it is of critical importance, may I say a matter of life or death, that my name not be associated with the police in any fashion. Absolutely not. Therefore I must insist that you not exhibit any concern to the authorities. Should my house have been entered, you must emphasize how fortunate it is that I am off island. And that"—her usual cheery tone returned—"will take care of that. Now you and Annie get right back to sleep. Ta-ta." The connection ended.

"Ma!" He stared at the receiver.

Annie bolted toward the door. "I'll check the caller ID."

But when they reached the kitchen, Max right behind Annie, and looked at the blinking light, Annie slapped her hands on her hips. "She used her cell phone. She could have called from anywhere."

They looked at each other, faces strained, hair tousled with sleep, and turned to hurry upstairs, both talking at once.

". . . better go and check . . ."

". . . so she's not there. But maybe we'll find out . . ."

Annie flipped open her purse, felt about for her Chap Stick. "Why does she think her house has been broken into?" As she traced her lips, the Ferrari careened out of their drive. "Better slow down a little."

Just as Max braked, a white-tailed buck loped across the road. "Yeah. Annie, I don't get it. She says somebody shot at her and her house may be broken into. Now what's the cause and effect? I mean, I know Laurel's . . ." His voice trailed away. "Wait a minute. Somebody shot at her and she thinks whoever did it will still be out to get her, so her house may be broken into. My God, what do you suppose she's gotten herself into?" He gave a spurt of irritation. "Dammit, why was she so vague?"

Annie didn't bother to answer. If a man didn't know his own mother by now . . . Laurel was a grand master of vagueness, misdirection and obfuscation. There was always, of course, a reason. Not, perhaps, a reason that would suffice for the great majority of rational beings, but a reason.

Annie stared into the pitch-dark gloom of the un-lighted road. The turnoff to Laurel's house was not far, but it would be difficult to see. "Running lights. What did that mean?"

Max's head jerked toward her. "Running lights! Annie, she must have been on the boat. Maybe we should check the marina first."

A siren sounded. Annie pointed up the road. "Look, Max, flashing lights. That's a police car and it's turning onto Laurel's road."

Max gripped the steering wheel and pushed on the accelerator. The Ferrari bolted ahead and careened onto the dusty road only a car length behind the police cruiser. Both cars jolted to a stop in the crushed-oyster-shell driveway in front of Laurel's dark house.

Annie and Max piled out of the Ferrari as the door of the cruiser opened, slammed shut. A burglar alarm wailed from the dark house. A sharp white flashlight beam swung toward them.

"Annie, Max." Billy Cameron hailed them. "The alarm company called us. Did they call you, too?"

Max, true to his legal background as well as his Boy Scout oath, never deliberately lied. Annie found it quite endearing as well as mystifying. She, however, was neither a lawyer nor a Boy Scout. "We got a call, Billy"—certainly that was true and there was no law that she had to identify the caller—"so we came as fast as we could. We'd better check everything out."

Billy rested one hand on his holster. "I'll see. You stay here."

But Annie was starting up the front walk toward the house built high on arched supports. "Probably a squirrel triggered the alarm and Laurel's not here to turn it off. She's shopping in Atlanta."

Max made an inarticulate sound in his throat.

The tension eased from Billy's shoulders. "Oh, she's not home? Okay, I'll take a look around. You and Max wait here."

Annie pointed at the pot of geraniums on the front porch. "There's a key tucked in the middle of the flowers. And the code's 5555. Laurel said 1955 was a very good year." Annie had an inkling that whatever Laurel had enjoyed in 1955 would not be an appropriate topic for dinner-table conversation.

Billy hurried up the broad steps. He shook his head as he fished for the key. He found it, opened the door, and stepped toward the alarm box. The siren stopped in mid-wail.

Max jammed his hands into the pockets of his chinos, paced back and forth by the broad front steps. "Listen, we can't lie to Billy. Somebody shot at Ma."

"Max, she told us to keep quiet about it." Annie moved toward the steps.

Slamming doors marked Billy's progress through the house. In a few minutes his heavy footsteps sounded on the heart-pine floor of the entryway. He poked his head out the front door. "The glass is broken on a patio door and it's open. Nothing's disturbed. I'll look upstairs." The front stairs creaked beneath his weight.

Max started up the front steps.

Annie reached out, gripped his hand. "You heard Laurel—a matter of life or death. Max, she meant it."

Max's unshaven face was drawn with worry. "That's the problem. We need to find her. And the police can look for her." He held the door for Annie. They stepped inside, looked around the charming entryway, the pink-and-white-striped wallpaper, ivy twining from a cut-glass punch bowl on a wrought-iron table, an original oil of a seaside Greek village clinging to a cliff.

Annie squeezed his hand. She kept her voice low. "Max, she's okay. That's why she called. We have to do what she asked. For some reason it is very important that she not be linked with the police."

Max stared up the curving stairs. "Life or death . . . that's what she said." His tone was thoughtful. He took a deep breath. "Okay. We'll play her game—whatever the hell it is. But I wish we had some idea of what she's up to."

Doors banged upstairs.

Max frowned. "Sounds like Billy's slamming into every room. What's he looking for?"

Annie walked to the end of the hall. Billy had left the lights on as he went. The long, cheerful terrace room glowed. The heap of broken glass by the French window was easy to see. The breaking of the glass must have triggered the alarm. Annie frowned. The door was ajar. That meant the intruder, despite the alarm, reached inside to unlock the door. Of course, everyone ignored alarms. Still, it would take enormous coolness or utter desperation to enter a house with a burglar alarm ringing.

Steps thudded in the upper hallway. Billy started down the stairs, stopped when he saw them. "Hey, come on up. Nobody's here, but somebody's made a hell of a mess."

Max took the steps two at a time. Annie was right behind him.

Billy stood by the open door to the bedroom that overlooked the pond. It was Laurel's bedroom, a lovely room with floor-to-ceiling glass doors that opened onto a balcony, a huge canopied bed with ice-blue silk hangings and spread, cream walls, a grass mat on the wooden floor. Billy's big face creased into a heavy frown. "Look at that."

Chairs were overturned. The doors to the balcony flung open, many of the glass panes shattered and cracked. Cosmetics atop the dresser had been swept onto the floor. The torn canopy of the bed hung in shreds. Ugly gashes scored the posters of the French Provincial bed. A machete protruded from the center pillow.

*   *   *

Water slapped against the pilings. Max stared at the empty slip. "So she was out in the boat. Annie, why the hell? In the middle of the night, she was out in the boat. And she's still out somewhere. Where could she have gone—and where is she now?" He glanced at his watch. "My God, it's almost five o'clock."

"She was fine when she called us." But Annie, too, was puzzled.

Max swept the flashlight back and forth. There was nothing to see but the dark water. "Dammit, we should have told Billy."

Annie slipped her arm through his. "Max, she didn't want us to do that. And she's okay, we know that. Yes, somebody tore up her room, but it wasn't anything more than a bully trying to scare her." Or was it? The slashed furnishings argued unsatisfied fury. If Laurel had been there . . . Annie took a deep breath. "Anyway, Laurel was smart enough not to come home. She's lying low. And if we can't find her, Mr. Machete can't find her either." Annie tugged on his arm. "Come on." She smothered a yawn. "Let's go home. There isn't anything else we can do tonight."

As the Ferrari pulled away from the marina, Annie leaned back against the headrest, welcoming the soft sweep of air through the window. Window . . . Tomorrow she'd have to see about her car window. Smashed glass. Smashed glass at Laurel's house, too. Somebody didn't like them very much. Tomorrow . . . It was already tomorrow, the faint tendrils of pink presaging sunrise. But she had to get some sleep. Laurel was probably sleeping like a baby at this very moment.

* * *

Laurel stirred in her sleep. So wonderful to relax for a while. No hurry to get up. Surely there was some coffee in the pantry. And there was the bike in the carport. Not even locked. Dear Pudge. So trusting. And the dock was quite private. There was no reason for anyone to note the presence of the boat. Oh yes, she was secure for the moment. After tonight . . . well, she'd worry about the morrow when it came. She'd spend the day quietly. She'd spotted a raft of mysteries in the living room. Pudge was quite up-to-date in his taste, books by Robert Crais and Harlan Coben and Gar Anthony Haywood. Mysteries—why had that person shot at her? Her eyes opened for an instant. There had to be a reason. But that could wait. The coming night was what mattered. Her eyes closed, she gave a little sigh and slipped into a favorite dream of a darkly handsome man walking toward her across a sparkling expanse of marble while an orchestra played, the violins sighing. He wore a tuxedo with a red cummerbund. Perhaps paisley? And her blue—ice-blue, of course—dress swirled over her silver slippers as she ran to meet him. . . .

Rachel burst into the breakfast room, her cerise backpack dangling from one arm. She darted to a cupboard, opened it. "I'll grab a PowerBar. Got to run to catch the bus." She paused in the doorway, eyes shining. "Annie, you have super ideas. Everything's totally tight. The senior girls are wild about this threat to Diane—and they think I'm like a wizard." She flapped the reward sheets. "See ya." She plunged into the front hall and banged through the door.

Max touched the red line where he'd cut himself while shaving. He looked at Annie, his dark blue eyes somber and weary.

She understood. He didn't have to speak. "Max, Laurel's okay." Annie turned her hands palms-up. "I believe it. I believe"—she heard her words with a sense of surprise—"in Laurel. Yes, she's mixed up in something bad, but she's handling it. We have to trust her and do what she's asked. We have to act like nothing's wrong. We can't run around the island looking for her or acting worried."

Henny Brawley loved having her morning coffee and dish of applesauce on the deck. As she sipped the strong Colombian brew, a female hawk—a little larger and darker than her male counterpart—glided toward the marsh, calling, "Chit, chit, chit." Henny lifted her mug in salute. From one flying lady to another. She finished the coffee, still smiling. What a lovely way to start the day. Through the open window, she heard the chime of her small Dresden clock. Seven o'clock. It was early to call, but she wanted to catch Kay before she left for school.

Henny picked up the portable phone, punched the familiar number. Perhaps she'd drop by school. Have lunch with Kay. It was always pleasant to visit there. It had been a while since she'd substituted. Of course, her area was English and Kay taught social studies and American history. Kay knew more about the New Deal than anyone Henny had ever known. A good teacher. Henny frowned. No answer. Surely Kay hadn't already left? Of course, she may have had a special meeting, some reason to reach school early. Henny clicked off the phone. She stared out at the marsh, not seeing it, hearing once again Kay's troubled voice. Henny pushed back her chair, hurried inside.

Annie poked Max with her elbow. "Smile, smile, smile." They stood in front of the door to Confidential Commissions.

Max forced a grin. "Okay. Can't let down the side."

"Laurel always lands on her feet." And such prettily shod feet. Annie was willing to bet that whatever Laurel's costume of the moment, her shoes would be a perfect match. It was a good thing Annie didn't aspire to stylish greatness. She would never match her mother-in-law.

Max unlocked the door. "Even a cat only has nine lives. But"—now his smile was genuine—"you're right. Besides, she can't have tangled into anything too serious. She probably just hacked a good old boy, ran her boat in front of his, something like that."

So he brought a machete when he came calling? But Annie didn't voice her thought. It was good to see Max relaxing. And in any encounter with the ungodly, as Leslie Charteris's The Saint always dubbed the bad guys, Annie's money would be on Laurel.

Annie felt a rush of happiness. On a sparkling morning such as this—and not even heaven could be lovelier than a sea island—everything had to be fine. After all, Laurel had called to reassure them and no one but they knew she was on the island. By Annie's own energetic efforts, the fake flyers had been thoroughly discredited. What had looked to be sheer social disaster for Rachel was turning into a tour de force that might well win her an elite status at school. And—Annie crossed fingers on both hands—no doubt when she went into Death on Demand, there would be a message that Emma's new books were en route. Buoyed by optimism, Annie stood on tiptoe, kissed Max's cheek.

Instantly, his eyes gleamed. "Hey, maybe we should have lunch at home today."

Her peal of laughter rang across the silent boardwalk. Dear Max. Dear irrepressible, sexy, man-of-one-mind Max. "I'll take it under advisement." She'd never really known what that meant, but it had a nice positive ring. She evaded his seeking hand and hurried up the boardwalk to Death on Demand.

Henny drove a little faster than usual. It wouldn't hurt to go by Kay's house and check on her. She was much younger than Henny, but not young. In fact, Kay planned to retire next year. She would miss teaching. Henny knew that. There was enormous pleasure in seeing a mind thrill to learning, a pleasure unlike any other. And there was also the joy of youth—fresh faces, unquenched spirits, vitality, eagerness. The flip side wasn't so pleasant—sullen resistance to effort of any kind and the darkness of bigotry, the cruelty of rejection, the downward spiral of drugs. Most chilling of all was the uncertainty of what might happen on any given day. No teacher would ever forget Columbine.

As Henny turned into Clapper Rail Lane, a blue Mustang convertible swerved around a curve, narrowly missing Henny's old black Dodge. The driver tossed blond curls, lifted her shoulders, smiled an apology.

The car eased to a stop, as did Henny's Dodge. The driver of the Mustang leaned out her window. "Sorry, Mrs. Brawley. Nobody ever comes this way so early."

"That's okay, Meredith." Henny's voice was warm. She'd substituted in senior English often enough last fall to know that Meredith Muir was a superb student, though there was a hardness in her young eyes that worried Henny. "I'm going to Mrs. Nevis's house. Did you happen to notice if her car's there?"

Meredith brushed back a strand of long blond hair. "Mrs. Nevis's car?" Her face still and thoughtful, Meredith stared at Henny. "Yeah. I think so. Is something wrong?"

Henny wished she'd said nothing. There was no reason to alarm the girl. Obviously, Meredith had picked up on Henny's worry. Meredith had always been empathetic, quick to understand characters and motivation. There was always one in every class who understood the horror of Lady Macbeth's ceaseless hand washing.

Henny forced a smile. "I'm sure everything's all right. She didn't answer when I called a few minutes ago, but she may not have heard the phone."

Meredith glanced at her watch. "Would you like for me to come with you to see?"

Kay surely would not appreciate a delegation that included the student who lived in the house across the marsh. And there was no point in making Meredith late for school. Henny smiled. "No, that's fine. You scoot along. But thank you, Meredith."

When Clapper Rail Lane reached the marsh, it curved north to the Muir house and south to Kay's house. The

Muir house was a rambling three stories with skylights and porches. A long pier led out to the deeper water. A white clapboard cabana overlooked a shamrock-shaped pool. Kay's gray wood house on the other side of the inlet was much more modest, built on stilts, like Henny's, with a deck that overlooked the marsh.

Henny turned left. She'd already spotted Kay's tan Camry on the oyster-shell drive next to the house. Henny pulled up beside the small car. She glanced toward the car as she parked and saw—could not miss seeing—an irregular X, perhaps three inches tall, scratched deeply on the driver's door. Henny sat for a moment, frowning. The defacement had to be deliberate. This was not a careless smash from the door of the next car in a parking lot. Some hand had scratched that X. How ugly . . .

Henny slammed out of her car and the sound was loud and intrusive in the serenity of the marsh. A Louisiana heron, spectacular with its purplish-blue neck and back, white chest and brownish plumes, flapped into the sky. A black anhinga low on a cypress limb dived into the water. As Henny clattered up the wooden front steps, hundreds of fiddler crabs scampered along the mud banks.

It was quiet, so quiet. Henny reached the deck. The front door was ajar.

"Kay? Kay?" Henny pulled open the screen, pushed the door. She stepped inside. Her eyes adjusted to the gloom. "Kay . . ."

Henny reached out, held the doorframe for support.

∻ *Eleven* ∻

"THERE SHE IS!" Annie pointed at the somber figure standing next to the old Dodge. Henny's dark head was bent, her hands plunged deep into the pockets of her coral linen skirt. Her car and a tan Camry were hemmed in by two police cruisers, a paramedic van, and Dr. Burford's old Ford pickup. The caduceus symbol on the rear window was faded, as were the stickers denoting his status as medical examiner and hospital chief of staff.

Max slowed. "There's no place to park." He glanced across the marsh. The tide was out and the marsh mud glistened. Two great white egrets, their plumes shiny white in the morning sun, waded in the shallow water, long yellow bills poking down to snare a seafaring snack.

Annie twisted in her seat. "We can park on the other side of the inlet."

Max put the Ferrari in reverse, stuck his head out the window. When he reached the fork, he turned and drove fast, dust roiling, toward an open area by the pier. He glanced toward the huge yellow house as he jolted to a stop. "Doesn't look like anybody's home. In any event, we aren't in the way here."

Annie was already out of the car and running down the road. She waved. "Henny. Henny!"

Henny's head lifted. She walked swiftly toward them. "Annie, Max." Her face pale and drawn, she reached out, gripped Annie's hand. "Thank you for coming."

"Of course we came." Annie glanced toward the small, attractive, well-kept house. "Would you like for us to take you home? We can get your car later."

"Home?" Henny's tone was absent. "I hadn't thought about getting home. I'd better stay, I think. I've got to call Kay's daughter. Charlotte lives in California. I'll have to help her with everything, the funeral, cleaning the . . . house." Henny took a deep breath. "They're going to"—she paused, pressed her fingers briefly to her lips—"take Kay away in a little while. Dr. Burford said she was shot. They found some cartridge cases. I didn't see those." Henny shuddered. "I found her in the front hall. She was lying on her back. She'd been dead for some time. The blood was dark and thick. I didn't see a gun. I came out to my car and called 911 and you."

The front door opened and attendants maneuvered a laden gurney across the threshold.

Annie slipped her arm around Henny, tried to turn her away as the procession bumped down the steep wooden steps.

Henny stood quite stiff and straight, staring at the covered form.

Annie tugged. "Come on, Henny. You can call from your house."

"No." Dark eyes moved slowly toward Annie. "You don't understand. You've got to talk to Pete."

Annie was startled. The young police chief would be deeply engaged in his investigation. "Henny, Pete won't talk to me. I scarcely knew Kay. I don't know anything that would help him."

Henny grabbed her arm. "Those flyers, Annie. The fake flyers." Her voice was scarcely audible. "They were thrown around the foyer, hundreds of them." Henny loosed her grip. "You've got to talk to Pete."

Emma Clyde glanced at her watch and gave an impatient shrug. "I'm right in the middle of Chapter Seventeen." She paced back and forth, her flaming orange caftan swirling, her stubby-heeled white shoes clicking on the heart-pine floor of Max's office.

Henny's dark eyes flashed. "Very inconvenient of Kay to be murdered when you have a deadline."

"I'm here," Emma snapped. "Though Kay certainly should have expected trouble. Those flyers were designed to upset people."

"I don't believe Kay made those flyers." Henny threw up her hands. "I don't care if the flyers were there. Kay would never do something like that."

"Nice of you to stick up for your friend." Emma's smile was cold. "I knew Kay. She was not a woman who welcomed diversity."

Henny sighed. "True. And untrue. Yes, she had definite values in which she believed, but she was kind and good."

Annie glanced at Max. He was staring moodily at the indoor putting green, hefting a putter in one hand. He wasn't paying any attention to the bickering between Emma and Henny. Annie understood. Pete Garrett was on his way to Confidential Commissions and Max had a decision to make.

Annie took two steps, leaned close. "Don't tell him."

His reply was equally soft. "Ma must have been in the Sound last night. She must have seen the murderer getting away. That's what she said—no running lights."

"But she couldn't identify him." Annie ran her fingers through her hair. "Or her."

Max's eyes were troubled. "Annie, we have to tell Pete. It might make a big difference to know the murderer came by boat."

Annie folded her arms. Her voice was as light as the rustle of cordgrass in the breeze. "We can't. Laurel said it was a matter of life or death."

Max wrapped both hands around the shaft. "What if it's Ma's life?"

Annie recalled Laurel's firm—yes, firm, determined, decisive—tone when she ordered them not in any way to permit her name to be associated with the police. Annie heard the front door to Confidential Commissions open. Barb's voice rose in greeting. "Hi, Chief. They're waiting in Max's office. Go right through there."

Quick, quick, Annie knew she had to be quick. She whispered, "Something's going on. Look, Laurel will be fine. She's . . ." What was the right word for Laurel? Unsquashable? Irrepressible? ". . . unstoppable. And nobody's fool." Laurel had run into trouble and she had gone to earth faster than a marsh rabbit running from a gray fox. "As soon as Pete catches the person who killed Kay, Laurel will be safe. Besides, Pete's okay, but if we told him your mother was out in the Sound near the time of the murder and she refused to say why and she's hiding out ..." Annie watched Max's expressive face, saw worry, uncertainty, and rapid calculation.

Pete Garrett strode through the doorway, Billy Cameron right behind him. Sprigs of wiry blond hair poked from beneath Garrett's cap. His round face gave him the aura of a choirboy, but his blue eyes, though young, were cold and tough. He'd worked hard since taking over from the island's longtime police chief Frank Saulter, but he wasn't their old friend, not like Frank. Annie resented Garrett's brusque manner. Was he compensating for his youth? Or did he have a tendency to bull to a quick conclusion because any hesitancy might be equated with weakness?

Garrett nodded at them. "Appreciate your taking time to meet with me." The words were polite, but his tone was formal. Exceedingly formal.

Billy flipped open a notebook, studied the blank page, avoiding Annie's eyes.

Max frowned, tossed the putter onto the green. "Sure, Pete. Glad to help." He folded his arms, lounged against the end of his desk.

The young police chief marched to Annie, stared down at her, his blue eyes measuring. "You got pretty mad when somebody played a trick with flyers headlined just like the ones from your store."

Annie stood up as tall as her five feet five would allow. "Wait a minute, Pete Garrett. Sure I got mad. I also got busy and took care of it. I made it clear to

everybody on the island—or darn near everybody—
that those flyers had nothing to do with me or my store
or Emma's signing. Are you accusing me of shooting
Mrs. Nevis?"

Garrett folded his arms. His eyes glistened. "How
did you know she was shot?"

"Pete, for heaven's sake"—Henny's tone was dis-
gusted—"I told Annie. I heard what Dr. Burford said.
Now you stop being silly—"

Garrett's neck turned bright red. "There are witnesses all over town who heard Annie say she was
going to find out who put out those flyers. Well, maybe
she did."

"Hold up, Garrett." Max moved toward him.

Henny slapped her hands on her hips and glared.
"Annie never shot anyone. That's absurd."

Barb poked her head in the room. "I've made some
coffee." She edged inside with a tray.

Garrett waved Barb away. "Someone shot Mrs.
Nevis and those flyers in her house make it pretty clear
she's the one who put them all over the island. Where
were you from eleven to one last night, Annie?"

"At home. With me. All night." Max butted up to
Garrett like a baseball manager confronting an umpire.

Annie loved it, but enough was enough. "Down,
Max. It's okay." She gently pulled him away from the
red-faced police chief and looked at Garrett. "I know
you have to talk to everyone, and you're right, I was
hunting for the person who put out those flyers. But I
doubt"—and now her tone was thoughtful—"that I
was searching half as hard as the people accused of
everything from adultery to murder."

Henny slipped off her glasses, dropped them into the pocket of her skirt. "Annie, Pete, you've got to listen to me. This is crazy. Annie didn't shoot Kay. And I don't care how many flyers you found at her house, Kay had nothing to do with them. We were supposed to play bridge last night and she left a message canceling the game, saying she had something she had to attend to. When I got home from Savannah, there was another message. She sounded worried. She said"—Henny frowned in concentration—"that she'd made a stand and she couldn't back down. That has nothing to do with those damn flyers."

"No?" Emma sniffed. "What were those flyers but a very public attack? I think they certainly would qualify as taking a stand."

Henny threw up her hands. "I heard the message. I heard the way she sounded. I'm telling you that she was worried, that she was waiting to receive some kind of assurance about some matter. I'll tell you further that Kay was never devious. She would never have stooped to putting out scurrilous flyers."

"Maybe she didn't see the accusations as scurrilous." Max's voice was gentle. "If she believed everything in them to be true . . ."

"Never." Henny clapped her hands together. "Never."

"To the contrary"—Emma's gravelly voice grated—"she fits my profile perfectly."

Pete Garrett raised a hand. "Mrs. Clyde, I'll get to you if you'll be patient."

Emma simply lifted her voice to its rock-crusher level. "When you study the flyers, it becomes clear to the meanest intelligence . . ."

Annie whispered to Max, "That's us. She, of course, is brilliant."

". . . that no personal knowledge was required to mention the deaths of Ricky Morales or Laura Fleming. At first glance, this would seem to be true also concerning the hit-and-run death of Bob Tower. There is, however, a significant revelation in the second flyer." Emma's bright blue eyes swept from face to face. "The red Jeep." She paused for emphasis. "There was no mention of a search for a red Jeep in any of the public accounts. I checked to be certain. However"— that broad, stubby hand chopped the air—"the second flyer cites a red Jeep belonging to the Littlefield family. That argues personal knowledge on the part of the person who created the flyers."

Annie hesitated, then knew she had to speak. "Diane Littlefield . . ."

Everyone looked at her.

". . . drives a red Jeep. She's a senior in high school."

"Hey." Max's voice was eager. "Bob was hit early in the morning. And he lived on the same road as the Littlefields. What if Diane was on her way to school and going too fast?"

Garrett's face was still several shades too red, but he was busily writing in a small notebook.

"School! There it is. That explains everything." Emma spoke with finality, moved to a nearby chair and picked up her huge white straw purse. "Or almost everything. It particularly explains the inside information necessary for the accusation that Frank Saulter framed Jud Hamilton. Colleen Hamilton was also a teacher."

"Oh my God, so it wasn't a coincidence at all!" Annie exclaimed.

Again every face turned toward her.

"Frank." She looked at the inquiring circle of faces. She didn't want to recount her conversation with Frank and her frightened feeling that Frank was prepared to shoot Jud Hamilton if he came. But . . . "I talked to Frank. He said Jud Hamilton's been paroled. I'll bet people at school knew that." There would be those who remembered Colleen Hamilton and kept up with her family. They would know that Hamilton was now free and they might well have heard whispers about Jud's alibi at the time of Colleen's death.

Emma slung her bag over her shoulder. "Kay fits the bill in every way. She would be able to use a computer to draw up the information about the drownings. She could easily know that Diane Littlefield drives a red Jeep. She certainly knew Colleen and Jud Hamilton." The writer's broad face creased. "The only accusation we can't link to the school is the adultery at Least Tern Lane. However"—she swung toward the doorway to the anteroom—"I'll wager some mother drives a Range Rover."

Annie stared at Emma's retreating back in awe. Damned if the wily writer hadn't scored again. Yes, indeed a mother did. Lily Caldwell's mother, if Rachel was correct.

Emma paused in the doorway. "Obviously, the prime suspects in the murder of Kay"—her cool glance at Annie combined amusement and dismissal—"other than Annie, of course, are the driver of the car that killed Bob Tower or anyone wishing to protect that driver; the resident on Least Tern Lane . . ."

Annie knew it wouldn't take Garrett five minutes to track down Paul Marlow, the very handsome Paul Marlow.

". . . and his lover who drives a Range Rover." She paused, then continued in a clipped voice, "Former police chief Frank Saulter, anyone present on the *Leisure Moment* the night Laura Fleming drowned, and"—her smile was bleak—"*moi*. I will state for the record that I did not shoot Kay. And now I must get back to Chapter Seventeen." Her brisk steps clipped across the anteroom floor. The front door slammed.

"The Range Rover." Annie's voice was reluctant. But Pete needed to know. "Rachel told me that Lily Caldwell's mother drives a Range Rover."

Garrett wrote fast, his face intent.

Barb moved about the room, offering mugs of coffee. Garrett declined.

Henny gripped a mug in one hand and yanked her glasses from her pocket with the other. She used the folded glasses as a pointer. "Someday somebody's going to shoot that odious woman. Of course she shoved her husband off that pretentious yacht. *Marigold's Pleasure.* Why not *Emma's Kingdom*? That's how she sees the world. Arrogant, impossible, infuriating!"

"But smart." Annie cradled the mug in her hands, sniffed. Hmm, a mixture of vanilla and almonds. Barb made wonderful coffee. "Smart as hell." She sipped from the mug, welcomed the old familiar coffee magic. "Thanks, Barb," she called to the secretary.

"You're welcome." Barb smiled as she carried the empty tray out of Max's office.

Max wandered to the indoor putting green, retrieved the putter. He took a swallow of coffee and put the mug on the edge of his desk. "Emma summed it up all right." He looked at Garrett. "It shouldn't be hard to find the murderer. You've got the names or good leads to everyone accused in the flyers. All you have to do is figure out which one doesn't have an alibi."

Annie understood the relief in Max's voice, but would it be that simple? She swept a hand through her hair. "How did the murderer know Kay did the flyers?"

"But she didn't!" Henny plunked her coffee mug on Max's desk and the dark liquid spattered over the rim. "Nobody's listening to me. I don't care what Emma says. Sure, Kay could use a computer and she knew everybody at school. But let me tell you what happened at the library Monday night . . ."

Henny concluded, ". . . it all fits together with the flyers—somebody climbing up to the second floor and getting into the library and using Edith's computer. I can tell you that Kay never climbed up a trellis to the second floor of any building. She had rotator-cuff surgery last fall and there's no way she could have done that." Henny slipped her glasses on, moved to the bookcase behind the desk and grabbed the phone book. She held it out toward Garrett. "Call Edith. She'll tell you."

Garrett tapped his pen on the notepad. "I'll see about that in due time. But maybe Mrs. Nevis got in the library another way. Maybe she had a key."

Henny clapped her hands together. "Of course she

had a key. She was the treasurer of the Friends. And since she had a key, she wouldn't have needed to climb up the trellis."

Garrett's smile was patronizing. "She used her key and opened the window on the second floor to make it look like someone came in that way."

The phone rang. Max leaned across his desk, picked up the receiver. "Confidential Commissions." He listened, nodded. "Yes, she's here. Just a moment." He looked toward Henny. "Charlotte Kendall."

Henny hurried to the desk. "Charlotte. Yes, of course . . ."

Garrett poked the small notebook and pen in a back pocket. He dropped his voice. "I'll be in touch." His glance at Annie still held a soupçon of suspicion. "You won't be leaving the island." It was a command, not a question.

Max glowered. "Garrett, you're out of line."

"Nobody gets special treatment from me." The chief's voice was gruff. "Not you. Not your wife. Not Frank Saulter. Nobody." He gave glare for glare, then walked away.

Annie patted Max's arm. "It's okay."

Henny still held the phone, her face sad. "I know . . . it's a terrible thing . . . you know I want to do everything I can to help. . . ."

The front door slammed. Barb poked her head in Max's office, her good-natured face outraged. "I heard all that. Well, I wouldn't worry about Pete Garrett for long. He's got big-time troubles with the town council. My cousin Alma takes notes for the council secretary. The secretary, Herman Whiteside, is Alma's boss. He owns Whiteside Appliances. Alma got a great deal on a new Kitchen Aid. Anyway, Alma takes everything down and writes up the minutes, but Mr. Whiteside makes her take a lot of stuff out. Anyway, she told me the council members are all mad at Pete Garrett. Mr. Whiteside says there hasn't been a cop downtown for weeks and he wants to know where everyone is. He says they're probably lollygagging around the beach instead of patrolling like they used to. And Mrs. Abernathy's mad because Pete wouldn't let her put up posters for the Methodist Easter Sunrise Service at the police station. Pete told her it was town property and couldn't be used for religious purposes. And Mr. Grady—he's the retired pharmacist—wants the town to buy a speedboat and put up a twenty-four-hour patrol. He claims a guy at the Down and Out. . . ." Annie recognized the name of a bar she'd never visited. It was not, Max said, a place for nice girls. Annie thought this sentiment so enchanting and otherworldly and endearing, she'd never mentioned the place again. ". . . told him there were drugs being run into Broward's Rock on a regular basis." Barb wrinkled her nose. "'Course, how much can you believe from a guy who always smells like bourbon? But that's not in the minutes. My cousin told me Mr. Whiteside—he's a teetotaler—holds his handkerchief to his nose when he has to sit next to Mr. Grady. And Billy Cameron gave Mrs. Jones a ticket for speeding and she wanted Pete to fire Billy and Pete refused. And Mayor Cosgrove wanted his no 'count nephew to have a summer job at the police station and Pete said he'd already promised the job to another boy and the mayor's frosted." Barb took a deep breath. "So Pete better solve this one quick. Any-body want a refill?" She lifted the coffeepot.

Henny replaced the receiver, shook her head at Barb. "No, thanks. I've got to get back to Kay's house. There's so much to do and I told Charlotte I would take care of everything—people to call, the funeral to arrange. I'll pick Charlotte up at the airport tomorrow. She'll get in touch with Kay's brother and sister. Annie, if you'll give me a lift to Kay's . . ."

"I'll drive you." Max pulled his keys from his pocket.

Annie shook her head. "Max, why don't you take us to our house and I'll get my car. It's on the way to the Nevis house. And you know you were going to make some calls." Annie had given him a list of Laurel's friends, making no comment about the fact that the list was 90 percent male. Whatever, as Rachel might say.

"Oh yeah. Those calls." Worry darkened his eyes.

Henny was starting for the door.

Annie fell into step with Max. "Remember, just say you forgot what she had planned today and you thought she'd mentioned . . . whomever."

"Right. I'll take care of it." As they stepped out onto the boardwalk, he murmured, too low for Henny to hear, "Ma's okay. I'm sure she is."

"Eighteen lives," Annie whispered. She gave Max a thumbs-up.

The police van and two cruisers were still parked in front of the Nevis house near Henny's old Dodge and Kay Nevis's Camry. Annie pulled up behind the Dodge. She looked toward the modest frame house.

The red shutters had been recently painted. Pale pink begonias bloomed in a three-foot terra-cotta pot at the top of the steps. A V of pelicans skimmed near the porch. The tide was coming, flooding to the tips of the spartina grass. A motorboat spanked across the mouth of the inlet. "It looks so serene." There was no hint from the outside of the careful investigation under way within.

"Serene. Yes. Kay was a serene woman. Annie, she didn't have anything to do with those flyers." Henny looked toward the Camry. She cleared her throat. "Annie, I want to show you something."

Henny led the way to the Camry. They stopped beside it and Henny pointed at the uneven, ragged X. "Do you think the same person broke your car window?"

Annie felt cold, even though the breeze off the inlet held the faintest hint of warmth. Spring was coming. "I don't know. What do you think it means?"

"Somebody was mad at her." The breeze stirred Henny's dark hair. "We have to find out who did this."

Was defacing a car a predictor of murder? Annie shivered despite the warmth of the sun. She hoped not. "I thought whoever did the fake flyers broke my window because I'd told everyone the flyers were phony. But this . . ." She stared at the ugly scrape. Actually, didn't a scrawled X on Kay Nevis's car suggest anger by one of the persons defamed in the fake flyers?

Annie didn't want to say so, but no matter how difficult it was for Henny to accept, it certainly looked as though Kay Nevis had used Annie's contest as an excuse to go after people of whom she disapproved. The proof seemed ample: the flyers in her house, the connection with the school, now this jagged X. "She was pretty uncompromising, wasn't she?"

"She was"—Henny looked toward the inlet, lovely in the late-morning sunlight—"a moral woman. She expected people to meet their responsibilities." Henny pressed her fingers briefly against her temple. "There's so much I have to do. I must get started. But I can't let Kay go to her grave with everyone believing she's the one behind those flyers." Henny reached out an imploring hand. "You've got to help me, Annie. Look, you've known me for a long time. I'm not sentimental or easily duped by people. Don't you agree?"

Annie stared into tired dark eyes. Henny was smart and quick and kind and funny and clever. She had lived a long and interesting life, which was another way of saying she'd known happiness and heartbreak, good times and bad. She was a world-class mystery reader with all the knowledge and expertise that that suggested. Henny knew human frailties, she knew wickedness, she knew the fruits of the seven deadly sins. Henny, in short, was nobody's fool.

"You are certain." Annie made it a statement, not a question.

Henny's gaze never faltered. "I am certain. As certain as if it were you or Max or Laurel. Even if I found the file for those flyers in your computer, I'd know someone else put it there."

Annie understood that kind of certainty. She knew Henny well enough to know what she would or would not do. When Henny was found unconscious near a murdered club woman, Annie knew her friend was innocent, no matter how appearances might suggest otherwise.

Appearances can deceive. In this instance, information contained in the flyers was accessible at the high school where Kay taught. The flyers had been found in her house. The flyers, if they were true, provided obvious motives for murder. Most damning of all, Kay had been murdered. That was the bedrock, inescapable fact: Kay Nevis had been shot to death in her house.

Annie glanced at the neat, well-kept Nevis house. "Okay, Henny, let's say for a moment that she didn't do those flyers. Don't you see what that means?"

"It means someone wanted her to be blamed—" Henny stopped, shook her head. "Oh no, wait. No. The point was to make it look like Kay wrote the flyers so that when she was killed, it would be obvious someone mentioned in the flyers committed the murder. The point of the flyers wasn't to bring people guilty of one crime or another to justice. The point of the flyers was to make it possible for someone to kill Kay and never be suspected. That means no one accused in the flyers had anything to do with her murder. Annie"—Henny's eyes gleamed—"that has to be what happened! We've got to tell Pete." Slowly, the excitement eased from her face. "He won't believe me, will he?"

"No." Annie's tone was troubled. "You've got to have more than that. Why would anyone kill Kay Nevis?"

Henny's thin face was drawn and weary. "I don't know. That's what's crazy. I've thought and thought. She didn't have any money. Besides, her daughter will inherit what there is and I spoke to her in California this morning. She couldn't have been on the island last night. Anyway, Kay and her daughter were best friends. Kay was planning to go out to San Diego as soon as school was out and she was so excited and happy. All right, there's no money motive, no family motive. Her personal life? She was a widow and not involved with anyone. I would have known." Henny's glance was quick and defiant. "I know, you're thinking that if there were some reason to keep a relationship secret, I might not have known. But you can't have it both ways. She most emphatically would not have engaged in a hidden affair. It's simply impossible. The same qualities that convinced Emma that Kay wrote the flyers are the very qualities that make an adulterous affair unthinkable. I keep saying, not Kay, and I mean every word. Neighbors?" Henny looked across the smooth green water of the marsh. "There's only one other house on this inlet, and I never heard Kay say anything negative about the Muirs, other than the fact that they're off island so much. He's a CPA and he travels all the time. You know Louise Muir, don't you? She does the gardening books and she's all over the South. Louise"—Henny's tone was dry—"never met a plant she didn't adore. Can't say the same for people. Kay said if she'd spent a fraction of the time with her daughter and husband that she spent photographing azaleas, they might have been a happier family. But"— Henny shaded her eyes, studied the big, quiet pink house—"Kay was certainly on good terms with her neighbors. There was no quarrel there. In fact, I know Kay made a special effort to be friendly with Meredith, the daughter. Meredith's a nice girl. I've subbed in a senior English class several times and she's a good student, a pleasant person. So, not the neighbors."

Annie didn't bother to look toward the house. A neighbor across the inlet would not need a motorboat to reach Kay's house. That was the extra fact known only to Annie and Max. And to Laurel, of course. Someone in a motorboat tried to shoot Laurel on the night Kay was killed. On the night, in fact, that Kay was shot to death. That could not be a coincidence. Laurel must have come near a motorboat carrying Kay's killer.

Max was hoping Pete Garrett would quickly solve the murder, then Laurel would be safe.

"If Kay didn't do those flyers . . ." Annie realized two facts at once, two terrifying realities: If Kay Nevis didn't have anything to do with the flyers, Pete Garrett was looking in all the wrong places for a determined, clever and canny murderer and Laurel was in deadly danger. But who had reason to kill Kay? "All right, Henny. You knew Kay Nevis, knew her well. If no one in her family wanted to kill her and if there isn't a secret in her personal life, what's left?"

✧ *Twelve* ✧

ANNIE WALKED FAST. It was her natural gait. Moreover, the faster she walked up the crushed-oyster-shell path, the less time it gave her to think about (a) getting thrown out of Broward's Rock High School, home of the Island Cougars; (b) ending up in jail for messing in a police investigation; and (c) carrying out a brazen plan that depended on chutzpah worthy of Selma Eichler's Manhattan P.I. Desiree Shapiro.

Annie's heart thudded. Why had she ever agreed to do this? But it wasn't simply that Henny was persuasive and an old friend and a woman whom Annie respected. Annie was motivated by a cold edge of fear. Pete was ferreting out everything there was to know about the people accused in the flyers. What if Pete was wrong? What if Kay Nevis had nothing to do with the flyers? What if the teacher's death was, as Henny insisted, orchestrated by the person who created the flyers, thereby providing the subsequent murder investigation with a list of suspects? If that was so, the murderer might go to great lengths to make certain Laurel didn't divulge her knowledge of the boat without running lights.

Annie reached the main walk to the school, an L-shaped, two-story buff brick building. The parking lot was behind her. A soccer field stretched to her left. Built in the fifties, the school looked old-fashioned, not much different from the one Annie had attended in Amarillo, except for the row of palmetto palms and the softly green water of the Sound. Annie had been inside the building several times since Rachel came to live with them. Most recently, she'd helped out for a fund-raiser for the tennis team. The bake sale, used books and collectibles had been in the gym, which made up the short stem of the L.

A circular drive curved in front of the main entrance. Bright red tulips bloomed in a round bed. High in the air, Old Glory and the South Carolina flag rippled sluggishly in the gentle breeze. Annie reached the top of the wide shallow front steps and stopped, staring at the big red doors. She glanced at her watch. Twenty minutes to eleven. Rachel had mentioned there were two lunch periods. Annie was pretty sure she'd arrived before the first one. She took a deep breath, pulled open the door.

A poster sat on a tripod in the vestibule. The message was clear:

ALL VISITORS REPORT
IMMEDIATELY
TO THE OFFICE
Rm. 101

A red arrow pointed to the right.
Annie obediently turned into the hall to her right.

None of her earlier visits to the school had included a stop at the office. At the first door, another poster on a tripod announced: OFFICE.

Annie opened the door, stepped inside. On the other side of a brown wooden counter, three desks were occupied: a bony woman with iron-gray hair peered intently at a computer, a faded redhead flicked through a stack of cards and a plump, round-faced woman with mounds of dark curly hair tapped her desk with a pen while she listened on the phone. There were several offices on either side of the open work area. Nameplates were attached to the doors.

Annie remembered Henny's instructions: ". . . decent guy . . . treats women with great courtesy . . . don't hesitate to ask for help . . . big on family . . . let him see you're stressed . . ."

Annie had no difficulty looking stressed. She was there under totally false pretenses, despite Henny's assurances that Kay's daughter had given Henny carte blanche and Henny was deputizing Annie. As Henny saw it, all Annie had to do was announce she represented Kay's family and everything would be easy.

Annie cleared her throat. It was easy to fall off the Empire State Building if you climbed over the guardrails and jumped from a parapet. "Hello."

The plump woman looked up, smiled, waved her pen at the redhead. "Janine, will you help her?"

The slender redhead gave Annie a languid glance. "Yes?"

"I wonder if I might speak with Dr. Allensworth?" There, she'd done it, asked to see the principal. Annie was committed now to playing out the charade that she was at the school on behalf of Kay's daughter. "Mrs. Nevis's daughter asked me to come." Annie was so immersed in her effort that it took her a moment to realize all three women were staring at her.

The dark-haired woman tugged on a curl, spoke rapidly into the phone: "Yes. Please tell Mrs. Thornton that the high school called about her son's absences. Please ask her to call us at her earliest convenience. Thank you." And she plopped down the receiver and pushed back her chair. "Is something wrong with Mrs. Nevis? We called the house this morning when she didn't arrive, but there wasn't any answer. I left a message."

It had never occurred to Annie that the school didn't yet know about Kay's death. Annie had assumed the police would have been to the school. Perhaps that would yet take place. But Kay Nevis died at her home and the investigation was focused there. The fact that the school hadn't been contacted was simply more proof that the investigation was directed toward the people accused in the flyers. Henny was not only confident that Kay had nothing to do with the flyers, Henny believed the creator of the flyers was quite likely someone at the school and that Kay's murder must have grown out of some incident at school. Henny had put it somberly, "School was her life, Annie. That's where she spent most of her time. She had no family on the island. She lived on an isolated inlet. The answer has to lie at school. And we've got to find it."

Right this minute Annie scrambled for an answer to the secretary's question. Annie couldn't simply announce that a teacher well known to these women had been shot to death.

The round-faced woman, who had a face made for laughter and good times, slowly rose, walked heavily toward the counter. "Something's happened, hasn't it? Something bad."

Annie's hand tightened on the strap of her shoulder bag. "I'd better—please, I should speak with Dr. Allensworth."

In the silence, Annie was terribly aware of the worried faces turned toward her. The secretary swung about, hurried to the principal's door. In the tense silence, the sound of the knock was shocking. She opened the door. "Dr. Allensworth. There's a woman here to see you. Something's happened to Mrs. Nevis."

The gray-haired woman, her dark face creased with concern, hurried from her desk to open the gate at the end of the counter. She stood aside for Annie.

When Annie reached the open doorway, Gerald Allensworth was coming around his desk, a tall, angular black man with a narrow, sensitive face. He was a little over six feet tall and fence-rail thin, his gray suit coat loose on his shoulders, his trousers flapping around his ankles. He pushed horn-rim glasses higher on a bony nose above a thin black mustache flecked with silver. "Is there illness? This is most irregular. Someone should have called."

"Dr. Allensworth." Annie stepped inside, pulled the door shut. "I'm Annie Darling." Annie didn't give him a chance to respond. She wanted this moment over with. "Mrs. Nevis's daughter asked me to come. I have bad news. Mrs. Nevis was shot to death last night at her house. The police are looking for the murderer."

And so am I, she thought. But you aren't to know

that. Annie didn't know what to do or say next. She hoped for inspiration and wished her heart would stop pounding as if she'd run a race.

Allensworth lifted long, thin hands as if in protest. He stared at her in disbelief.

"I'm sorry," she said awkwardly.

He fumbled to pull a chair closer to his desk, gestured toward it, then walked slowly to his chair, sank into it, his face stricken. "Kay's dead? Murdered?"

"I'm sorry." Annie perched on the hard edge of the yellow oak chair. "It happened last night. Henny Brawley found her body this morning. Henny's spoken with Mrs. Nevis's daughter, Charlotte. Henny is handling everything until Charlotte arrives. She's flying in tomorrow. I've been asked to talk to you, to ask for your help." It was scary how a little piece of truth could be stretched like taffy on a warm day. Or like a rope pulled from a coil. Annie envisioned a noose dangling above her head, pushed the thought away, hurried to speak while Gerald Allensworth was in a state of shock and unlikely to question her status. "The memorial service is scheduled for Monday. If you could direct me to the teachers who knew Kay the best . . ." She let her voice trail away.

"Oh, of course. I'll be glad to help." He sat up a little straighter in his chair. "I would be proud to speak on behalf of Broward's Rock High School. I've known Kay for almost thirty years. A fine woman. A caring teacher. A woman of high moral principle who always met her responsibilities."

Annie wondered what he would think of the possibility that Kay had authored the scurrilous flyers. Perhaps that question could be asked later. She smiled. "The family will be honored to have you as a speaker. Could you suggest one or more of the teachers who knew her well?"

Allensworth picked up a paperweight, turned it over and over, the leaping cougar within appearing to fly through sea-green space. "Possibly Mrs. Riley, who teaches art. And Mrs. Thompson, algebra. But"—he frowned—"we need to have an assembly. The students mustn't learn of this terrible tragedy through the media. And I need to speak with someone in authority. I don't understand why I haven't been contacted." Frowning, he placed the crystal weight on the desk and flipped open his Rolodex, found a card. He picked up the phone, punched a number. "Gerald Allensworth here. Broward's Rock High School. To whom am I speaking?" He listened. "Oh, hello, Billy"—Allensworth's voice was friendly. Had Billy been a favorite student?— "May I speak with the officer in charge of the investigation into the death of Kay Nevis? Oh, I see. Will you ask him to call me, please? We had not been informed of this dreadful occurrence. I wish to confirm the information I've received . . . oh, a representative of the family is here to make plans for the memorial service . . ."

Annie managed to keep a look of pleasant interest on her face. If only Allensworth didn't feel compelled to identify that representative. She didn't like to envision Pete Garrett's expression if he learned Annie was at the school.

". . . and I intend to call an assembly to inform our faculty and students. Can you please give me the details about Mrs. Nevis's death?"

Annie wished she could hear what Billy was saying.

Allensworth picked up a pen, began to make notes, muttering as he listened ". . . No evidence of a break-in . . . died as a result of several gunshot wounds . . . believed to have occurred between ten P.M. and two A.M. . . . Investigation is continuing. . . . Oh yes, of course, I'll be glad to make that request." He glanced at his wristwatch. "I'll call an assembly at two o'clock and ask anyone with information concerning her death to contact the police department. . . . Yes, of course I will do that. . . . Problem here at school? Absolutely not, Billy. Kay got along well with both faculty and students and certainly had no enemies here. I'm quite certain of that. I know all of us will do everything we can to help in the investigation. Don't hesitate to call on us. . . . Yes, Billy, thank you. And I'll expect to hear from Chief Garrett." Allensworth was frowning as he hung up.

Annie scooted the heavy chair forward. The legs screeched against the floor. "Trouble at school—that's one reason I came, Dr. Allensworth. We know Kay was upset about something here at school—"

Allensworth's pointed chin jutted forward, his thin shoulders stiffened. "That seems highly unlikely. Kay would surely have spoken with me had there been a serious problem. And we don't have the kind of problems . . ." His voice trailed away. His gaze dropped to his desk.

Once that might have been true. Schools in the not too distant past had been havens of safety and rationality and order. No more. And no one knew that better than the principal.

The blinds were closed behind Allensworth, probably because the sunlight would put a glare on the computer screen that sat to the right of his desk. He was computer-literate, a graceless term that everyone in the new century understood. Computer-literate—Emma Clyde saw that as another black mark against Kay. Everyone in a high school knew computers. Even more damning was the information in the flyers that seemed clearly linked to the school: the red Jeep that may have killed Bob Tower, the sad death of Colleen Hamilton.

Colleen Hamilton. Always a creature of impulse, Annie blurted, "I suppose Kay was worried about Jud Hamilton's parole."

Allensworth's thin fingers brushed at his mustache. "All of us were worried. I don't know what we'll do if he shows up here. He's a violent man. But that can't have anything to do with Kay's death. She and Colleen weren't close. Jud wouldn't have any reason to be angry with her." There was the faintest emphasis on the pronoun.

Annie spoke in a matter-of-fact tone. "No. I guess he's mad at Chief Saulter."

"That's what they say," Allensworth agreed. "Amy Mendoza—she teaches biology—was close to Colleen. Amy said the fellow who claimed to be with Jud, then changed his testimony, was telling everyone there wasn't any cocaine in his car. I don't know the ins and outs of it . . ."

Annie heard the faint regret in his voice. Gerald Allensworth struck her as a man eager to know everything about those around him. But obviously those at the school knew a great deal more about the background to Jud Hamilton's conviction than had been reported in *The Island Gazette*.

". . . but that can't have anything to do with Kay's death. Murder . . ." His voice wavered.

"Yes, it's terrible." Annie stood. "I want you to know that the family appreciates your help. Now, I'd like to find Mrs. Riley and Mrs. Thompson."

He pushed back his chair, came around the desk. "Mrs. Jenkins will get you a hall pass and I'll have her show you to the rooms. You'll let us know when the service is set?"

"Yes, of course. At the assembly, please announce that services are pending and there will be an announcement in *The Island Gazette*." Annie reached out, shook hands.

As they stepped out into the office, three strained faces turned toward them. Allensworth cleared his throat. "I'm sorry to have to tell you that Mrs. Nevis was shot to death in her house last night. The police are investigating." He inclined his head toward Annie. "Mrs. Darling is here for Mrs. Nevis's family. They are in the process of arranging the service. Mrs. Jenkins"—he glanced at the pale redhead—"please issue Mrs. Darling a visitor's pass. I would appreciate it if you will show her to Mrs. Riley's room and Mrs. Thompson's. Mrs. Otis"—he nodded at the round-faced woman, whose fingers plucked at the silver chain around her neck—"there will be an assembly at two o'clock. Required attendance. I will announce the assembly during first lunch period."

"Yes, sir." She shook her dark hair, cut her eyes toward Annie, large, scared, saddened eyes.

Annie hurried to the redhead's desk.

Mrs. Jenkins picked up a red felt pen. "Your name, please?"

"Annie Darling."

The redhead printed the name in all capital letters on a small rectangular white card, slipped it into a plastic holder with a clip on the back, handed it to Annie.

Annie took the holder, clipped it to her blouse. "Thank you. Now, perhaps we can go."

"Mrs. Darling." Allensworth pulled off his glasses, gestured toward the hall. "We have a substitute in Mrs. Nevis's room. However, I can ask the class to move to the library if you wish to clean out Kay's desk."

"Her desk?" Annie had a quick memory of the late Cubs baseball broadcaster Harry Carey warning a pitcher against the opposing team's slugger when the bases were loaded, "Be careful here. Be careful here." She nodded judiciously. "That's a very good idea. But perhaps we'd better leave the desk unchanged until the police have had a chance to check everything. However, I'd be glad to take a quick inventory and give that to the family." How could Pete Garrett complain? Annie felt suffused with righteousness.

Allensworth nodded his approval. "That's a good idea. Mrs. Jenkins, please ask the substitute to take the class to the library. Mrs. Darling can inventory the desk, then meet with Mrs. Riley and Mrs. Thompson. And I"—he drew a deep breath—"shall prepare for the assembly."

As the students trooped out of Kay Nevis's classroom, a long-legged blonde in a cerise T-shirt and white shorts leaned close to Annie. "I'll tell Rachel you're here. Everybody's coming to the meeting after school." She was gone before Annie could answer. Annie decided the girl had to be Christy. The plan to enlist students to seek out the creator of the flyers now seemed like an innocent hope from another world. Annie would have to find Rachel, cancel that gathering. Annie had a gut-deep sense she didn't want any students poking into the mystery of the flyers. As for the flyers found in Kay's house, maybe the police would keep that quiet. It certainly wasn't information Annie intended to provide. Annie felt a flicker of anger. If Henny was right, Kay's murderer wanted to destroy both her life and her reputation. If Henny was right . . .

As the last student left the classroom, Mrs. Jenkins held the door for Annie. She stepped into the classroom, noting the open windows with a view of the marsh and a long pier that led out to a deeper channel. There was a red boathouse at the end of the pier.

A bell rang.

"Oh, first-period lunch." Mrs. Jenkins pointed at the golden oak desk. "There's her desk. I brought a master key for the locked drawers. Mrs. Riley's room, 126, is two doors down this hall. Mrs. Thompson is upstairs in room 203. But they both have first-period lunch, so they won't be in their rooms until noon. If you need anything else, you can come to the cafeteria or back to the office."

As the door closed behind her, Annie walked slowly toward the desk. *Be careful here*. She stopped behind the desk. Oh hell, she was here. She wouldn't touch anything. She'd tell Pete Garrett all she'd done was look and note the contents of the desk. What could he do about that? Put her in jail? Maybe she didn't want to know the answer to the second question.

Annie glanced around the room and felt for a moment as though she'd stepped into the company of distinguished ghosts. Famous faces from twentieth-century America looked down from the walls: Theodore Roosevelt, Charles Lindbergh, Amelia Earhart, Franklin Roosevelt, Eleanor Roosevelt, Jackie Robinson, Dwight D. Eisenhower, Martin Luther King, Jimmy Carter. Real faces, real people, real lives. Had Kay Nevis talked about the good that can be achieved by one life well lived?

Annie's gaze returned to the desk. A single pink carnation poked from a bud vase. A yellow porcelain frame held an eight-by-ten snapshot of a family on horseback: a dark-haired woman in her thirties, a chunky balding man with a ready grin and three teenage girls. A green leather appointment book lay next to an onyx pen set. An in-box brimmed with sheets of written-upon notebook paper. Annie bent to look at the title emblazoned in green ink on the top sheet: "Contrast the characters of Douglas MacArthur and George C. Marshall."

Annie reached into her purse for a pen. She used the pen to flip open the appointment book. She scanned the pages, noting the usual appointments—dentist, bridge games, Saturday lunch dates—but there was no hint of anything odd or unusual. Annie unlocked the center drawer: grade books, pencils, note cards, reading lists, a vial of prescription medicine. The side drawers held thick files, the tabs indicating subjects.

Annie glanced at a few of the tabs: "The Civil War Experience for Women in South Carolina," "The Influence of Yellow Journalism on American Political Decisions in the Early 1900s," "Roosevelt's New Deal and Huey Long," "Isolationism and the Beginning of World War II."

Annie pushed shut the last drawer. If there was anything here that pertained to murder, Annie had missed it. She dropped the desk key in her purse, glanced at her watch. Kay's best friends on the faculty were in the lunchroom. Rachel had first-period lunch. Maybe Annie could find her and Rachel could point out Mrs. Thompson and Mrs. Riley.

Max clicked off the portable phone, placed it on the countertop. He bent down, nuzzled thick white fur. Dorothy L.'s blue eyes looked at him curiously. Max picked up the plump cat, who ducked her head beneath his chin and began to purr. "Yeah, yeah, I know. I'm your favorite guy and where's the chopped liver." Max carried Dorothy L. with him to a cupboard. He plucked out a can of cat food—salmon, Dorothy L.'s favorite—opened it. He put the cat down by her bowl, emptied the can, gave her a final pat. He frowned as he glanced across the kitchen at the silent phone. Nobody—not a single one of his mother's friends—had heard from Laurel or knew where she was. Laurel, of course, could be ensconced at a friend's house and have sworn that person to secrecy. But Max didn't think so.

Absentmindedly, he made a sandwich—watercress, whipped cream cheese, lox, capers on a bagel. He held fast to one fact: Laurel had called, told him she was all right. Where was she now? The empty slip at the marina told him she had docked the motorboat elsewhere, quite likely tying it up to a remote dock on one of the curling waterways that meandered through the marshes. That must mean she intended another foray in the boat. But why and where? And what the hell had she been doing near the inlet where Kay Nevis died? Max took a bite of the sandwich, hurried into the terrace room. They had a map of the island in the desk. Maybe if he studied it . . .

The hum of voices was even louder than the bang of trays and the scrape of chairs. Rachel said loudly, "Do you want a hot dog or hamburger or pizza?" Her hand swept toward the food islands. Rachel didn't even bother to suggest the salad bar.

Annie felt chagrined. After all, she should be a role model. Rachel would certainly have pointed out the salad bar to Max. "Hmm, how about a salad?" After all, there would be olives and cheese and maybe even bacon bits to add a little substance. She was suddenly ravenous.

"Sure. The honey-mustard dressing's great." Rachel, her thin face eager and cheerful, waved hello to friends as she and Annie pushed their trays, filled plastic bowls with spinach leaves, endive, shaved carrots, celery, cherry tomatoes, radishes and pecans. Annie almost added bacon bits, decided that was overkill and certainly not worthy of a role model. She did pick up a poppy-seed muffin. So hey, she wasn't perfect.

Rachel leaned close. "Do you want to eat out on the terrace?"

Annie glanced around the red-walled cafeteria, which smelled like food, disinfectant and varnish. A long table near the hot-food line was filled with teachers. Annie jerked her head in that direction. "I see a table up front."

When they were settled, not more than fifteen feet from the teachers, Annie glanced at the table. Three women ranging in age from early twenties to late fifties sat on one side, two men and an uncommonly pretty young woman on the other. "Do you know Mrs. Thompson and Mrs. Riley?"

Rachel snapped the tab from her can of Pepsi. "Mrs. Thompson looks like a mouse. We call her Minnie. Mrs. Riley's the one with orange hair piled on top of her head and long dangly earrings."

Annie smiled. A small black woman ate with quick, dainty—mouselike?—bites. Her gray hair was drawn into a bun, emphasizing her sharp features. She wore a plain white blouse with her gray suit. Her jewelry was simple, a pair of small silver earrings and a silver brooch. She was absorbed in a paperback book. Two chairs down, Mrs. Riley gestured dramatically, long red fingernails flashing in the air. Her face beneath the mound of bright hair was large and amiable. Her fringed eyelashes were heavy with mascara. Bright spots of red decorated plump cheeks. An orange pattern—leaping fish?—spangled her purple silk dress.

Annie made her decision on the spot. There was an air of reserve to Mrs. Thompson. She would talk to Mrs. Riley first. "I understand Mrs. Thompson and Mrs. Riley were good friends of Mrs. Nevis's."

Rachel didn't note the tense. She nodded as she

stirred the dressing into her salad. "Yeah. I guess so. Anyway, Annie, we've got everybody excited about the flyers. Everybody's really mad that the police would suspect Diane."

Annie hated to tell her, but knew she must. "Rachel, listen . . ." She explained that Kay had been murdered.

Rachel pushed her salad away. Tears welled in her eyes. "Mrs. Nevis—Annie, that's awful. She was really nice."

"There's one thing more. And Rachel, you mustn't tell anyone about this." Annie glanced around, spoke so only Rachel could hear. "There were boxes of the flyers in her house."

Rachel's eyes widened. "Mrs. Nevis! I don't believe it."

Annie took a bite of salad. "I know. Henny insists she would never have done anything like that. Henny says someone else must have put out the flyers. Henny's convinced it has to be someone connected to the school. Anyway, you've got to cancel the meeting this afternoon." The salad was fresh and crisp. Annie ate quickly.

Ignoring her lunch, Rachel hitched her chair closer to the table, planted her elbows. "Wait a minute, Annie, wait a minute. No, we'll tell everybody that Mrs. Nevis's been framed—"

Annie put down her fork and reached across the table to grab Rachel's arm. "Definitely not. We don't want anyone to know about the flyers in her house. If that gets out, her reputation's smeared even if we ultimately figure out who did it." Annie scrambled for a plan to deflect Rachel. No way could she tell Rachel there might be danger for anyone nosing into the history of the flyers. Annie remembered that age well enough to know the possibility of danger would simply be an attraction. "No, we need to get everybody's attention away from those damn flyers. Say that you've received information and you can't reveal your source . . ."

That always added a cachet to any announcement.

". . . but it has been learned that the flyers are a complete hoax and that the authorities will be making an announcement shortly." Annie pushed away the cold little thought that Pete Garrett might not be thrilled to hear this. But that was going to be Pete's problem. If ever she was in a position to explain to him why she had come to the school, surely he would be pleased that she'd made an effort to keep the students from getting involved. Whatever happened, Annie didn't want Rachel or any of her friends pursuing the hand that wrote the flyers, because that same hand might very well have held the gun that killed Kay Nevis.

Rachel gripped her soda can. "Oh, but everybody's coming and they all want to help Diane."

"It will be great," Annie said brightly. "Everybody will be relieved that the flyers are phony and that Diane has been falsely accused. What you can do is even more important. Ask the kids to write tributes to Mrs. Nevis and bring them to their first hour tomorrow and turn them in. They will be a wonderful present to her family."

"Annie, that's a super idea." Rachel's face brightened. "Sure. Christy and I will handle it."

A shrill buzz sounded three times.

Rachel glanced toward a loudspeaker mounted above a small stage at the end of the room. "Some kind of announcement."

"Students and faculty, may I have your attention"— the sound was tinny—"for an important announcement."

Rachel's eyes darkened. "That's Dr. Allensworth. I'll bet he's going to tell everybody about Mrs. Nevis."

Allensworth cleared his throat. The room slowly quieted. "There will be a special assembly today at two o'clock. I regret to inform you that one of our own— Mrs. Nevis—has died." There was the sound of indrawn breaths, exclamations. "I further regret to inform you that she was shot to death at her home last night. At the assembly, I will report to you the facts as we know them and will issue a special plea to all students and faculty to contact the police if they feel they have any information that might be useful in the investigation. Thank you."

Annie was only dimly aware of the shocked silence in the long room. She studied the table of teachers. The book had slid from Mrs. Thompson's hand. She stared at the loudspeaker, her face stricken. Mrs. Riley clapped her hands to her cheeks, let out a shrill cry.

Annie pushed back her chair. "I need to talk to Mrs. Riley. Now don't forget what we decided about the meeting, Rachel."

❦ *Thirteen* ❧

MRS. RILEY'S HANDS trembled as she smoothed her hair against the breeze. "Of course I'll help. Will the service be on Saturday?" Her molasses-thick accent stretched each word.

"The time hasn't been announced yet. Mrs. Nevis's daughter and her family arrive tomorrow. I'm sure someone will call you. I know you were a very close friend." They stood at the end of the pier, the green water bright in the sun.

The teacher shaded eyes that glistened with sudden tears. "We often walked out here after lunch. I love the kids, but sometimes you feel like you're smothering!" She lifted her arms as if pushing away a burden. "Kay used to scold me, tell me I took everything too hard and that I shouldn't get so personally involved. Just last week, she said, 'Maureen, tell that boy'—one of my favorites, oh, it breaks my heart, he's so bright, so good, and he sees colors like jewels—'that he can do drugs or he can have a life. Tell him to talk to a counselor, but you let it go. If he doesn't listen, it's not your problem.' " Maureen Riley flung out her hands, gave a huge sigh. "How can I not care? Of course, Kay cared, too. But she was a bear for personal responsibility. Hard choices, that's how she saw the world—for herself, for everybody around her."

Hard choices.

Annie touched the weathered railing. Had Kay rested her fingers against this warm wood, welcomed the gentle sweep of wind off the water and thought about hard choices? "I know she was upset lately."

Red nails gripped Annie's arm. "What was that about? She wouldn't tell me. I knew something was wrong. She hadn't been herself for a week or more, so quiet and—well, almost grim."

Annie's flare of hope withered. "I thought you could tell us. All we know"—Annie doubted the editorial "we" had ever been used so loosely—"is that she was worried about something at school. We even wondered if it could have something to do with her murder."

Maureen Riley's grip eased. She lifted her hand, smoothed her hair. Her heavy face creased in thought. "Here? At school?"

In the silence, Annie heard the chug of a motorboat, the slap of water against the pilings, the cackling call of a clapper rail.

"Last Friday"—Mrs. Riley's sweet soft voice was thoughtful—"Kay and I were in the cafeteria. We were running a little later than usual. I'd had to stop and leave some papers in the office and she waited for me. At the end of the line, she picked up her tray and looked toward our table. She just stood there, frowning. I guess I was a little impatient. I said, 'Kay, get a move on.' She didn't budge. She took a deep breath and finally said, 'Yes. I suppose I must.' When we got to the table, she said hello to everyone, but after we sat down, I swear she didn't talk at all." Mrs. Riley lifted her plump shoulders in a shrug. "Of course, I have to admit I always have lots to say. But there's so much to talk about. We're all going to have to take more computer instruction. I swear we just learn how to do it one way and they make us learn another and now they want us to take roll on the computer and we have to click on a student's picture if they're absent and I don't see why we can't just send a slip to the office like we always have. But Kay was always up-to-the-minute. She liked learning more about computers. We were talking about the new software that day and everybody chimed in, everybody but her. I thought maybe she didn't feel well. Anyway, she ate real fast—her usual lunch, vegetable soup and two packages of crackers and lime Jell-O. But now I wonder." Big brown eyes looked earnestly at Annie.

Annie wasn't sure what she was supposed to take from Mrs. Riley's breathless report. "Wonder?"

"Yes. You see, when we were in the cafeteria line, she was looking at our table. I think she didn't want to go and sit down there. You see what that means!" She gripped her long amber necklace, held it tightly.

Annie imagined Kay Nevis in the cafeteria line looking toward the usual table. "Were the others already there?"

"Yes. Just like today." Maureen Riley spoke the names slowly. "Lois Thompson. Algebra. She's the tiny little black woman who has such bright eyes, shiny as polished chrome. Amy Mendoza. Biology. Masses of dark hair and an elegant carriage. She models on the weekends. And on the other side of the table . . ."

Annie nodded, recognizing the same-pew-every-Sunday syndrome, that human penchant for returning always to a particular spot.

". . . Jack Quinn. Chemistry and track. As you might expect, he's the tall skinny guy. He wears his hair longer than Dr. Allensworth likes, but"—a quick smile—"Jack pretty well does what he likes. Three state championships in a row for boys' quarter mile. And some of his top students always AP out of ChemOne. And next to him, you may have noticed the chunky guy with a carrot top and a big grin. George Wilson. Counselor." Her lips curved in a smile. "Everybody loves George. He could make Silas Marner laugh. Loudest man I've ever known. Talks a mile a minute and he knows something about everything—the latest quiz shows, the average high temperature in Manila in December, Clare of Assisi is the patron saint of television, a gross is twelve dozen—" She paused for breath, peered at Annie. "Really, you'd love him."

Annie's idea of male perfection was summed up in her tall, blond, agreeable, good-humored, sexy husband, who definitely didn't talk nonstop. "Hmm," she replied pleasantly.

Mrs. Riley plucked at her amber beads. "The kids adore George. And he's awfully good at getting them to really look at what they're doing. And next to him"—her tone was suddenly dry—"that terribly pretty girl, Nita Harris. Spanish."

Annie remembered the young teacher sitting with

the men, a tangle of blond curls, a hairdo that looks windblown and casual but is the result of art and care, a fresh open face with a merry smile, an aura of exuberance and enthusiasm.

"If anyone else wore a skirt that short . . ." Mrs. Riley lifted an eyebrow. "The men all go right to her, just like lemmings. It is lemmings, isn't it, that get all caught up in a swarm and try to cross the sea and drown? You know, propelled by a force they can't resist. Men will be men. They simply can't help themselves. And I swear, I don't think she does a thing. All she has to do is walk into a faculty meeting and there's a mass migration. But I have to say she's a nice girl." Her eyes squinted in thought. "If only I could remember exactly where Kay was staring. She might have been looking at that side of the table. But really, Kay liked Nita, said she was just one of those women men can't resist and it didn't matter whether a man was married or not. Jack and George are both married. Jack's wife is a very successful lawyer and George's wife is a pharmaceutical rep and makes a lot of money. And Nita has a boyfriend, so it doesn't mean anything."

Annie tried to sort everyone out in her mind: the precise teacher the students had nicknamed Minnie, the model, the lanky track coach, the ebullient counselor and the femme fatale. Had Kay quarreled with one of them? Was there some reason for her to avoid sitting at the lunch table? But the dead woman had taken her usual place on Friday, though she'd had little to say. Mrs. Riley had wondered if she was sick.

A bell rang.

"Oh, I've got to get back." Mrs. Riley started up the pier. "The more I think about it, the more I think Kay was looking at our table. There was a stillness about the way she stood, a reluctance to move. She didn't want to sit with someone at our table."

Max frowned at the map. Last night Laurel must have been in the Sound fairly near the inlet where Kay Nevis had lived. There were only the two houses there, the Nevis house and the Muir house. South of that inlet there was a long stretch of undeveloped marshland, part of a nature preserve. To the north, a thin finger of land poked out into the Sound. There was only one house there. It belonged to Eva and Terry Crawford, owners of Smuggler's Rest, the newest gift shop on the marina. Max picked up the phone. He'd call Ben Parotti, rent a motorboat and be out in the Sound tonight.

Max hesitated, remembering the crisp, imperative tone in his mother's voice when she had insisted that she had a matter to attend to. Max sighed. That meant—had to mean—Laurel would be abroad tonight. But if he took a boat into the Sound, he might—

The phone rang.

"Hello." Max pulled the map a little closer.

"Maxwell, dear." Laurel's husky voice brimmed with eagerness, goodwill, and affection.

Max felt a huge rush of relief. "Ma! Listen, you've got to tell me what you're up to." He talked fast, knowing the connection with his mother might be terminated any instant. "Were you near the Nevis house last night? Don't hang up. You've got to tell me. She was shot. What did you see?"

"I'm so glad I called." Her voice lifted with contentment. "I simply had an inkling you might be disturbed, a roiling of wavelengths when I envisaged you. Usually, dear Max, you exude the most soothing aura of mellow cream. My dear, you must learn to relax." Her tone was earnest and reassuring. "If you go out to your hammock and stretch out and breathe deeply, you will feel much better."

It was that old familiar feeling that often occurred when he spoke with his mother, like stepping into a cobweb, little tendrils of obfuscation twining around him. "Ma, stop fooling around. I'm going to get a boat and be in the Sound tonight—"

"Absolutely not." Her tone was sharp. "To put your mind at rest, let me assure you that I have no information of interest to the authorities except the fact that I was in the Sound around midnight not far from the inlet where Kay Nevis lived. I encountered a motorboat without running lights. To my surprise, the occupant shot at me. So, of course, I departed immediately. I cannot describe either the boat or my attacker. Therefore, we have no obstruction of justice here." A light tinkling laugh. "However, I do have a matter to which I must attend this evening. I promise that"—a thoughtful pause—"let's see, tonight is Thursday and tomorrow is Friday, ah yes, I promise that I will be home either Saturday or Sunday. I assure you that I am quite safe and well and that I will be in no danger unless"—now she was crisp and compelling—"there is well-meaning but terribly misguided interference. There is definitely a possibility of terrible danger if you contact the authorities. Please continue, should anyone inquire, to say that I am in Atlanta. It is, Maxwell, a matter of life or death."

"Ma—" The empty line buzzed in his ear. He clicked off the phone. *Terrible danger* . . . Max took a deep breath. All right, he had to do as his mother demanded. But he couldn't ignore what he knew. Max hurried toward the door. There were some of those flyers at his office. Who among those named could have been on the Sound last night at midnight? Certainly Pete was going to explore the people cited in the fake flyers. He was a careful, thorough and intelligent cop. But nobody was shooting at his mother.

"Class," Mrs. Thompson, a woman who felt no need to raise her voice, said softly, "we will have a short quiz. Please work the problems on page 89."

The students flipped open their books and set to work.

Mrs. Thompson held the door for Annie. She looked back to the class. "I shall return in fifteen minutes."

When they stepped into the hall, the door closing behind them, Lois Thompson fingered a silver filigree brooch in the lapel of her gray suit. Her shiny eyes studied Annie.

Annie decided Mrs. Thompson indeed looked like a dusky mouse, a highly intelligent, thoughtful and curious mouse. "I appreciate your willingness to take a few minutes to speak with me. We are planning the service for Kay and her daughter hopes you will agree to speak."

The teacher's shiny eyes blinked in her small, intense face. "Of course I will. Is there a particular aspect of Kay's life you wish for me to discuss?"

Slowly, Annie nodded. "The family wishes to remember especially her devotion to duty and her commitment to high moral principles. I understand she was presently engaged in a dispute here at school about some matter she found distressing."

Perfectly formed eyebrows rose a fraction. "Really? I was not aware of a specific problem." Mrs. Thompson clasped her smooth hands together, the nails shiny with colorless polish.

Annie almost left it at that. Obviously, Kay Nevis hadn't told her best friends on the faculty about any difficulty at school. If she hadn't told either Mrs. Riley or Mrs. Thompson, it was unlikely she'd told anyone else. Told them what? Mrs. Riley suggested Kay didn't want to sit at the lunch table. Why? What could Kay know about a teacher that would distress her enough that even a brief lunch period seemed intolerable? It would have to be a matter of great seriousness, something that could lead to the loss of a job, perhaps even criminal charges . . . *not aware of a specific problem* . . . Annie looked into bright, shiny, intelligent brown eyes. "Specific?"

Mrs. Thompson's small nose wrinkled. Annie had a quick vision of a mouse sniffing. A quick smile revealed even white teeth. "Kay was a forward-looking woman, but she was not comfortable with today's lax standards. Last week in the lounge, we were drinking tea and discussing the difficulties teachers face today—students who are overscheduled, undisciplined, exposed to endless corrupting influences, most especially senseless violence and promiscuous sex in every aspect of their entertainment—when Kay said, and I can only describe her tone as bitter, 'Parents have a responsibility. When they don't oversee a child, there will be trouble.' " Mrs. Thompson turned to look through the glass panes in the door.

Annie looked, too. It did not surprise her that Mrs. Thompson's students, heads bent, were writing industriously.

Mrs. Thompson gave an almost imperceptible approving nod, returned her calm gaze to Annie. "At the time, I noted Kay's tone was more exercised than usual. But now I believe—though it is perhaps easy to invest a momentousness to the event because of Kay's death and your question to me—that she might have been grappling with a decision regarding a student. She took a last sip of tea and gathered up her papers. Her manner was abstracted, as if she was deep in thought. That was the last conversation we had."

A student! Annie was jarred. Mrs. Riley insisted Kay wished to avoid sitting at the usual table with the other teachers. Mrs. Thompson suspected Kay was disturbed by some situation involving a student. Which was correct? Possibly neither. After all, Chief Garrett was at the moment trying to link one of the people impugned in the flyers to Kay's murder. Maybe that still made sense.

"I don't suppose"—Mrs. Thompson's voice was contemplative—"that we'll ever know. Kay was a very discreet woman."

Discreet and dead.

Annie was ready to give up, consign the search for Kay's murderer to the police, whose responsibility it was. Responsibility. Laurel. If Pete Garrett was wrong, if Henny was right, Laurel remained in danger. Dammit, why had Laurel been out in the Sound in the middle of the night anyway?

"Discreet." Annie studied the trim, competent-looking teacher, not a woman who missed much, not a woman who exaggerated or misstated. "I would think you are very discreet, too."

There was a flash of surprise in Mrs. Thompson's dark eyes. "I suppose that's true. But in this instance, if I had any idea what Kay meant, if indeed she meant anything at all, I would certainly tell you and the authorities as well."

"Mrs. Thompson, there has been a suggestion that Kay may have written those flyers that have been scattered around the island, the ones accusing some people on the island of crimes."

"Those scurrilous things?" The teacher stared at Annie in dismay. "That's absurd. Impossible. No, I'm quite certain Kay had nothing to do with them."

Annie said stubbornly, "Everyone has emphasized how morally upright she was."

"Morally upright, yes. But Kay was not a vigilante." Mrs. Thompson was adamant, her voice firm and determined. "I saw those flyers. If Kay had information about any of those incidents, she would have approached the authorities. I've no doubt of that. But to fling accusations about anonymously, to tarnish people's reputations publicly, no. Never. That would not be honorable and Kay was most emphatically an honorable woman."

"So you believe Kay would definitely have taken action if she were aware of . . ." Annie's voice trailed away. Aware of what? Annie turned her hands palms up. "What could Kay have known—especially about a student—that might end in murder?"

Mrs. Thompson rested her fingertips lightly on one smooth cheek. "It seems absurd when put like that. But the fact is, Kay was shot to death last night. If she had known perhaps that a student possessed a gun, brought it to school . . . No, she would have taken immediate steps. It can't be anything like that. What else could be involved? Drugs? Sexual abuse or misbehavior of some kind? Theft? Intimidation? Oh, we can spin ideas forever. The difficulty is that I don't see how Kay could gain information detrimental to a student unless the student in question informed her or perhaps"—her eyes narrowed—"perhaps another student came to Kay, told her of something dangerous, something illegal. . . . But we come up against the fact that Kay did not go to the authorities. I assume you asked Dr. Allensworth if he was aware of any problem?"

Annie nodded. "He was very emphatic that he knew of nothing at school that could be connected to her death."

Mrs. Thompson's eyes narrowed. "Kay always followed procedure. Dr. Allensworth would be the first person to be informed if there were a matter that posed danger to anyone." The teacher lifted her slender shoulders in a shrug. "I don't know what to tell you. She may have been concerned about a particular student that day. If so, I've no idea who that student may be. Kay never spoke of students unless she could speak

well." A sudden smile. "It was a dear trait. She was"—
and her bright eyes glistened with tears—"a dear and
kind woman."

Annie looked at the index card in her hand. Mrs.
Thompson's printing was as precise as her speech, the
small letters perfectly formed:

Amy Mendoza. Room 216.
Jack Quinn. Room 111.
George Wilson. Main office, room 101, office D.
Nita Harris. Room 202.

Annie glanced across the hall at room 202. First
come . . .

Henny Brawley slipped the soft gray plastic dust
shroud from the computer. A smile tugged at her lips
even as she blinked away tears. Kay was the only person she'd ever known who kept her computer covered.
All right, all right. No time to grieve now. The police
were finally gone and she had permission to clean the
foyer where Kay had died in a pool of blood. That
would be hideous, but someone must do it. Tomorrow,
she'd bring over a grass mat from her own living room
to hide the stains that she would not be able to remove.
There was much to do before the arrival of the family.
Of course, the guild would bring food. Pamela Potts
had already called twice. The house, beyond the crime
scene, was immaculate. Kay had kept a clean house.
But it would take only a minute to check . . .

Henny perched on the edge of the straight chair,

booted up, called up the list of files. Lesson plans, research, letters, saved travel pieces—but nothing, not a single scrap of information to link this computer to those awful flyers. Of course, Pete Garrett wouldn't be impressed. He'd simply cite Henny's own discovery of unauthorized entry into the library and use of a computer. But Henny felt better anyway. Dammit, Kay hadn't written those flyers. Henny shut down the program, took a deep breath. She'd put off this moment as long as possible. She walked into the foyer, glanced at her supplies, a bucket with sudsy ammonia, steel wool, rubber gloves . . .

Amy Mendoza beamed at the class, dark eyes glowing, white teeth bright. "Pop quiz."

The class groaned.

"Now, now." Her voice was good-humored. "Answer the questions at the end of Chapter Thirteen. Peter"—she nodded toward a blond boy in the first seat—"please take up the papers in fifteen minutes. Thank you."

The students rustled and squirmed behind long, scarred wooden tables. The classroom smelled of a combination of disinfectant and must. At least, Annie hoped it was must.

Amy Mendoza beckoned to Annie. "We'll visit over here by the door. I can't leave students unsupervised in a lab." Her royal-blue silk skirt swirling, she swept gracefully past Annie to a corner of the room just past the entrance. A matching silk tank top emphasized her willowy figure. She turned so that her back was to the students. She looked somberly at Annie, her face abruptly bleak and sad. She spoke in a tone too low for anyone other than Annie to hear. "This is awful. The kids are upset. We're all upset. I can't believe anything like this could happen to someone I know." Long slender fingers touched her throat. "Do you know what's going to happen at the assembly?" Before Annie could answer, she chattered on. "Oh no, of course you don't. You're here for the family. That's what someone told me. Well, I'll be glad to do anything I can to help."

"Thank you. We especially hoped you'd be able to come to the house after the service . . ."

Amy Mendoza was startled. She immediately smoothed out her face, managed a smile. "Oh yes, of course."

". . . since we wanted to honor her friends whom she saw every day. You always lunched together. Kay enjoyed that very much."

"Oh. Certainly. Lunch. Yes." Amy nodded energetically, though her eyes were puzzled. "I mean, we all had the same lunch hour."

Annie ignored the hint that lunchtime companions were a result of the fortuity of scheduling, not choice. "Since you saw her every day, I suppose you noticed that she was upset this past week?"

Amy folded her long thin arms. "Upset? Honestly, I didn't notice. She never had much to say." A quick smile. "Maureen and George and I are the ones who talk. Lois always has a book. Kay would make an occasional comment. Jack shrugs and looks sleepy. Except when Nita says something." Her voice was dry. "But this past week?" Her dark brows drew down. "Kay was quiet. What else was new?"

Annie ignored the curious stare of the skinny boy in the nearest seat. "Was Kay worried about Jud Hamilton coming up to school?"

Amy shivered. "I don't know. But I'm scared. I used to spend a lot of time with Colleen. Jud's mean and they say he's out to get the guy who sent him to jail. We all hope Dr. Allensworth gets some added security for a while."

"Everybody agreed?" So the topic had been explored at the lunch table. Here was more proof that Kay had the information to write the accusatory flyers, but proof as well that everyone at the table knew about Jud Hamilton.

"Oh yes. Nobody wants to tangle with Jud." Her eyes were wide.

Everyone at the table . . . "So you weren't aware of anything that upset Kay this past week?"

"I don't know if something was wrong." Amy's tone was uncertain. "She was awfully quiet. Even quieter than usual. But I don't know why."

Max paced in his office, head down, face intent.

Barb sat on a straight chair, hand poised above a legal pad.

"Here's what we need to find out." Max flipped out his fingers one by one, "Do the Littlefields own a motorboat? Where were the members of the Littlefield family last night at midnight?" He glanced at his notes. Ah yes, Least Tern Lane. "Ditto Paul Marlow, Teresa Caldwell, Frank Saulter and Emma Clyde. If no alibi, who had access to a motorboat? Ditto everyone connected with the *Leisure Moment*. Okay, we'll divvy it up. . . ."

*   *   *

Square face determined, Emma Clyde stared at the computer screen. All right. She needed to introduce two more characters. Now, why would Marigold need to talk to the druggist? Have to be a good reason. A prescription refill? No, no, that was contrived. All right, how about Marigold sees the pill bottle on the victim's nightstand, writes down the pharmacy name and phone number? Hmm, that might work. Okay, Marigold goes to the pharmacy. It's the old-fashioned kind, has a soda fountain. She decides to get a chocolate soda, definitely with a maraschino cherry, and she asks the kid behind the fountain if he knows Mr. Woolery, the guy who was knifed in his bedroom the night before. Turns out the kid delivers prescriptions. Oh hey, this is good. Emma hitched her chair closer to the keyboard. The kid—make him a skinny blond with a nose ring and a snake tattoo on his forearm—tells Marigold . . .

Emma stared at the screen where she'd typed: Smoke screen.

Dammit, smoke screen had nothing to do with Marigold Rembrandt and *The Case of the Curious Catbird*. Smoke screen, an effort to hide the true facts. Annie might be right. What if someone else did the flyers, left them at Kay's house? What if the objective of the flyers was to provide a convenient list of suspects in Kay's murder? Damn clever, if so. Had anyone thought to check and see whether Kay kept a diary?

Emma blinked irritably. Dammit, she didn't have time to worry about flyers and smoke screens. She had to get Chapter 17 finished. Pronto. But what if . . .

She whirled her chair around, reached for the phone.

*   *   *

Nita Harris fluffed her golden curls with a casual swipe. She exuded energy and restlessness, one foot tapping as she listened to Annie. "Oh, look, I don't do funerals. Sorry. Nice woman and all that, but I just knew her because we both had first-period lunch. Thanks, I'll give it a bye." A decided nod. "I'll donate to whatever, flowers or a charity. Anyway, thanks for thinking of me." She backed toward her classroom door.

Annie thought nothing short of a lasso was going to prevent Nita Harris's retreat from the hall. But maybe . . . "Just one thing more. Who was Mrs. Nevis mad at?"

Nita gripped the door handle. "Oh hey, who not? People who write nasty song lyrics, everybody in Hollywood, the NRA, the Pill." She gave a whuff of exasperation. "Honestly, did she think the world was better when Hester Prynne wore a scarlet letter? But"—a bemused smile—"she was nice at heart. Took the time to warn me against 'married men who should know better.' I wasn't sure whether she meant Jack or George, but I told her it was no sweat. My mama told me a married man was like a coon dog on a leash, always lunging, never a threat. But"—her dry tone warmed—"she really meant well. She told me I was a Nice Girl. Made my day." And with a bright smile she popped into her classroom.

The last pail of faintly pink water gurgled down the drain. Henny splashed a half cup of ammonia into the sink. She turned on the faucet, let the cold water pound against the porcelain. The water ran and ran. Finally, white-faced and trembling, she turned off the water. It was then that she heard a deep voice call.

She swung about, a hand at her heart.

Billy Cameron stood in the doorway of the kitchen. "Hey, Henny, it's just me. I didn't mean to scare you. I rang the bell." He shoved a hand through his thick sandy hair.

Henny peeled off the rubber gloves, looked at them with distaste. She took a step, tossed them into the garbage pail. "I had the water running. That's okay, Billy."

His big face creased in concern. "You okay? Listen, I can get Mavis to come over." He looked around. "Where are the ladies from the church?"

Henny smiled at him. "I told them to come tomorrow. They'll bring the food over starting early. Today"—she took a deep breath—"today I had to see to cleaning up." She nodded toward the front of the house.

He understood. "I could have come. I could have helped."

"All done, Billy. But thank you." She smoothed back a lock of hair. "What you are doing is more important." Her gaze sharpened. "Have you found out anything? Is there any progress on finding the murderer?"

"Not much. That's why I came. See, the chief's not having any luck. He thought it was going to be easy. I mean"—Billy gestured toward the front of the house—"all those flyers. He said no wonder she got killed. She made somebody mad big-time." His blue eyes were suddenly shrewd. "Or scared the hell out of them. I mean, how would you feel if you ran somebody down or pushed somebody off a boat and suddenly there's a big hint plastered all over town? But he's been checking everybody out and it looks like most of those folks are in the clear. Most of them weren't even on the island last night. Except maybe one, and the chief's keeping mum about that. But Mrs. Clyde called the chief and all of a sudden she's spouting the stuff you said, that maybe Mrs. Nevis didn't write those flyers, maybe somebody else did. She told the chief to check and see if Mrs. Nevis kept a journal or a daybook, that she was just the kind of woman to write down everything she was thinking about. The chief wanted me to ask you to give us a hand, seeing as how you're handling everything for the family." He rubbed his nose. "Do you know whether Mrs. Nevis had a journal?"

Annie's nose wrinkled at the sour, acidic smell. Was that an overlay of chlorine? Vials and test tubes glittered in shades of violet on long laboratory tables. A dozen or so students measured, poured, jotted notes.

Annie stepped inside, aware of quick curious glances. "Mr. Quinn?"

He stood with his arms folded, looking over a student's calculations. "Good work, Josie." Josie's lips spread in a pleased smile and she fingered the four tiny rings that clung to one ear. He turned, looked sharply at Annie. "Yes?"

"If we could talk for a moment . . ." She kept her hand on the door.

For an instant she thought he was going to send her away. Then, with a faint shrug, he jerked his head toward an alcove at the back of the room.

She followed him. He faced the room, his gaze

moving swiftly about the lab. When he looked at Annie, his glance was cool, his eyes quizzical beneath dark brows. "Yeah?" He had an Alan Alda face, but there was no nice-guy charm here. "Gerry says . . ."

Gerry? Oh, Gerald Allensworth. Now, why had Jack Quinn talked to the principal?

". . . that you think Kay had a problem at school. How so?" His look was brooding, intense.

Max always told the truth. Annie thought about that for a minute. Well, there were different ways to tell the truth and she didn't want this arrogant dude confronting volatile Maureen Riley. "We understand she was upset with someone at the lunch table. Would you know about that?" Was it you, buddy?

He frowned. "The lunch table?" His tone was puzzled. He looked sharply at Annie. "Who told you this?" He took a step toward her.

Annie realized Quinn was big, intimidating and worried. "I don't think that matters. What matters is Kay's quarrel with one of you."

He rubbed his face. "With one of us . . ." His tone was odd.

The bell rang. Students flowed out of the classroom, some of them glancing toward their teacher and his guest.

Quinn bent closer, spoke loud enough for her to hear. "So far as I know"—his gaze was steady—"Kay had no trouble with anyone at the lunch table." There was relief in his voice. "Maybe you got the wrong information. So"—he began to back away—"be sure and let me know the time of the service." And he turned and hurried out into the hall.

Annie wondered where he was going. Most of all she wondered at the odd tone in his voice when she'd suggested Kay was distressed by someone at the lunch table. Whatever problem he'd expected to be told about, it hadn't included the lunch table.

Annie checked her watch. It was already a quarter past one. The assembly was set for two o'clock. But maybe there was time for one last stop.

∴ *Fourteen* ∾

MAX RESTED comfortably in his reclining red leather desk chair. The vibrator hummed. He propped the phone between his head and shoulder. "This is Josiah Pilkington of Pilkington, Papillon and Porter. I wish to speak with Mr. Littlefield on a matter of some importance. . . . Oh, could you tell me when he will return? Next week. Is Mrs. Littlefield available? Oh, in Europe. I see. No, I will call again."

So the Littlefields were off island. But Diane was here. Annie had spoken with her at the antique shop yesterday.

Max punched a button. The chair rose. He pulled the legal pad closer, marked through Curtis and Lou Anne Littlefield. After Diane's name, he wrote: Midnight?

He tapped the pen on the desk. Who would know where Diane had been at midnight? Was she staying home alone although her parents were out of town? She might well be. She was, after all, a senior in high school. Hmm. In any event, she had no alibi so far.

Except for Diane, he was through with the Littlefields. Now for his next quarry. Max flipped through his Rolodex, found a number, punched it in. "Ben?

Max Darling here." Max leaned over, turned on the speakerphone, turned off the portable phone. "Is *Leisure Moment* in port?"

"Nope. Pulled out yesterday. Mr. Fleming's brother took it down to the Bahamas for some fishing." Ben sniffed. "Don't see how the fishing could get any better than here. They brought in a couple of fifty-pound king mackerels this week. The *Yahoo Sister* out of Charleston."

If *Leisure Moment* left the harbor yesterday afternoon for the Bahamas, neither the captain nor anyone aboard had been on the island at midnight. "Mr. Fleming's brother took it out. Is Keith Fleming aboard?"

Ben gave a snort of laughter. "Not likely to be for a while. He married himself a mighty young woman and they're off to some island in the South Pacific." He was scornful. "Here's the best island in the world and I don't see why anybody'd go anywhere else. Anyway, Captain Joe said the new Mrs. Fleming's not much for fishing. Except for fat wallets, is my guess."

"Ben"—Max's voice was dry—"you're such a romantic."

"Well now, Max, there's ro-mance and ro-mance, and some women don't think they's nothing as romantic as crisp new dollars. But maybe turnabout's fair play. They always said Keith Fleming married Laura Neville for her money, so now somebody's married him for his as what used to be hers, if you get my meaning."

Max did. But he was willing to consign the Flemings past and present to the world of their own making, since none of them were on Broward's Rock at the moment or had been at midnight last night. "What goes around comes around. Thanks, Ben."

On his sheet, he marked through Captain Joe, Keith Fleming and Fleming's wife.

Max studied Frank Saulter's name. That was a poser. Frank lived alone. There wasn't going to be an alibi for him. Max's hand hovered over the phone. No. His hand fell. What good would it do to call Frank? If he had nothing to do with Kay Nevis's death, he'd say he was home asleep. If he'd shot Kay Nevis, he'd say he was home—

The phone rang. Max punched it on and smiled as Annie's voice flowed into the room over the speakerphone.

"Max, listen, I just have a minute." She sounded breathless. "I'm at school."

He frowned. "School? Is Rachel okay?"

"She's fine. I don't have time to explain everything, but Henny's sure Kay Nevis didn't write those flyers. Henny persuaded me to come here to see what I could find out. Because if the people in the flyers didn't kill Kay Nevis, then Pete's not hunting in the right places. Anyway, I've got to hurry. There's an assembly, but I'll tell you all about it later." The connection ended.

Max clicked off the phone. The women in his life seemed to be making a habit of hanging up on him.

Barb trotted into his office, carrying a sheet of paper in one hand and a bowl of fresh fruit topped with a sauce in the other. "Want some fruit? I made a yummy dressing with vanilla yogurt, apple juice and poppy seeds."

"Sure." He smiled. "Thanks."

Barb placed the bowl and a napkin and dessert fork on the desk. "Here's what I've found." She placed the sheet next to the bowl. "The Littlefields have a motorboat. They keep it at a dock behind their house. Let me know if you want me to check on anything else. That didn't take long."

"Will do." Max speared a chunk of pineapple.

Barb's sheet contained a list of names with brief notations:

Paul Marlow played poker last night. The game broke up around one in the morning.

Teresa Caldwell left the island yesterday afternoon, taking her daughter with her on a trip to visit her mother in Birmingham. Arrived in Birmingham about seven o'clock, still there. According to his office, Ralph Caldwell is in New York and has been there all week. Frank Saulter was home alone. No confirmation.

At the end of the sheet, Barb had printed in large block letters: I'M LEAVING EMMA TO YOU.

Max grinned. So who's afraid of the big bad mystery writer? He reached for his Rolodex. Slowly his smile slipped away. Yes, he'd call Emma in a moment, though it was rather the same thing as calling Frank. People who live alone are not likely to whip out unassailable midnight alibis. More to the point was the dwindling list of suspects from the fake flyers. Diane Littlefield, Frank Saulter and Emma Clyde. That was not a great field of choices. If Pete Garrett was seeking a murderer there, Laurel might well be in serious danger from a hidden adversary. Dammit, what was she up to out in the Sound at midnight?

The faded redhead—Annie tried to remember the name—James? Jennings? Jenkins?—leaned on the counter. Cutting her eyes toward the principal's office, she whispered, "Mr. Wilson's in with Dr. Allensworth. I don't know when he'll be free. I guess they're talking about—well, you know."

The murder? The assembly? Annie didn't know, but she understood that nothing would be running on schedule this day. In the open office area, the other secretaries murmured into telephones. Had calls from worried parents begun? More than likely news of the murder was now out on radio and television.

A freckled arm pointed toward a narrow hallway. "The counselors' offices are back that way, Mr. Wilson and Mrs. Heaston. I think she's available. Would you like to see her?"

"No, but thanks. The family is contacting the teachers who knew Mrs. Nevis well." Annie had offered this story for so long, it almost seemed true. She checked her watch. A quarter to two. Perhaps Wilson would return to his office before the assembly. Annie could use the time to wonder about Jack Quinn. She couldn't quite define his attitude, but he was concerned about something. Apparently it had nothing to do with the lunch table. Or was that the impression he meant for her to receive?

". . . one student already waiting. But you're welcome to take a seat." Mrs. Jenkins nodded so vigorously, her lank red hair quivered. "I'm sure he'll see you first, since you're from the family."

"Thanks, I'll do that." Annie smiled and turned to the corridor, which was an extension of the long narrow space that ran along the counter of the main office. There was a wall with trophy cases to her left and office doors to the right. She passed a frosted door and realized it was likely another entrance to Dr. Allensworth's office. A plaque beside the next door announced: SYLVIA HEASTON, COUNSELOR. The plaque by the last door read: GEORGE WILSON, COUNSELOR.

A long green wooden bench was tucked between two trophy cases. A red nylon backpack was slung carelessly at the far end. A slender girl in a softly woven turquoise blouse and white capris stood at the end of the hallway, staring out the window at the long sweep of grass and marsh and green water. As Annie's shoes scuffed on the cement floor, she swung around, a hand at her throat.

The girl was strikingly lovely—long curling blond hair, deep-set violet eyes with dark lashes, smooth golden skin, high cheekbones, a rounded chin, lips that were made for laughter—and she was quivering with distress, her eyes huge with fear, her breath coming quickly, her face flaccid.

Annie reached out her hand.

The girl whipped her arms tightly together, hunched her shoulders, turned away.

Annie hesitated. There was trouble here and certainly this girl should have first call on seeing the counselor. But the other counselor was free. . . .

Brisk steps sounded behind them. Annie turned and

realized the girl, too, was swinging toward the doorway to the office.

George Wilson paused on the threshold. His round face was furrowed and grim. His sporty white polo shirt and pleated khakis weren't the right costume for heavy drama. He looked stunned, a man far out of his element. His gaze noted Annie, moved past her. His fair, freckled face changed, softened. "Meredith." There was concern in his eyes.

The girl darted past Annie, skidded to a stop in front of the stocky red-haired counselor. He'd called her Meredith. Was this Meredith Muir, the girl who lived across the inlet from Mrs. Nevis? If so, no wonder she had come for help. The shock of learning that a neighbor as well as a teacher had been murdered was certainly enough to bring her here. The counselors were surely going to have to deal with distraught students in the coming days.

"Meredith, you've heard the bad news?" Wilson had a nice tenor voice, light and clear. "I know it's a shock. The last thing anyone would expect."

"I came because . . ." Her high, soft voice trailed away. She glanced toward Annie, a vacant, frightened look.

Annie took a step toward the main office. This was no place for her. This girl needed help and Annie was in the way. "Mr. Wilson, I'll speak with you later. I'm Annie Darling and I'm here from Mrs. Nevis's family. We're making plans for the service."

Quick steps clattered into the hallway. Curly-haired Mrs. Otis, her round face red and worried, heaved a sigh of relief. "Oh, here you are, Mr. Wilson. Dr. Allensworth needs you. He wants you and Mrs. Heaston"—she was knocking on the first door—"right now."

The door opened. A middle-aged woman with frizzy black hair, a horselike face and bright green eyes stepped into the hallway. She held up a sheaf of notes. "I've got some ideas. It had occurred to me that Dr. Allensworth might expect us to be ready. Come on, George." She moved quickly, her navy patterned silk dress swirling around her ankles.

Wilson hesitated. "Meredith's here. I need to speak with her."

Mrs. Heaston looked back. "Later, George. Meredith, you don't mind, do you? We've some serious matters to discuss."

Meredith took a step back, another. "Oh no. It doesn't matter. That's all right."

In only a moment, the hallway was empty except for Annie and Meredith. The girl stared at the empty doorway, her face bleak. Abruptly she whirled, dashed to the bench and grabbed the backpack. She ran past Annie, head down.

Annie stared after her. Someone should have spoken to this girl, reassured her. Reassured her? Yes, Meredith Muir needed reassurance. It was fear that had permeated this long silent corridor, fear that had emptied the strength from the muscles of that beautiful face, fear that had leached all vigor from her voice. Annie took two quick steps, then stopped. She had no idea where Meredith had gone and the girl would very likely rebuff an approach from a stranger. Maybe she would be at the assembly. If so, Annie would try and catch her, speak with her.

*   *   *

Henny finished her careful survey of the library shelves. "I don't see anything that looks like a journal or daybook. I suppose she might have a desk in her bedroom. Let's try there, Billy."

She didn't look toward the scrubbed patch of wood in the entry hall but her memory of the morning was indelible in her mind: Kay, the most immaculate and carefully dressed of women, sprawled on her back, arms outflung, robe agape, nightgown drenched with blood, sightless eyes staring from a dead gray face. As Henny moved down the short hall, she tried to push the picture away. Kay would have hated being seen that way.

The bedroom door was open. Henny stopped on the threshold. This room must be straightened before the family arrived. She'd change the sheets. It wouldn't be hard to find clean bed linens. Her efforts had focused on the entryway and the kitchen. She had not thought this far. For the first time, she began to imagine the events of the night.

The bedroom was small but cheerful: bright yellow chintz on a love seat, a painted pine bed with a soft white chenille spread, old golden wood floors with a patchwork throw rug of red and blue and orange, more bookcases and, in a window alcove, a small white desk. The night lamp on the bedside table glowed, the covers were flung back. "Look, Billy, she'd gone to bed." Henny pointed at the lamp. "It's on. Kay must have heard the bell ring and gone to answer the door."

Billy's big face was somber. "That's what the chief thinks, too. It figures from where she was found. It

looks like she opened the front door and pow! somebody shot her. Except for those flyers tossed around
the hall, nothing seemed to be out of place."

Those damn flyers . . . Henny skirted the narrow
bed, reached the white desk. "It looks like Emma's
right." An annoying habit of Emma's, but sometimes
useful. "Those have to be journals, Billy." Henny
pointed at the small books with floral covers.

Emma Clyde gave a bark of laughter, a cross between
the guttural cry of a sea lion and the creak of a dungeon
door. "Max, is that a delicate way of inquiring whether
I was gunning down my old friend last night?"

Max blinked at the speakerphone. "Your old
friend?"

"Oh yes." Emma's tone was pleasant. "I liked Kay.
I suppose I sounded a little snappish at your office
today. She did seem a natural to have done the flyers.
But I gave it some thought and you'll be pleased to
know I've urged our young police chief to see if Kay
kept a journal. Serious people so often do, you know."

Max fought down the desire to ask Emma if she
kept a journal.

"No," came the crisp declarative, answering the
unasked question. And another bark. "But about midnight at my house . . ." There was sheer delight in her
voice. "My dear, I do have an alibi. Actually, I'll have
to use this in a book someday. I was working—I've got
to get this damn book done—and I finished for the
night at just past twelve and, of course, I saved the
chapter. You will be pleased to know—or perhaps not,
if you've cast me as chief villain—that the time the

chapter was saved is quite clear in my file index. Twelve-oh-four A.M. You can come over and look if you like. I started a new chapter this morning, so that file hasn't been touched. I'll definitely use that in a book one of these days. And if that's all, my dear Max, I must get back to work." The connection ended.

Max crossed through Emma's name. Only two names left. Diane Littlefield and Frank Saulter. Yes, it was possible that one of them was guilty. Even now, if he was persisting in this line of inquiry, Pete Garrett must be closing in on these names. Max had an empty feeling. The flyers—what had Emma muttered when they first discovered them? Smoke screen? Yes, that was it. Smoke screen. Somewhere, hidden in swirling mists of subterfuge, had a clever murderer outfoxed them all?

Students filled the hallway, but it was uncannily quiet, the only sounds the shuffle of feet, an occasional soft comment. Annie reached the wide double doors to the gym just as outside doors across the wooden expanse opened. The stocky police chief, his khaki uniform crisp, strode through, followed by a uniformed policeman. From Annie's point of view, it was unfortunate that the crowd in front of her thinned at that moment and Pete Garrett looked across the basketball floor directly at her. His frown was quick and intense.

Annie simply nodded, forced a smile and moved to her left, stopping beside the blue steps to the bleachers. Running footsteps sounded and Rachel arrived beside her, grabbing her arm. "Annie, you can sit with us." Over her shoulder, Rachel announced, "This is my sister, Annie. Come on, everybody."

Annie hesitated, then moved with a swarm of girls, looking around for Meredith Muir. But there were too many people, too many blondes, too many girls. Rachel led the group up the bleacher steps to a top section. Annie took the last seat next to the stairs. At the far end of the gym, Dr. Allensworth shook hands with Chief Garrett. The principal introduced Garrett to the counselors. George Wilson, his round face somber, leaned forward and spoke to Garrett. Mrs. Heaston tossed her head like a fractious horse, pointed at her watch. Dr. Allensworth nodded.

The assembly reminded Annie of her high school days: women teachers in summery print dresses; men in short-sleeve shirts and slacks; students of all backgrounds—black, white, Hispanic, a smattering of Asians—and every style of clothing from preppy to high fashion to grunge. The only difference from a usual high school assembly was the somber quiet that pervaded the gym.

Annie looked for familiar faces in the bleachers. One by one, she found Mrs. Nevis's daily lunch companions. Lois Thompson was almost lost from sight among the bigger, taller students, but her erect carriage and gray suit made her noticeable. Her small dark face was thoughtful and attentive. Nita Harris moved impatiently, her eyes darting restlessly around the gym. She perched on the edge of a seat, as if ready to jump to her feet and race away the minute the assembly ended. Lean and muscular Jack Quinn hunched his shoulders and stared toward the podium, his face abstracted. Amy Mendoza's slim fingers plucked at the neck of her silk tank top. Her lovely face was somber. Maureen

Riley's bright orange hair and vivid makeup emphasized the paleness of her face. Occasionally she lifted a shaking hand to her lips.

And there, finally, was Meredith Muir, a few rows below Mrs. Riley. Annie was relieved to see that Meredith was talking—and talking fast—to a girl . . . Oh, hey, Meredith's companion was Diane Littlefield. The girls were deep in conversation, Meredith clutching Diane's arm, bending close to listen. Both girls looked upset. Annie shifted on the hard seat. She wished she were near enough to hear. What were they talking about with such intensity? Maybe talking to Diane would help Meredith. Annie wished she'd spotted Meredith earlier, sat on that side of the gym. The girl was a long way away.

Abruptly, she turned to Rachel. "Rachel, are Meredith Muir and Diane Littlefield close friends?"

Rachel broke away from the girl next to her, peered across the gym floor. "Oh, sure. Big-time." She held up two fingers pressed together. "I heard that Diane was over at Meredith's last night and she's really spooked to think Mrs. Nevis got killed right across the way. I mean, everybody's just knocked out. And"—she hunched closer to Annie—"I've got the word out and everybody's coming to the meeting after school and they think it's a swell idea to plan tributes to Mrs. Nevis." Suddenly she was very still. "Ohh."

Her change of tone was so sudden, Annie looked at her sharply.

Rachel's face softened. "Gee, look, Annie. Up there two rows behind Meredith and Diane. The guy in the blue Oxford shirt next to Mrs. Riley. That's Ben. Doesn't he look sad?"

Annie didn't have any trouble picking out Ben Bradford, the senior who had invited Rachel to the prom, the boy who loved Meredith Muir, the editor of the school paper. He sat with his chin on his chest, arms folded, as he watched Meredith, the pain in his face easy to see.

Dr. Allensworth picked up the microphone. It gave a shrill beep. "Students and faculty, as I unhappily informed you earlier today, our own Mrs. Nevis was shot to death at her home last night. We have with us Police Chief Peter Garrett. We appreciate his taking time from the ongoing investigation to provide us with the facts of Mrs. Nevis's death. Chief Garrett." The principal handed the microphone to Pete.

The chief didn't look much older than many of the students, his blond hair thick and unruly with a noticeable cowlick, his round face cherubic, but his youthful voice was quick and precise. "Mrs. Nevis's body was discovered this morning by a friend, Mrs. Henrietta Brawley."

There were stirs and murmurs. Henny often substituted at the high school.

"Mrs. Brawley immediately contacted us. Our investigation has revealed that Mrs. Nevis was shot to death. There is no evidence that the house was broken into. The position of the body near the open front door suggests that Mrs. Nevis admitted her assailant. Death is believed to have occurred between eleven P.M. and one A.M. Possible motives are under investigation, though no arrests have been made."

Annie leaned forward. Would Garrett mention the flyers?

The chief gazed soberly around the gym. "If any faculty member or student has information about Mrs. Nevis or her murder, please contact me, come by our office or call our Crime Stoppers hot line." He gave the hot-line number twice and returned the microphone to Dr. Allensworth.

Annie wondered whether the omission meant Garrett had changed his mind about Kay Nevis as the author of the flyers. It could equally well mean that the chief preferred not to reveal details about the crime scene. Whatever the reason, Annie was glad she could report to Henny that her good friend's reputation had yet to be sullied. Of course, word would ultimately get out. But if they could discover the truth about the flyers soon enough, perhaps Kay Nevis would rest in peace.

Dr. Allensworth moved slowly to the podium. He poked the microphone into a holder. He surveyed the gym, rocked back and forth on his heels. "I would like for us to take a moment to remember Mrs. Nevis, the place she held in our world, our debt to her as a wonderful teacher and a good person."

The kindness and sincerity in his voice rolled through the huge quiet gym like soothing balm. Annie heard the sounds of indrawn breaths, sighs and occasional sniffles.

Dr. Allensworth bowed his head, folded his thin dark hands together.

Up and down the bleachers, students and teachers followed his example, some with rigid faces, others uneasy, a few indifferent, most respectful. Annie's gaze darted from face to face, faces she was beginning to know: the small dark teacher with the aura of dignity, the impatient blonde who didn't do funerals, the angular track coach, the lovely Hispanic model, the blowsy art teacher, the stocky counselor. Tears slipped down Lois Thompson's cheeks. Nita Harris moved restlessly. Jack Quinn rubbed his knuckles against his chin, slowly bowed his head. Amy Mendoza shivered. On the gym floor near the podium, George Wilson stared at the golden floor, head down, hands clasped behind his back. Maureen Riley clasped her hands, bowed her head.

In a moment, a long, sad, powerful moment, Allensworth cleared his throat. "Out of all sorrow, some goodness comes." There was a marked cadence to his voice and Annie wondered if he'd grown up a preacher's son. "I have been told that one of our students—Rachel Van Meer—has invited everyone to come together after school on the soccer field . . ."

There was a gasp from Rachel. Her fingers dug into Annie's arm.

". . . because Rachel wants to invite everyone who knew Mrs. Nevis to bring a written piece to school tomorrow. Rachel has volunteered to take these writings and put them into a scrapbook for Mrs. Nevis's family. Rachel"—his dark face lifted, his eyes searched the gym—"I commend you."

Two rows down a boy in an oversize football jersey twisted to shout, "Stand up, Rachel."

"Here she is." Christy yanked up Rachel's arm, waggled it.

Rachel, her face burning, reluctantly came to her feet. She wavered unsteadily on the narrow metal

walkway. "Yes. Please. Everybody come. Mrs
Nevis—well, we can do this for her. Thank you." She
sank down on the bench.

"Thank you, Rachel." Dr. Allensworth folded his
thin arms. "The service for Mrs. Nevis is scheduled a
four P.M. Monday at Saint Mary's by the Sea. Severa
members of the faculty have been asked to speak. It is
always difficult to understand when our lives are dis
rupted by violence. Man is never reconciled to evil.
urge all of you—students and faculty—to take advan
tage of the caring and support we have here at school
Our counselors, Mrs. Heaston and Mr. Wilson, stand
ready to speak with you—today, tomorrow, next week
Both counselors will be in their offices following thi
assembly. Thank you."

Rachel jumped to her feet. "Annie, I'd better hurr
out to the soccer field. Come on, Christy." Rachel
squeezed past Annie, thudded to the steps and ra
down.

Across the gym floor, as the students began to fil
down the bleacher steps, Meredith Muir moved fast.

Annie moved fast, too, but she had to cross the gym
She'd lost sight of Meredith by the time she reache
the outside doors. Annie shaded her eyes against th
bright sun. Some students were gathering aroun
Rachel and Christy on the soccer field. Car door
slammed in the parking lot, motors roared. Many of
the younger students converged at the covered walk
way, where buses waited. Of course, not all student
would be personally acquainted with Kay Nevis.

Annie didn't see Meredith Muir. She hesitated
glanced toward the soccer field. Rachel didn't nee

er. She glanced toward the building, then shook her
ead. She wanted to talk to George Wilson. He was the
nly lunch-table occupant she'd not yet contacted, but
iis was not the time. He and Mrs. Heaston were wait-
ig in their offices to help students. But definitely it
as important to see Wilson. He was trained to listen
id understand. Perhaps he might have picked up on
me look, some word, some act from Kay Nevis that
ight reveal a problem at school. A problem with a
acher? Or a student? Perhaps tomorrow . . .

Annie started toward the parking lot. She was al-
ost at her car when she saw Meredith Muir. Meredith
ood by the open driver's door of a bright blue Mus-
ng. She glared up at Jack Quinn, shaking her head
olently. She flung her purse and backpack into the
ir, jumped into the seat, slammed the door. The Mus-
ng jolted back, narrowly missing a green pickup,
inned forward.

Dust swirled around the track coach. He stared after
ie Mustang, his sharp features grim. Then he
rugged, jammed his hands in the pockets of his
acks. Head down, he walked swiftly back toward the
hool.

Annie almost started after him. But Quinn's attitude
id been antagonistic when they spoke earlier. She
dn't expect he would be any more forthcoming if she
ied again. Now she was intrigued. He'd followed
[eredith Muir out of the assembly. Why?

∿ *Fifteen* ∿

ANNIE PACED up and down the kitchen. "Nobody answers at the Muir house. All I get is voice mail."

Max grated a final curl of cheese, fished a box of mushrooms from the refrigerator. "I don't know what else you can do, Annie. Meredith's not a little kid. Didn't you say she's a senior? She's got a family, friends. If she's upset, there should be plenty of people who can help."

"Oh, I know. It's just . . ." Annie walked slowly to the cabinet, lifted down two plates. Funny, how she'd got so easily in the habit of setting the table for three or, when her father was here, for four. Tonight, it would just be the two of them, since Rachel was having dinner and spending the night at Christy's. The girls had already been to the gift shop on the marina and found a big scrapbook with a green leather cover. Annie carried the plates to the white wooden table. ". . . that I think she's scared. Max, you know how a lost animal looks?"

Max chopped the mushrooms. "That bad?" He cut the top off a green pepper, lifted out the seeds, rinsed the pepper, sliced it.

236

"That bad." She yanked up the portable phone, unched "redial." "Damn. I followed her home. Her ar was there, but she wouldn't answer the door."

The buzzer sounded at the back door. It opened and Henny poked her head inside.

Annie clicked off the phone as the Muir voice-mail message sounded. "Henny." She hurried across the itchen, pulled her old friend into a swift embrace. Hey, stay for dinner. Max is fixing omelets."

Max flashed a grin at Henny. "Tell me what you ke. Cheese, onions, mushrooms, sweet peppers? Or ow about some green chilis? Best omelets on the land."

"Modesty becomes him, doesn't it?" Annie took Henny by the hand. "Come on, sit down. Join us."

Henny sank into a chair at the kitchen table, ropped her purse on the shining wood floor. "I came y to find out what you learned at school. But if you're re it's okay, I'd love to stay."

"We're sure." Annie swiftly pulled out another place at, added a third plate.

As Annie described her day, Henny listened and Max swiftly made three omelets to order: onions, eese, and green chilis for Annie; mushrooms, nions, and cheese for Henny; mushrooms, green peppers, and onions for Max.

Annie talked and ate, finishing her omelet as she oncluded.

Henny frowned. "Nothing's clear-cut, is it? Maureen Riley thinks Kay was angry with someone at the unch table, but Lois Thompson believes Kay was oset about a student. Jack Quinn brushed you off and

Meredith Muir won't answer her door." Henny took a last bite. "That was wonderful, Max." She picked up her tea. "Someone at the lunch table. Or a student." She sighed. "If only we'd found the journal."

Annie leaned forward. "What journal?"

"Didn't I tell you?" Henny gave a tired sigh. "It was such a long day. Late in the afternoon, Pete Garrett sent Billy over. Apparently Emma Clyde called Pete and suggested he check and see if Kay kept a journal. I'm surprised Emma did that."

"You'll be pleased to know that Emma's come around to your viewpoint, Henny." Max grinned. "I called our esteemed novelist to ask if she had an alibi. Damned if she didn't." He explained the late-night work and the file time in Emma's computer.

"That should make her Suspect Number One." Annie's eyes glinted.

"Only in her books." Henny almost managed a smile.

"According to Emma, the murder investigation"— Max's tone was dry—"is interfering with the book. To be precise, Emma is distracted. She is fascinated by the possibility of the flyers' being fobbed off on Kay Nevis to throw up false suspects."

"Of course she's fascinated." Henny's eyes glinted. "The murderer and Emma have similar thought patterns, though I'd better not tell her that. But I'm glad Emma has an alibi. Even if it should turn out that Kay did the flyers and that the flyers provoked her murder, I know Emma wasn't involved. Emma never panics. She's lived with the story about Ricky for too many years to worry when it turns up again. No, not Emma. That's another reason I'm sure those flyers were cre-

ted to divert attention from Kay's life. There's no way
here could be any evidence about Ricky's death that
would threaten Emma. That makes all the accusations
n the flyers suspect. Those flyers have nothing to do
with someone seeking justice and everything to do
with confusing the search for Kay's murderer. Anyway"—she leaned back in her chair—"Emma called
Pete and he sent Billy over to the house. We searched
and Kay did keep journals, but we couldn't find a journal for this year. Billy and I looked everywhere. Kay
kept the journals in her bedroom. There was one for
each of the last twenty-two years. But not this year."
Henny's voice was grim. "I talked to Pete and he
doesn't think it matters. Pete says the murderer took
the journal because Kay spelled out the facts behind
the accusations in the flyers. I don't see it that way at
all. If we ever find that journal"—she glanced toward
the windows overlooking the lagoon—"and we won't,
not with water all around us, I'm sure there's no mention of those people. But there would be Kay's
thoughts about the problem she'd encountered." Henny
looked sharply at Annie. "Something at school! It has
to be something at school, but Pete's not even looking
there."

"We'll keep trying tomorrow." Annie hoped she
didn't sound as discouraged as she felt. After all, she'd
looked today and she hadn't turned up anything definite. All she had was Maureen Riley's certainty that
Kay's worry centered on the lunch table and Lois
Thompson's belief that Kay Nevis was concerned
about a student. Could Meredith Muir be that student?
Maybe Annie could find out tomorrow.

*   *   *

Annie gave a final swipe with the dishcloth and hung
it above the sink to dry. She looked through the window. The lights around the pool glowed. There was no
light on the pier that jutted into the lagoon. She could
barely see a dark form near the railing.

Annie turned toward the back door. She reached for
the handle, then paused long enough to pick up the
phone, punch "redial." Ring and ring and ring and ring.
Click. "You have reached . . ." Annie shook her head,
punched off the phone. If Meredith Muir was home,
she still wasn't answering the phone.

Annie pushed through the door, welcomed the soft
cool March night air. She hurried to the pier. Her steps
echoed on the wooden planks.

Max turned to meet her.

She slipped her arm through his. "Don't worry. Laurel's okay." Laurel might be flaky and fey, but she always landed on her feet.

"Annie, she's out there somewhere." Max nodded in
the direction of the Sound.

"I know. But look at it, Max, whatever she's up to,
she's given it a lot of thought. And she's involved in
something that matters. Besides, Kay Nevis was shot
last night. Nothing will happen tonight."

Laurel smiled at the thick cloud cover. It was a very
dark night, nice for her and no problem for her dear little nightscope. She throttled back the motorboat, maneuvered it on the lee side of a substantial hummock.
She put down the anchor. Almost midnight. She
glanced at the backseat—two knapsacks and, of

course, an assortment of dowsing rods. She was especially fond of the bright pink rod studded with fake rhinestones. Actually there had been a distinct pull the other night when she'd held the rod above this very hummock. Could it be . . . Well, no matter. If Blackbeard's treasure rested there, it could rest a hundred years more. That kind of discovery always led to trouble for everyone involved. She picked up the maroon knapsack and pulled out the nightscope-equipped video camera, held it steady, looked through the viewfinder. The Crawford dock jutted clear and distinct above the dark water.

She rested the camera in her lap. All was in readiness. The second knapsack was new. She'd handled it with gloved hands. No fingerprints there. Tonight she'd carefully polished the camera and viewfinder and she was wearing soft and supple dark leather gloves. She wouldn't leave any prints on anything she touched. As for the note in the new knapsack, she'd written it wearing the gloves. She nodded in approval as she recalled the printed message:

Cocaine shipment delivered to Eva and Terry Crawford Thursday night. The bricks of cocaine will be picked up Friday night during a party at the Crawford house. There will be a number of guests from the mainland.

Crisp. Clear. To the point. Wouldn't Max be proud? And to think she'd never be able to tell him. Not that Max wasn't discreet. Of course he was, but there must never be a single hint that she had been instrumental in the capture of the Crawfords. That would pose terrible danger for Rosa, the only link between Laurel and the Crawfords. Oh, well, there had been other adventures she'd never been able to share. She smiled.

A dark shape moved in the Sound. Laurel lifted the camera and the film began to whir.

Frank Saulter's fingers lightly rested on the rubber-boot grip of his Smith & Wesson Airweight .38 Special. No moon tonight, so the ivory handle wasn't visible. If he moved his hand, he could touch the gold-edged initials, "FJS, Francis John Saulter." He was sure it was Billy who'd gone to the extra trouble to order the initials. They'd given the revolver to him at his retirement party. It was a swell gun. The cylinder held five rounds of .38 lead hollowpoints. Billy had shrugged away Frank's thanks, saying the initials were just an idea they'd all kicked around, he and the other guys, a little something for Frank to remember them by.

He remembered them, all right, Billy and all the fine young men who'd been on his force through the years. Frank moved restlessly on the air mattress. Would Jud come tonight? Frank felt sure Jud was coming. Jud feasted on hatred.

Anger . . . Deep in the night, truths pluck at the mind. He felt the hot ugly core of anger pulsing within—raging fury at Jud, icy grief for Colleen. But he'd made certain that Jud didn't get away with murder. He had put Jud in prison.

Wasn't that enough?

Frank heard the light tinkle of breaking glass, saw

the window rising. Rolling to his knees, he lifted his arm, waiting. He was a good shot, an excellent shot. Framed within the open window, a darker form moved against the dark of night. A thin spear of light winked on just long enough to reveal the motionless lump beneath the bedcovers—and the dark glint of a steel revolver pointing at the bed.

Frank pressed the trigger.

Darkness cloaked the island at night, making stars vivid and bright when the sky was clear. Laurel drove slowly, glancing occasionally at the rearview mirror to be certain no one followed. The road lay black and silent in front and behind her. She drove past the checkpoint for the residential development. The exit was open. The guard at the entrance would have no reason to note her car. It wasn't far to the main streets of Broward's Rock and the police station that overlooked the harbor.

Laurel smiled serenely, glancing at the new backpack lying on the passenger seat. Now it held the film cassette and her brisk note. She wished she could be present when dear Chief Garrett viewed the film. Wouldn't he be surprised! Wasn't it a shame, actually, that one couldn't just for a few moments take another form? Such as a butterfly! If she could be a butterfly— perhaps a zebra, for zebras loved passion fruit and that surely seemed congenial; or perhaps a swallowtail, for they had quite good taste, cruising round and about magnolias—she would hover near that nice young man and flap her wings in pleasure when he realized what the cassette contained. Oh, the phone wires would zing, calls to the DEA and to the sheriff's office and perhaps even to the FBI. Did phone wires zing? Wasn't everything just a pulse through space now? Hmm. Oh, well, whatever. But, sadly, she could not be present when the chief set in motion the actions that would culminate in breaking up a heretofore exceptionally successful smuggling ring. She would simply have to read all about it in *The Island Gazette* when the Crawfords were arrested along with those picking up the cocaine Friday night. It surely should be exciting. Would it be inappropriate to take the motorboat out that night, just for a ride in the moonlight? Hmm. No. She must be sensible and she'd already arranged for her surreptitious departure from the island tonight. Discretion was surely the better part of valor in this instance.

Sirens shrieked.

Laurel's hands tensed on the wheel. Without a pause, she turned the car into the first cross street. She stopped, turned off the lights and motor, and turned to watch.

Two police cars and an ambulance streaked past. Red lights whirled. The sirens' wails rose and fell. Was the Sea Side Inn on fire? No, they'd gone past Bay Street. In any event, the night was once again dark and silent. She drove quickly to the police station. It took only a minute to dash up the walk and leave the knapsack on the front steps. A few minutes later, she nosed her Morris Minor onto the ferry. Ben Parotti gave her a quick salute.

When the ferry was well away from the island, she left the car and climbed the metal ladder to the wheelhouse. "Ben, you are simply wonderful." Her husky voice radiated admiration. "I appreciate your making this special run for me. And it will be our secret, won't it?" She smiled, looked deep into his eyes.

Ben turned a peculiar rust color, cleared his throat. "Sure thing, Mrs. Roethke. Anytime."

The phone rang Friday morning at almost the same moment the alarm pealed. Max rolled over, flailed for the phone and the alarm.

"Max, do something." Annie pulled a pillow over her head.

Max knocked the alarm on the floor, reached over to try and find it, shoved the receiver next to his chin. "H'lo."

"Maxwell, my dear. I do believe you sleepyheads are—what is that wailing noise?" Laurel yawned.

"The damn alarm. Wait a minute." Max found the alarm, turned it off. "Ma." He sat bolt upright. "Where are you?"

Annie pulled the pillow off her head. "Is it Laurel?"

Max nodded, held a finger to his lips.

"In Atlanta, of course." Laurel's voice was sleepy but cheerful. "Don't you remember?"

Max covered the receiver, pointed toward the door. "Go down and check caller ID. Hurry."

Annie popped out of bed and ran.

Max looked appreciatively after the slim legs revealed beneath the shorty nightgown. "Okay, Ma, I want the truth."

"The truth." A reverent pause. "My dear, we all seek truth every day. It is the human—"

"Ma."

A sweet laugh. "Maxwell, I do believe you are grumpy. Poor Annie. Are you always so bearish when awakened?"

"Ma!" It was short but not sweet.

"Do have a nice breakfast. Perhaps some oatmeal. That's always so strengthening, and yes"—she spoke fast—"I am definitely in Atlanta, as I have been most of the week." The last words were clear and distinct.

"You damn well better stay there. You didn't give me a chance to tell you when you called before, but somebody broke into your house on Wednesday night. They left a message. They trashed your room. If you'd been there—"

"But I wasn't." She was serene. "However, I see your point. One would think, however, that the intruder might have relaxed by now. After all, had I been able to identify the person, I would already have transmitted that information to the police."

"Killers don't rest easy, Ma. Stay in Atlanta until we give you the all clear." This time Max hung up, which cheered his morning considerably.

Sunlight splashed into the breakfast room. "Oatmeal?" Annie held up the Quaker Oats box.

"No. Definitely not." He cleared his throat. "I'm going to fix French toast. Do you want some?"

Annie nodded happily, returned the oatmeal to the shelf. "Sprinkled with shaved almonds?"

"Sure." Max picked eggs from the refrigerator, broke them into a mixing bowl. He chose oatmeal bread.

Annie poured orange juice into two glasses. "Do you think she'll stay in Atlanta?"

"She'd better." His voice was grim.

Annie set the table, shot him a worried look. "Do you suppose Pete is getting close to finding the murderer?" But Pete wasn't checking out anyone at school. Was Pete right? Or Henny?

"Maybe. But we can't stop looking." Max flipped two pieces, watched them turn golden brown. "She won't stay in Atlanta for long."

Annie walked fast. It was too bad she hadn't arrived a little sooner. The bell had already rung and only a few students still hurried across the school grounds. Annie slowed when she reached the slot where Meredith Muir had parked yesterday. Today there was a beat-up circa 1960 Chevy in that parking space, not the sporty blue Mustang. Annie glanced up and down the row, but she didn't see Meredith's car.

In the main hallway, Annie headed for the office. No one had questioned her credentials yesterday, but she was relieved when she stepped into the main office to see that Dr. Allensworth's door was closed and that Mrs. Otis wasn't at her desk.

Annie reached the counter, spoke to the languid redhead. "Good morning. We're still settling some details for Mrs. Nevis's service. I'd appreciate a visitor's pass. Annie Darling."

The redhead pulled the sheet with nameplates nearer, began to print.

"I'll start with Mr. Wilson." Annie nodded toward the corridor branching off the main office. "Oh, could you check for me, see what class Meredith Muir has now?"

The secretary turned to her computer, punched in a name. "Mrs. Whiteside. Room two hundred."

Annie smiled her thanks as she took the pass, clipped it to her blouse. She felt a flash of triumph. One-two-three. This was going to be easy, George Wilson, Jack Quinn and Meredith Muir, here she came, ready or not.

Putter dangling from one hand, Max wandered back and forth by the putting green. He didn't try to keep the irritation out of his voice. "I know the chief's busy, but can't I talk to somebody, Mavis? How about Billy? Or Lou? *Somebody?*"

At the Broward's Rock Police Station, the dispatcher hesitated. "Max, I'm sorry. Everybody's busy."

Max dropped a ball on the green. "What if I said I knew who killed Mrs. Nevis?"

There was a pause. "Max, honestly, everybody's out. We had a big stakeout last night at Frank Saulter's. They got that guy—you know, Jud Hamilton—the one who killed his wife and Frank got him convicted. Anyway, everybody knew he was gunning for Frank and he broke into Frank's house last night, and Max, you wouldn't believe it, but Frank shot the gun out of his hand before Billy could even get inside. Billy's just worn out. He was there every night this week and then the Nevis murder and—well, things are pretty wild over here."

Max dropped the putter and flung himself into his desk chair. "Wait a minute, Mavis. Are you telling me Frank's house was under surveillance every night this week?"

"Yes. That's exactly right." Another phone rang in the background. "Max, I'm sorry, I got to go."

Max pulled his legal pad close. On it were two names:

Diane Littlefield.

Frank Saulter.

Max picked up his pen, crossed out Frank Saulter.

George Wilson's broad face, spattered with freckles, was made for smiling, with a generous mouth above a rounded chin. He wasn't smiling this morning. Annie judged him to be in his forties, but he had a jaunty youthful air. His small office was a mixture of staidness—scholarly books, green metal filing cabinet, framed diplomas—and bold mementos—a multicolored parachute splashed against the wall behind him, a weathered fossil bone, a lump of coal encased in a clear plastic container. Maureen Riley had described him as something of a rapid-fire comedian. He wasn't making Annie laugh, but he certainly talked a mile a minute.

". . . certainly be glad to be of any help I can. We are all absolutely shocked. I can still scarcely believe that Kay is dead. Really a lovely woman. I didn't know her all that well." A swift grin. "She was lots older, a different generation, though the students respected her. We all did. But today you can't tell what's going to happen anywhere. If students can be gunned down at school . . ." He shook his head in disbelief. "Anything can happen. Our students are going to have a tough time dealing with this."

Annie leaned forward in her chair. "That's what I wanted to talk to you about. Who was the student Kay

Nevis was worried about? Could it have been Meredith Muir?"

There was utter surprise on his face. "Kay? Meredith?" He looked at her sharply. "I can't imagine a problem there." But for once he spoke slowly, his face creased in a thoughtful frown.

The idea was obviously a shock to him. Annie hurried to explain. "Yesterday I saw Meredith here." She nodded toward the corridor outside his door. "She was very upset. I know you and the other counselor had to help Dr. Allensworth, but it's a shame no one talked to Meredith. I watched her during the assembly, and I could see she was scared. I tried to catch her after school, but Mr. Quinn was talking to her, and whatever he said, it upset her even more and she jumped in her car and drove away. I followed her home—"

"You followed her home?" Wilson's tone was shocked, his stare probing.

Annie realized she was treading on uncertain ground here. Her status as an emissary from the family scarcely included reassuring students. But . . . "I was worried about her, if you want to know the truth. She wouldn't come to the door. I kept trying to call her last night but there was no answer." Annie scooted forward in her chair. "Look, Mr. Wilson, I'll be frank with you. The family knows that Kay Nevis was disturbed by something that happened at school and they don't know whether it involved a student or another teacher. We want to be able to tell the police all about this. We are hoping that someone who knew her, who spent time around her, someone such as yourself, may have picked up on the problem, whatever it was."

He tapped a pencil on the metal desktop, his face furrowed. "This is all a surprise to me. I'm afraid I won't be able to help. If Kay was upset about something, she didn't share it with me." He gave a helpless shrug. "But if I can be of assistance in any other way, do let me know." He rose, started around the desk.

It wasn't exactly a bum's rush, but Annie knew her time was up. She stood, but she didn't move toward the door. "You'll talk to Meredith?"

"I definitely will." He strode to the door, held it for her. "It's good of you to take the time to help a student."

Annie paused in the doorway. "Have you ever talked with Meredith before? Do you know if she has any problems?"

He gave a firm head shake. "I'm sorry, Mrs. Darling. Our contact with students is strictly confidential. But"—he hesitated, shrugged—"I think I can fairly say that Meredith is a well-adjusted student, a successful student, and that you need have no long-term concern about her. Either Mrs. Heaston or I will speak to her today."

As the door closed behind her, Annie frowned. Dammit, did the man get it? Did he have any inkling of the girl's deep distress? Would he do something? Okay, okay, if he didn't, she would.

Max drove slowly past the Littlefield house, one of the island's earliest homes, frame on a brick foundation. Wide porches extended along the front and sides of the house both on the first and second floors. Old live oaks, wisteria, crape myrtles and azaleas pressed close.

Max craned to see. No cars were visible. No red Jeep. He reached a dead end, backed, turned, retraced his route.

The dusty road curved. It was just about here where Bob Tower died, thrown a half-dozen feet to lie bleeding and broken in the ditch. Longleaf pines threw deep shadows. The morning sun had yet to pierce the gloom of the narrow lane. Diane Littlefield drove this way to reach the main road.

If a car came around the curve too fast early in the morning, it might be hard for the driver to see a jogger.

Max was thoughtful as the road straightened out. There was the Tower house, a shabby gray wooden house on pilings. No cars there either. The next house was a low-slung ranch style built flush to the ground. Max pulled in the drive behind a sleek green Jaguar. Obviously, there was money here. He wondered if the owners had come to the island from a landlocked state. Didn't they realize Broward's Rock could be under four feet of water from a storm surge if a category-3 hurricane struck? For that matter, who had built this and similar houses on the island? A contractor from Montana? Mars, maybe.

A woman in a sleeveless denim dress knelt beside a bed of impatiens, a trowel in one hand. An oversized floppy yellow straw hat shaded her face. She looked around as he slammed the car door shut.

Max walked swiftly across the yard, noting the nameplate that dangled from an iron stanchion next to the front porch: MARK AND IRENE HUDDLESTON.

She rose to face him. Tendrils of auburn hair poked from beneath the hat. A tiny woman, she had bright dark eyes, sharp features and the restless impatience of a hummingbird. She jiggled the trowel in a gloved hand.

Max assumed his most genial expression. "Hello, I'm Max Darling and I'm looking at houses in this neighborhood. If you'd give me a minute I'd really appreciate it. Realtors always suggest checking with the neighbors."

"What's for sale?" She poked up the wide brim of her hat with the tip of the trowel.

"We're interested in the Littlefield house." That was true enough. "Perhaps you know the family?"

"In passing." A whisper of laughter. "They aren't home much. He's off on business and the mother's an antique hound. The girl's there during the school year. I know I wouldn't have gone off and left my children at home alone when they were in high school. I doubt the house would have been standing when I got back. Of course, we have three boys. Our youngest just turned thirty. I think maybe we're home safe. But Diane's a quiet one. Except when she drives. Roarrrrr—there she goes in that Jeep. Must think she's at Daytona." She waggled the trowel. "I know who you are, of course. Known your mother in my garden club for some years. Not that she grows anything. But she's a joiner, isn't she? You want to know about that Jeep, don't you? I saw those flyers, heard your wife was really upset about them. That's clever of you, saying you're interested in the house, letting me think you want to buy it. I know it's not for sale. Lou Anne Littlefield would sell Diane before she'd sell that house. 'The house' "—her tone clearly mimicked Lou Anne as she quoted—" 'is a shining example of the classic Adam style, with lavishly designed decorations that recur throughout.' " Irene Huddleston sniffed. "But about those flyers, once I thought about it"—she cocked her head to one side like an attentive sparrow—"it makes perfect sense. Diane probably ran right over Bob, not meaning to, you know, but she drives too fast and that time of morning it's hard to see on that road. Is that what you wanted to know?"

Max folded his arms and lounged against an urn with a mass of gladiolus. He grinned. "My disguise penetrated! Yes, you're right on all counts. I am trying to find out more about Diane Littlefield. I want to know if Diane was at home the night before last at midnight."

"You have a good reason for asking?" The dark eyes peered at him intently.

Max's smile eased away. "Yes, ma'am, I do. One of Diane's teachers—Kay Nevis—was shot that night near midnight."

Mrs. Huddleston drew her breath in sharply. "I know Kay. How dreadful."

"Yes, ma'am." Max waited. This woman would not be hurried or led.

She turned away, walked to a wooden bench, sat down. "Why would you think I might know where Diane was at midnight?"

Max strolled nearer, turned over his hands. "It never hurts to ask."

She took off her hat, laid it beside her. "I saw her car coming home at just after eleven. I'd brought Regis out." She pointed at a fat cocker, face resting on his paws, in the shadow of a crape myrtle. "The Jeep roared by. That's all I can say."

Max looked thoughtfully at the road. So Diane arrived home at just after eleven. But Kay Nevis's killer came by water and the Littlefields had a motorboat.

Students hurried past. Through an open window came the raucous *ca-ca-ca* of a flock of pileated woodpeckers and the drone of a single-engine plane. Jack Quinn's eyebrows were drawn into a tight dark line, his lips pressed into an equally tight line. He stood outside the open door to his classroom, arms folded, glaring at Annie.

Annie tried again. "Look, Mr. Quinn, Meredith Muir's scared to death. I'm trying to find out why."

"She's scared?" His voice was surprised. "But I thought . . ." He stopped, shook his head. "Look, I don't know anything about Meredith or her connection to Kay Nevis. I suggest you talk to Meredith." The bell rang. He stepped toward the door. "I've got to get to work."

Annie called out, "Why was Meredith angry with you—"

The door to his classroom closed.

Max steered the motorboat out of the marina. It was a beautiful day. He wished he were heading out to the Snapper Banks with his trolling rig and plenty of cut bait. He'd get himself a mess of grouper and fix a great dinner. But not today. He reached the Sound, turned north. Shading his eyes, he searched for the entrance to the waterway that led to the Littlefield house.

*   *   *

Annie pushed in the classroom door. A ginger-haired
teacher stood at the blackboard, energetically writing.
Annie stepped inside. "Mrs. Whiteside," Annie spoke
softly, "if you don't mind"—Annie's eyes scanned the
class, white and black and brown faces, clothing of all
sorts, one head with pink hair, one head with no hair—
"I'm looking for Meredith Muir . . ." Annie's voice
trailed away. Her gaze sped up and down the rows.

She knew before Mrs. Whiteside spoke. "Meredith?
She's absent this morning."

∴ *Sixteen* ∾

DUST PLUMED beneath the wheels. Annie knew she was driving too fast. Worse, she was steering with one hand while she held the cell phone in the other. She was doing everything she most loathed in other drivers. But . . .

"Mavis, Annie Darling. Listen, it may be nothing"—oh, if only it would turn out that Meredith was skipping school, if only that would be all—"but please, ask Billy or the chief, ask somebody to go to Meredith Muir's house. That's the house across the inlet from—"

"Hold on a minute, Annie. Got a nine-one-one here." The phone line went on hold.

Annie reached the fork, wrenched the wheel. Oh, God, there was the Mustang, parked where she'd seen it yesterday afternoon. Annie jolted to a stop near the bright blue car. She slammed out of the Volvo, swung toward the house, then stopped, peering out at the water.

Max stood at the end of the pier. Their motorboat was moored near the ladder. He held a cell phone, spoke into it with a grim face. As he clicked it off, he saw her. "Annie."

When she heard his voice, Annie knew she was too late, knew that no one now could help Meredith Muir. She walked with leaden, reluctant steps toward the pier, stopping once to look past the marsh at the sodden lump that floated not far from the wooden pilings. She still held the silent phone to her cheek. The phone clicked on.

"Annie . . ." Mavis's voice was gentle.

"Yes. I'm here." Annie pushed words from a throat that ached with sadness. "Yes, we'll wait."

Horace Burford knelt by the girl's body. She lay facedown. The medical examiner gently spread lank, wet hair. "See the swelling? Probably unconscious when she went in the water. Drowned." He pushed up a little unsteadily, wincing as his right knee straightened. "Look for"—his bulldog face creased in thought—"something like a board. Maybe an oar, something like that." He glanced toward the murky green water. "Fat chance you'll find it. Anyway, she's been dead about twelve hours, give or take a few either way."

Billy Cameron made a final note, stuffed the small spiral in his pocket. "Okay. Thanks, Doc."

Dr. Burford lumbered away, anger in every heavy step.

Max and Annie stood on the wooden deck near the swimming pool, out of the way of the homicide detail. Max watched Dr. Burford slam into his old black car. "Hates it, doesn't he? Hates death. Hates wrongful death most of all."

"If I hadn't left here yesterday . . ." Annie's voice quivered.

Max swung toward Annie, gripped her arm. "No. You did what you could. She wouldn't open the door."

Annie shivered. "I should have called her parents. I should have got in touch with the counselors. I should have done something!"

Max glanced toward the big rambling house. "Her parents aren't here. I've already been up to the house. No answer. Nobody home. You couldn't have called them. As for the counselors"—his grip tightened— "Annie, look at me." He waited until her pain-filled eyes met his. "What would have happened if you'd called them?"

Some of the misery drained from her face. "I guess . . . I think they'd have said they'd talk to her this morning. Nobody would have imagined anything like this could happen. But, dammit, I should have asked somebody to help. I saw her. She was scared, scared to death."

"Annie"—his voice was soft—"you did your best."

"None of us did enough, that's obvious." Annie jerked away from him, paced to the edge of the deck. "Where's Pete Garrett? What's he doing that he's so damn busy he's put Billy in charge of this? Billy's a good guy, but my God, the girl's dead."

Max hurried to join her. "Shh. Billy and the others are doing everything that can be done. There's not a hell of a lot to do. Look at it"—Max swept his arm toward the water—"I came up in the boat and saw her floating there. She must have been on the pier last night and somebody hit her, knocked her out and she fell into the water."

"Out on the pier . . ." Annie squinted against the

sun. "If she was scared, why did she go out on the pier with somebody? Max, I'm sure she was scared."

Max hunched his shoulders, stared at the water. "Why?"

"Why did she go out on the pier?" Annie shrugged. "I don't know. I doubt we'll ever know."

"No. Why was she scared? And was she scared or upset?" Max's dark blue eyes were thoughtful. "It makes a difference."

Annie took her time answering. Yes, it did make a difference. She tried to remember with precision the feeling that had permeated the narrow corridor in front of the counselor's office. Was Meredith scared or upset?

Annie looked across the inlet at the Nevis house. The front blinds were open. A woman bustled up the steps carrying a casserole. There were several cars Annie didn't recognize. Kay Nevis's tan Camry was there, but not Henny's old black Dodge. Henny was probably on her way to the Savannah airport to pick up members of Kay's family. "I think she was scared." Annie threw up her hands. "I can't be certain. She definitely was distraught. There's no doubt about that." Once again Annie looked out at the green water, her gaze moving on to the modest house on pilings. "Max, maybe Meredith saw something"—Annie pointed toward the Nevis house—"Wednesday night. But if she saw the murderer come to Kay's house, why didn't she tell somebody? Kay's murder was announced during the lunch hour. Meredith had the whole afternoon at school to go tell somebody—the principal, one of the counselors, somebody." Annie's eyes widened. "Maybe hat's why she was waiting for George Wilson. I told you about him. He's a counselor. I saw him this morning and he promised to talk to Meredith." Annie ook a deep breath. "Max, why didn't Meredith tell someone?"

Max jammed his hands in the pockets of his khakis. 'Okay, we can be sure she would have told someone if, say, she saw somebody leave the Nevis house carrying a gun. But"—he squinted against the sunlight—"it seems likely that she saw something that puzzled her and she began to wonder and worry."

The steps to the deck creaked. Billy bounded toward them, his big face creased in a frown. "Okay, you two. How come you're here?" Behind him, the ambulance with Meredith's body backed and turned, drove slowly away.

Annie took a deep breath and started with Henny's insistence yesterday that the flyers had been planted on Kay Nevis, that there had to be some other reason for Kay's murder and that school was Kay's life. ". . . I went to school yesterday and talked to Kay's best friends and both of them said she had been worried about something recently. One thought it had to do with one of the teachers Kay lunched with every day. The other thought Kay's distress was over a student. I tried to talk to the teachers at Kay's lunch table. When I went to see George Wilson, the counselor, Meredith Muir was waiting for him. Anybody could see the girl was upset. But she didn't get in to see Wilson. I saw Meredith later at the assembly. She was talking to Diane Littlefield. Diane's the girl who drives a red Jeep, probably the one mentioned in the flyers."

Billy held up a hand. "Wait a minute. Wait a minute." He wrote fast. "This Diane Littlefield, tell me about her."

Diane Littlefield. Annie pictured the two girls as she'd seen them during the assembly yesterday, Meredith's blond head bent toward Diane's bronze curls, the two of them deep in conversation, their faces strained and intent. "Diane was a good friend of Meredith's. We need to find out what Meredith and Diane were talking about. Rachel told me she'd heard that Diane was at Meredith's Wednesday night."

"Diane Littlefield." There was an odd tone in Max's voice. "That's why I came." He pointed out at the pier and the motorboat bobbing in the swells. "Because if Pete's right, if Kay Nevis did those flyers and got killed on account of them, well, Diane Littlefield's the only person connected to the flyers who has no alibi for the night Kay was killed."

Billy blinked eyes red-rimmed from fatigue. "Yeah, and she was probably driving the Jeep that killed Bob Tower. Maybe Kay Nevis knew it. Hey, maybe this girl knew how Tower died." He jerked his head toward the Muir house.

"Meredith. Her name's Meredith." Annie's tone was sharp. Dammit, she wasn't just a girl. She'd been Meredith Muir, beautiful and scared and now dead, with all the long years that should have been discarded like a crumpled paper cup. "Listen, Meredith was mad at one of the teachers, the track coach, Jack Quinn."

"Oh, sure, I know Jack." Billy's tone was admiring. "Great guy. Well, I'll check that out. But you say she and this Diane Littlefield were friends. Maybe Merelith knew about the Jeep, and when the teacher gets killed, she's afraid her friend did it and she talked to her at this assembly." Billy flipped his notebook shut. "And if Diane Littlefield was over here Wednesday night, hey, this is beginning to make sense." He glanced at his watch. "Yeah. I'll get over to the school."

His face darkened by a frown, Max sliced open the box of books.

"Careful," Annie cautioned. "If the covers are scratched, the collectors go berserk."

"Oh, sorry." He lifted the flap, peered at the bright orange covers with the crimson letters WHODUNIT cascading from the tip of a smoking gun. "No problem." He picked up the ten hardcovers, added them to the towering stacks ranged behind a card table next to the coffee bar.

"That's the last box. So"—her voice was tired—"everything's set for the signing Sunday afternoon. If, of course, our prima-donna author can tear herself away from Chapter Seventeen. But"—and there was grudging admiration in Annie's tone—"Emma had the right idea, asking the police to look for Kay Nevis's daybooks. Just think, Max"—Annie jammed her hand through her thick blond hair—"if we had Kay's last daybook, we'd know why she was murdered."

Max leaned against the coffee bar. "Yeah." His voice was thoughtful. "I wonder how the murderer knew she kept a daybook. That's not the kind of thing a kid would think of. Is it?" It was a challenge.

"I don't know. That's a good point, Max." Annie

stepped behind the coffee bar. She glanced at the rows of mugs reflected against the mirrored wall. Each mug carried the title of a mystery and the author's name. Without hesitating, Annie selected *Who Saw Her Die?* by Patricia Moyes and *Frame-Up* by Andrew Garve. She poured steaming Kona coffee in each mug, handed the second one to Max.

"That's what I'm afraid of." Max ran one finger over the bright red letters of the Garve title. "I feel like we handed Diane Littlefield over to Billy tied up like a lamb for slaughter." He drank the coffee, put down the mug, frowned at it.

Annie knew he wasn't frowning at the wonderful coffee. *Frame-Up*. Maybe so, maybe no. "Maybe with good reason," Annie said quietly. "No matter where we look, there's Diane. She drives a red Jeep. She's Meredith Muir's best friend. She was at Meredith's house Wednesday night. At the assembly, Diane and Meredith had an intense conversation. But who knows?" Annie shrugged. "Maybe Diane has an alibi for last night when Meredith died."

"For her sake, I hope so." Max reached for the coffeepot. "If not, she's in deep trouble."

The front door to Death on Demand banged open. Rachel's high voice called out, "Hi, Ingrid. Is Annie here? In back?" She clattered down the central aisle, her backpack dangling from one hand. "Oh, Annie, I'm so glad you're here." Rachel tossed her backpack onto the table, flung herself into Annie's arms. "Have you heard about Meredith? Oh, Annie, it's awful. I tried to talk to Ben, but he left right after they told us about Meredith. He just walked right out of school, but I don't think he'll get in trouble. Dr. Allensworth's pretty nice, really. And the police came and talked to Diane. They say she was white as a sheet when she came out of the office and she ran to her car and left. Annie, it's so awful." Rachel burrowed her head against Annie's shoulder.

Annie held her tight. "I know. I know."

Rachel slowly pulled away, swiped at her face. "Everybody says they're going to arrest Diane. They say the police told her not to leave the island and they called her dad in Honolulu and as soon as he gets back they're going to talk to her. She's supposed to have a lawyer with her." Rachel's eyes were huge. "You know what that means! And they say Diane was over at Meredith's Wednesday night. You know, nobody's ever home at their houses. I guess it was like when I was at Aunt Marguerite's after Mom died, nobody caring where you were or what you did. Some of the kids thought it was cool. I mean, Meredith and Diane could do whatever they wanted, stay up all night or look at anything on the Net or drink a lot. Meredith and Diane used to do that, stay up all night in the cabana at Meredith's. It's the separate house right by the pool. Everybody thought Meredith was so lucky, doing whatever she wanted to do, she and Diane both. But it isn't cool. It's like being out in a blizzard and you can't see anything because the snow's swirling around you and you ache inside because you're so cold. And now Diane's in big trouble." Rachel took a deep breath. "I told everybody you could help." She stared at Annie with huge, hopeful eyes.

"Help? Me? Rachel, I don't know anything that will help Diane." Everything she and Max knew, Billy knew, too.

Rachel reached out a thin, wavering hand. "Please, Annie. You will help, won't you? Diane didn't hurt Meredith. She wouldn't do that. Not ever. And all this stuff about Diane shooting Mrs. Nevis—why, that's just crazy. It would be"—Rachel's narrow face tightened, the cheekbones jutting out—"like Mom, wouldn't it? Lots of . . . blood?"

"Oh, Rachel." Annie stepped forward. She held Rachel tight once again, stroked the dark curls pressed against her shoulder.

Rachel lifted her head, her stricken face determined. "But that's true, isn't it? Wouldn't there have been lots of blood when Mrs. Nevis died?"

"Yes." Annie left it at that.

Rachel stepped away, gripped the back of a wooden chair. "Then"—she gave a decided nod—"Diane didn't do it. One day last fall, somebody ran over a dog in the parking lot. Diane screamed and screamed and somebody told me she's like that about seeing blood. She can't stand it."

Annie almost spoke, then didn't. There would have been blood when Bob Tower died. Was it the fact the dog was hit by a car that upset Diane?

"Anyway, I promised the girls that you'd talk to Diane tonight." Rachel's eyes fell. She didn't meet Annie's gaze.

"The girls?" But Annie knew what was coming.

"Some of the seniors." Rachel's muttered answer was hard to hear. Head down, Rachel swung away and reached into her backpack. She pulled out her cell phone. "I'm sorry, Annie. I shouldn't have said you'd do it. I'm supposed to call Diane and tell her what time. I'll just say you can't."

Annie spoke fast. "Ask her to come at seven, Rachel."

Rachel jerked to face Annie, her thin face alight with joy. "Oh, Annie, I know you can help her."

A chuck-will's-widow skimmed low near the edge of the lagoon, its repetitive cry a harbinger of dusk. A flock of pine warblers swarmed near a stand of loblolly pines. In the shadows of the crape myrtle, a dimly seen raccoon observed the terrace and, of course, the wooden enclosure where the snap-lidded garbage pails were kept.

Max clapped his hands. "Go on, fella. Snack bar's closed."

The raccoon didn't move.

Max grinned. "Have to admire a man who stands his ground."

"Wait a minute." Annie drawled the words as a challenge. "Aren't you being just a tad sexist?"

"Who, me?" Max's face exuded angelic innocence. "How could you even think it? So, okay, maybe this is a mama raccoon. Whichever, I'll lay odds the minute we leave the terrace he/she is alley-oop up and over the stockade fence."

Smiling, Annie relaxed against the cushions of the swing. This was fun. This was how life should be after dinner (somewhat early because of their expected guest) on a lovely spring evening with the moon edging up behind the pines and the male frogs creating a vigorous chorus of barks, shrieks and grunts in their romantic efforts to attract lady frogs. "A guy will do what a guy has to do," Max had been known to remark in a sympathetic tone.

They both heard the slam of the car door, shattering the peace of the night, silencing for an instant the song of the frogs. Where the raccoon had stood there was now only the shadow of the bush.

Annie sat bolt upright.

Max reached out, took her hand. "It will be okay."

"Oh, Max, will it?" Annie twisted to look toward the French doors. "I shouldn't have agreed to see her—" She broke off as one of the French doors opened.

"Out this way, Diane." Rachel held the door.

As they stepped onto the illuminated patio, the girls looked summery in T-shirts and shorts and sandals. Diane's bronze hair was pulled behind a red calico bandanna. Rachel's flyaway dark curls stirred in the breeze. She moved fast, then stopped and looked back, waggled an encouraging hand. "Come on, Diane, it's okay."

Annie wished everyone would stop saying it was okay. Nothing at this moment was okay. Kay Nevis and Meredith Muir were violently dead and the tall, slender girl walking so reluctantly across the flag-stones might soon be sitting in a jail cell charged with those murders.

When Diane was only a few feet away, she stopped and stared helplessly at Annie. "You came to the store Wednesday. About . . ." Her voice trailed away. She pressed the back of her hand against trembling lips.

Annie patted the cushion beside her. "Come sit with me, Diane."

Max stood up so suddenly, his chair scraped on the stone. "I'll bet you girls would all like to have a Brown Cow. Come on, Rachel, you can help me fix them."

Diane edged toward the swing, tentatively perched at the far end.

"Max and Rachel love to pretend we have an old-fashioned soda fountain. They . . ." But there was no answering spark in Diane's strained blue eyes.

The girl hunched her shoulders, wrapped her arms tightly together. She shivered. "I'm so scared." Her voice was a whisper of sound. "Oh, God, I'm so scared." She turned toward Annie. Terror burned in her eyes as wild as a fire roaring through mountain timber. Tears slipped out of those hot eyes, ran unchecked down ashen cheeks. "I didn't do it. I didn't do any of it. The police asked me about Mrs. Nevis and Meredith and they looked at me like . . . I hated the way they looked at me. They called my dad and told him they wanted to talk to me and I'm supposed to have a lawyer. Dad's flying home but he doesn't get into Savannah until real late and he's mad. He called and told me he didn't know what I'd been up to but I damn sure better be able to get it all taken care of because he had a big deal and he had to get back to Honolulu. And Mother's in London." Her arms fell away from her body and her hands lay open and helpless on her slim tanned legs. "I have to talk to the police tomorrow and they'll ask me those questions. I told them the answers and all they did was look at me, that terrible look. Rachel said you'd help me, but what can you do?" Her tone was hopeless.

Annie gently touched her arm. "I don't know, Diane. Maybe together we can figure something out. You were over at Meredith's Wednesday night, the night Mrs. Nevis was shot."

Diane nodded. "Yes, ma'am."

The oh-so-Southern courtesy touched Annie, made her want desperately to help this frightened child. "Did you know that Mrs. Nevis lived across the inlet?"

"Oh, sure." Diane tucked a strand of hair beneath the bandanna. "Mrs. Nevis was nice. She's one of the teachers I liked. She was . . . fair, you know? And she made the dullest things kind of fun. There was this general named Stilwell and she told us all about him and how he was treated . . ." Her voice faded away. "I used to always wave at her when I went to Meredith's." There was a tone of remembrance.

"Used to wave at her?" Annie repeated. "Did you stop waving at her?"

Diane sighed, slumped back against the cushion. "I hadn't been over for a while, but I had to talk to Meredith Wednesday night. I had to. I didn't know what else to do. Those flyers talked about my . . . about a red Jeep." She stared at Annie, her eyes hot with fear. "But nobody else knew. Only Meredith." She lifted a shaking hand, pressed it against her temple.

"Only Meredith knew"—it was as if the truth hovered in the air around them—"that you accidentally hit Bob Tower?"

The girl reached out, clutched Annie's arm. "Oh, God, I didn't mean to hit him. It was so awful"—horror bubbled in her voice—"and my folks were gone. I drove to Meredith's. She was just leaving for school.

And she went and . . . looked. She came back and said it was too late, we couldn't do anything for him. We left my car at her house and went to school. The next week we took my car and drove to Savannah and found a place that would fix the bumper. I told them I hit a deer. We got the car back when it was done and nobody ever knew—so how did it get in those flyers?"

The flyers. Everything came back to the flyers. "What did Meredith say?"

Diane sat up straight, clenched her hands. "She said I must have told somebody. But I never did. Never, never, never. Why would I? I've tried to forget but I can't. I dream about the way he went through the air like it was slow motion. I wake up and I want to run, but there's no place to go." She buried her face in her hands. Her words were muffled. "Oh, God, I can never get away."

Annie gently touched a trembling arm. "Diane, you can make it better."

Slowly that ravaged face lifted. "I have to tell them, don't I?" Her voice was dull. "They'll put me in jail"—she shuddered—"and jails are so awful. We went to see one on a civics trip. . . ."

"I wouldn't think about that now." Annie wished she could insist that wouldn't happen. But no one could make that promise. "Tell your parents. Will you do that?"

Diane pulled off her bandanna, used it to wipe her face. "The police will think I killed Mrs. Nevis and Meredith to keep it quiet about Mr. Tower. That's not true! I swear I didn't do it. I swear!"

Annie had a cold sense the girl was absolutely right.

That was exactly what the police would believe. To keep it quiet . . . Annie lifted a hand. "Wait a minute, Diane. You say that no one besides Meredith knew about the accident. Is that right?"

Diane twisted the bandanna in her hands, turning it tighter and tighter. "That's right. Nobody knew. Just Meredith."

But the deeply incriminating suggestion of the red Jeep was included in the flyers. Meredith knew, but Meredith's murder proved she was not behind the flyers.

Annie studied the nervous, distraught girl, her hands tight on the bandanna. "Do you think Mrs. Nevis knew about your Jeep?"

Diane looked at Annie with dull, hopeless eyes. "She saw me at Meredith's lots of times in my Jeep. But she couldn't have known about Mr. Tower. Not unless Meredith told her. And that would be crazy. Anyway, Wednesday night Meredith kept saying the red Jeep in the flyers had to be just a fluke or maybe somebody'd known about my car all along and maybe this was some kind of queer game somebody was playing and I should just keep my mouth shut. But the next day, she was real upset . . ."

Annie leaned toward Diane, listened to her faltering, puzzled voice.

". . . at the assembly and she told me that Mrs. Nevis being killed had changed everything and she didn't know what to do but she was going to see what she could find out and she asked me not to tell anybody. I asked her what she meant, but she just shook her head. She looked kind of sick. Then she ran away from me and I never saw her again." Diane began to cry, great gulping sobs. "We used to have so much fun together. She was my best friend. Then everything changed."

Max opened the kitchen door. He held a tray with four tall ice cream soda glasses.

Annie shook her head.

He turned away and the door closed.

Diane shook out the bandanna, scrubbed her tear-streaked face. "We used to spend the night in the cabana down by the pool. It was so neat. We'd play music and we could play as loud as we wanted to. There's a little kitchen and we'd make fudge. I used to spend the night there a lot because her folks are mostly gone, like mine. Starting a couple of months ago, she didn't invite me over anymore, and when I'd call, she didn't answer. I knew she was there and I thought maybe she and Ben . . . But Ben was real sad because she stopped going out with him, and pretty soon, nobody saw her much except on the weekends. She'd still hang out with everybody at Spooky's . . ."

Annie recognized the pizza parlor that, according to Rachel, was the place to be from Friday afternoon to Sunday night.

". . . on the weekends but she didn't have anybody over on school nights. She treated Ben like he was some kind of little kid. And Ben"—Diane's pale face softened—"he's the neatest guy. Everybody would like to go out with Ben, but he never saw anyone but Meredith. She just blew him off."

"Do you think she was depressed?" Annie knew that avoiding contact with friends was a classic symptom of depression.

Diane's lips twisted. "Oh, no. She seemed happy as anything. She just didn't have anything to do with us anymore. Now"—Diane rubbed her temple—"she's dead. It doesn't make any sense. Why would anybody kill Meredith?"

There seemed to be one easy answer. "Maybe she was up late and looked across the inlet and saw the person who shot Mrs. Nevis. What time did you leave Wednesday night?"

"About eleven." Diane took a quick breath. "I went straight home and I stayed there until I went to school Thursday morning."

"Where was Meredith when you left?" A shadow moved not far away. Annie glanced toward the crape myrtle. She and Diane had sat so still, spoken so quietly, the raccoon had returned to reconnoiter.

"Oh, in the cabana. Meredith always had her friends there. She was out on the deck and she watched me drive away." She pressed the back of her hand against trembling lips. "Just like always."

Annie recalled the cabana. It took only a quick glance to look across the inlet at Kay Nevis's house.

"And last night?" Annie kept her tone casual, but she watched Diane's pale, drawn face with careful attention.

"I called her and called her." Diane hunched forward, knotting her fingers together. "I was so mad I could have—" She broke off with a startled gasp. "But that was all. I was just mad. I didn't go over there. I just kept calling. I had to do something about those flyers. If my folks ever saw one . . . But I didn't know what to do. That's what was so awful. I didn't know what to do." Her hands sagged loose in her lap. She stared at Annie with despair in her eyes. "Now I don't know what to do about"—she shuddered—"Mrs. Nevis and Meredith. It's like when you know something awful's going to happen and you can't do anything to make it stop."

∽ *Seventeen* ∾

ANNIE WRINKLED HER NOSE. "Hmm, that coffee smells wonderful."

Max tilted the pot, poured.

Annie raised her mug, savoring the aroma and treasuring the rich, fresh taste. But when she put the mug down, her face drooped. "I feel terrible."

"I know." Max sighed and leaned back in his chair. He glanced toward the clock. "What time do you suppose Diane will be interviewed by the police?"

Annie lifted her shoulders, let them fall. "Sometime this morning." She looked through the terrace windows at the sparkling morning—the sky Wedgwood-blue, the azaleas such a vivid pink they dazzled her eyes, the lagoon emerald-green. "Max, they'll arrest her. I know they will. It all fits together—the flyers in Kay Nevis's house, the red Jeep, Diane at Meredith's house, Diane and Meredith having that terribly intense talk during the assembly."

Max drummed his fingers on the kitchen table. "Diane has a motorboat. I saw it. If Pete ever finds out that Kay's murderer came in a motorboat . . ."

Running steps clattered down the stairway. Rachel

burst into the breakfast room. "Hey, I'm going over to Christy's. Everybody's coming. We're going to see if we can figure out a way to help Diane." She trotted toward the garage door. "I'm taking my bike—" The door slammed behind her.

Annie half rose. "She hasn't had any breakfast."

Max grinned. "I imagine Christy's house runs to sweet rolls and Pepsi."

Annie dropped into her chair. "Well, it will keep her out of harm's way."

"Yes." Max's tone was grim. "That's important."

Annie shivered, though the coffee was good and strong and hot. "I'm scared, Max. I don't think Diane killed either Kay Nevis or Meredith. Can you see Diane breaking into Laurel's house and trashing her bedroom? Max, if it comes to it, we'll have to talk to Laurel, explain how important it is to tell Pete about sighting that motorboat the night Kay was shot."

"Telling Pete about the motorboat might just be enough to clinch Diane's arrest. And he won't be impressed at our linking Laurel's late-night excursions with the vandalism at her house." Max frowned. "Damn, what do you suppose will happen when Laurel comes back to the island?"

Annie sipped the robust coffee, wondered if it would be piggy to eat a second poppy-seed muffin. "If Diane's arrested, nothing will happen. The murderer won't worry about Laurel at that point."

Max moved restively. "I don't see how we can be sure of that."

Annie didn't answer. They couldn't be certain of anything. "What a mess." Annie shoved her hand through her hair. "I thought Diane would be able to help us. But obviously she hadn't seen much of Meredith recently. If we knew why Meredith stopped hanging out with her, maybe that would help." Annie paused, her face crinkling with thought. "Mrs. Thompson"—Annie pictured the teacher's dark, intelligent, thoughtful face—"said Kay Nevis was angry that some student's parents weren't paying enough attention. What if that student was Meredith?"

Max quirked an eyebrow. "Could be. But wouldn't that apply equally to Diane? Her dad in Honolulu, her mother in London, Diane left pretty much to do what she wanted to do."

Annie ran her finger around the rim of the mug. A circle. Everything seemed to come to a circle when what she wanted was a nice straight line leading to the stealthy figure that nosed a motorboat into a lagoon Wednesday night and shot a defenseless woman. Had Kay Nevis been worried about Meredith or Diane? "Right. It could be either one of them, so that doesn't get us anywhere. Maybe we should concentrate on Mrs. Riley's idea about the lunch table." Abruptly, Annie sat very still. "One of the teachers at the lunch table was Jack Quinn. I told you about him. He's the track coach, a tall, lanky guy with a bony face. Damn sure of himself. Anyway, he and Meredith had an argument in the parking lot Thursday afternoon. Yesterday morning I tracked him down, but he clammed up, told me to ask Meredith. What do you suppose that was all about?"

"An argument?" Max's face brightened. "Hey, that could be important."

"Meredith can't tell us now." Her tone was quiet. "So he damn well better." She popped up and hurried to the counter. She flipped open the phone book, ran her finger down the column. When she found the listing, she punched in the numbers. As the line rang, she switched on the speakerphone.

The phone was answered on the third ring.

"H'lo." The voice was young and could have been either a little girl or boy.

"Is your daddy there?" Annie's hand tightened on the receiver.

"S'minute. Daddy? Hey, Daddy . . ."

In a moment, the track coach answered. "Hello." His voice was good-humored, held the reflection of laughter.

"Mr. Quinn. This is Annie Darling. I spoke to you yesterday morning at school." A flock of pelicans swept past the terrace windows, heading for the harbor to feast upon menhaden and mullet. Annie loved the ungainly birds with their huge bills and snowy heads and silvery-brown bodies. One of her favorite pleasures was walking out on the pier to watch the birds glide toward the wavetops.

The flock was out of sight before Quinn said gruffly, "Oh." And nothing more. His voice now held no warmth, was wary and distant.

Maybe that was why she went straight to the point. "Why did you quarrel with Meredith Muir in the parking lot Thursday afternoon?"

Max pushed back his chair, joined Annie beside the speakerphone.

"Why do you ask?" Quinn's question was sharp.

Annie glanced at Max.

He understood. His nod was swift.

Annie traced a *D* on the counter next to the phone. "Because Diane Littlefield may be arrested for Meredith's murder and for Kay Nevis's murder and I don't think she's guilty."

"Oh, shit." Squeals rose in the background, were suddenly muffled. "Just a minute." Steps sounded, a door slammed. There was the distant burr of a leaf machine. "What's the deal about Diane?"

Annie told him all of it, starting with the red Jeep in the flyers.

Quinn spoke slowly. "I saw Meredith run away from Diane at the assembly. Anybody could see Meredith was upset." He stopped.

"You followed Meredith out to the parking lot." The more Annie thought about Quinn's pursuit of Meredith, the odder it seemed. "Why?"

"Because Kay Nevis was murdered." He blew out a spurt of air that rasped over the speakerphone. "Oh hell, I didn't think Meredith could be involved, but I thought I had to talk to her. Now . . ." A chair scraped on concrete. ". . . well, now it's pretty clear poor little Meredith didn't have anything to do with Kay's murder. Meredith must have seen something the night Kay was killed and she didn't have sense enough to tell anyone. Anyway, nothing I say can hurt Meredith now. It was Monday afternoon. I'd gone down to the parking lot to get some stuff out of my car before sports. I had on running shoes and I cut across the field. I was walking behind a line of willow trees along the near boundary of the lot. The point is, I wasn't making any noise. Nobody could hear me coming. When I ducked around one of the willows, I saw Meredith on the driver's side of Kay Nevis's car. She was bent over and her hand made a quick, slashing movement. She looked around, but she didn't see me. Then she took off running, back toward the area where the seniors park. By the time I got to Kay's car, Meredith was gone. I looked at the door. There was a jagged X scraped on the side."

Cars were parked on both sides of the road leading up to the Nevis house. Some of the overflow had encroached on the lane leading to the Muir house.

As Max cautiously eased his red Ferrari into a depression near a stand of firs, Annie shaded her eyes and looked toward the Muir house. "There are some cars there." Cars meant people and heartbreak, parents in pain. "Oh, Max."

He reached out, squeezed her hand.

Annie didn't want to look at the rambling house or at the cabana where Meredith and Diane had played music as loud as they wanted or at the pier where Meredith had walked out to meet death. "Max, if only Meredith had talked to me Thursday."

Annie felt that Meredith walked with them up the dusty, rutted road. When she and Max stood beside Kay Nevis's tan Camry, Annie had a sudden vision of a beautiful blond girl, head ducked, keys gripped in her hand, lifting her arm, scouring a rough X on the unblemished paint.

Annie pointed at the six-inch-long gashes in the pale paint. "Ugly. If Meredith did that, she must have been very angry with Kay Nevis. You know, when I saw this the morning Henny found Kay, I thought maybe the murderer had done it. But now we know Meredith scraped the car. Why on earth . . ."

Max rocked back on his heels, hands in his pockets. "Nobody has mentioned a quarrel between Kay Nevis and Meredith."

Annie scarcely heard him. She was shaken by the anger implicit in the vandalism. If Chief Garrett had known about the jagged scratch on the Nevis car, wouldn't he immediately have wondered if Meredith had reason to murder the teacher?

"A quarrel between Kay and Meredith . . ." Annie glanced at the Nevis house, filled now with friends and mourning family. She looked across the inlet at the Muir house. Soon there would be cars overflowing there, too, as friends came to call, bringing food and flowers, offering love when love was needed most. "I don't get it. We all thought Meredith was killed because she saw something—"

Annie broke off as she stared across the inlet at the cabana and the pool and the long rambling yellow house. Her gaze returned to the cabana with its inviting deck, a brightly striped folded umbrella over a table, a half-dozen webbed chairs. The cabana was Meredith's little kingdom, far from the house. There was a dusty path that led from the pier to the deck of the cabana. This view could clearly be seen from the deck of the Nevis house or through the windows that faced the inlet. Suddenly everything clicked into place for Annie—Kay Nevis's distress in the days leading up to her death, the information in the flyers that was clearly linked to the school, Meredith's anguish after Kay's murder.

"Oh, Max! Maybe it wasn't what Meredith saw." Annie pointed across the bright green water, barely stirred by a sluggish breeze. "Maybe it was what Kay Nevis saw!"

Annie walked behind the pines that screened the tennis courts at the country club. She heard the *thwock* of balls, smelled the sweet scent of water splashing onto an empty clay court. The clerk behind the desk in the tennis center said Ben Bradford was raking Court 16.

Annie reached the entrance to the court. A young man in tennis whites pulled a rake across the far court. His back was to Annie. His head was bowed, his shoulders slumped. There were pain and sorrow in every step.

Annie steeled herself, walked quickly across the court, the soft clay deadening her footsteps. She stopped a few feet away. "Ben."

He jerked around. His eyes were red-rimmed, his features hard, his skin splotchy. He stared at her and there was a flicker of recognition. "You're Rachel's sister."

"Yes. I wanted to talk to you. . . ." She didn't want to do this. She wished she were far from the beautiful tennis court with its pinkish clay and the huge green pines that rustled ever so slightly in the breeze and this terrible grief. "Ben, I'm so sorry about Meredith."

His face twisted in a spasm of pain. He gripped the rake, leaned his head against his hands.

She had nothing to offer except "Ben, you can help catch the person who killed Meredith."

Slowly he looked up. His eyes glittered. "How?" His voice was deep and harsh. "What can I do?"

Annie hated to ask this question, but everything hinged on Ben's answer. "Ben, please tell me why Meredith stopped seeing you."

His mouth trembled.

Annie wondered if he could bear to answer.

"Why"—he cleared his throat, stared at her with anguished eyes—"does it matter?"

Annie took a deep breath, forced out the words. "Was she seeing someone else?"

His eyes fell. His words were ragged, uneven, could scarcely be heard. "She told me I was just a kid and she didn't have time for kids anymore. I know there was some guy. I thought maybe a friend of her parents. Some goddamn old man."

. . . didn't have time for kids anymore.

Ben was probably eighteen. Anybody over twenty-five would seem old to him. And Thursday afternoon, Meredith slammed her car door and her Mustang jolted out of the parking lot, leaving a grim-faced Jack Quinn staring after her.

Annie pushed the Volvo horn, held it.

Max poked his head out of the back entrance of Confidential Commissions and waved. He held up an index finger, ducked back inside. In a moment, he returned, slamming the door and hurrying down the steps. He carried a folder in his hand.

As soon as Max had settled in the passenger seat, the Volvo zoomed up the alley. "Did you get anything on Quinn and Wilson?"

Max tapped the folder. "Some stuff. I got to work as soon as you called. Didn't Ben have any idea who the man might be?"

"Not really. He thought it might be some friend of the family. I didn't suggest anything about Quinn or Wilson—"

"I hope not." Max gave her a worried look. "We don't have anything definite to link anybody to Meredith, Annie. We can't go around accusing either Quinn or Wilson of having an affair with Meredith."

Annie paused fleetingly at the stop sign—her driving habits seemed to be deteriorating, but dammit, she was in a hurry and there wasn't anybody coming—and accelerated onto Sand Dollar Road. "Well, I can sure tell Pete exactly what Ben told me. Pete will have to check it out." Annie slowed to let a heavily pregnant doe lumber across the road. "Max, I don't know what's going on at the police station. I've called and called. Finally I got Mavis and she said if I didn't have an emergency I should call back Monday. I told her I had important information about the murders and she said she'd take my name and somebody would get back to me." The Volvo picked up speed. Wind rushed through the open sunroof. "Get back to me!" Annie's voice rose. "I mean, what the heck is going on? There was so much noise and hubbub behind Mavis, I could barely hear her. It sounded like a cross between an Elks convention and the midway at a carnival."

Annie sped through the residential checkpoint with a wave for the guard. Almost there. Only a few more blocks to the police station. Annie marshaled facts in her mind. All she had to do was present them, make everything clear to Pete. . . . She turned onto Main Street, slowed, and pointed toward the one-story cinder-block police station, its cream paint gleaming in the mid-morning sun. "Max, look!"

There wasn't an empty parking spot anywhere on the block and cars were parked three deep in the dusty lot north of the station, including pickups, vans and sedans, all black. Television vans were double-parked in front of the station.

Annie turned right and made an immediate left into a narrow lane. "We can park by the Littlefield shop. You can bet it's closed today." They slammed out of the car and Annie hurried to match Max's long stride. "Do you suppose they've arrested Diane?"

"I don't know what's going on." Max walked faster. "It looks like the television stations from Savannah and Charleston are here."

By the time they reached the police station, a pha-lanx of cameramen waited on either side of the shallow front steps. The door opened. Cameras swung that way. Lights flashed. Reporters pressed forward.

Annie gripped Max's arm. "Look. It's the circuit so-licitor. Something big's happened." Wherever there were news cameras, Circuit Solicitor Brice Willard Posey was sure to be found.

Posey paused at the top of the steps, his florid face exuding overweening pride. "Ladies and gentlemen of the press . . ." Was there a flicker of unhappiness that a mass of listeners wasn't arrayed before him? Bearing up to the disappointment, Posey clapped his hand on the shoulder of Chief Garrett, whose face was drawn with fatigue. "I am proud to announce that the great

tate of South Carolina has arrested smugglers at-
empting to transship more than a hundred kilos of cocaine from this fair island to the mainland. Thanks to
the excellent work of our local police"—Posey moved
his shoulder in front of Garrett, blocking him from the
view of the cameras—"and the magnificent assistance
of our federal Drug Enforcement Agency, I am an-
nouncing the arrest of"—he glanced at an index card in
his hand—"Terry and Eva Crawford. DEA agents in-
filtrated the island last night and, working with local
authorities, staged a surprise raid at the home of Mr.
and Mrs. Crawford, arresting not only the Crawfords
but more than a half dozen of their associates who had
arrived on the island to pick up portions of the shipment. This shipment is estimated to be worth a mini-
mum of three point six million dollars. My office will
make a news release available"—Posey, resplendent in
a navy suit just a little too tight in the chest, a blue Oxford cloth shirt and a rep tie, lifted his well-tailored
arm to check his watch—"at two o'clock this afternoon."

Max leaned close to Annie, whispered, "Requiring
the reporters to hotfoot it to his office on the mainland
where, of course, he will be happy to pose for further
photos."

"So that's why Pete's been so hard to get in touch
with this week. Max, do you suppose that Laurel . . ."
Annie shook her head. "No. How could she possibly
have known anything about the Crawfords?"

"I don't know." Max's tone was bemused. "But,
Annie, I checked the map when I was trying to figure
out why Laurel was near the inlet where Kay Nevis

lived." His dark blue eyes were wide. "The Crawford house is on the next point."

"I'll be damned." Annie brushed back a tangle of hair. She tugged at Max's arm. "We'd better get out of the way."

The reporters, shouting questions, swarmed after Posey as he strode toward a waiting car. In a moment he was gone, and the reporters headed back into the police station, following Chief Garrett.

"Come on, Max." Annie jerked her head toward the pier a half block away. "There's no point in getting involved in that mess. I'll use my cell phone."

Annie tried three times, then, her face determined, she punched in 911. "Mavis? This is Annie Darling. Listen, I have to talk to the chief." Annie frowned. "Left? My God, how could he have left?"

Max was pointing up the street at the police car rolling out of the parking lot.

"Look, I know you've got a lot going on. We saw the news conference. You'd think Posey captured them all single-handedly"—Annie nodded in agreement—"that's for sure. Nobody's had any sleep? Everybody's calling in congratulations?" Annie smiled. "And the mayor said he'll put out a proclamation for Chief Garrett Day. Oh hey, that's great, Mavis." Annie hesitated. "Was it a big undercover operation?" Annie looked at Max. "Oh, information received. A video of the stuff being landed! That's amazing."

Max bent closer and Annie tilted the phone so he could hear.

Mavis's voice was high and breathless. "The most exciting day I've ever had! The video was here Friday

morning. And that was after everybody'd been up all
night watching Frank's house for Jud Hamilton. You
know what happened there! Frank shot the gun out of
Jud's hand before anybody could get to them. Frank
just did a marvelous job. Everybody's so proud of him.
But that had all happened and then Friday morning
there was this video and Pete got busy and called the
DEA and the circuit solicitor and the sheriff's office
and everybody coordinated and last night the Crawfords were having a party and there were a bunch of
people who'd come over from the mainland and they
caught them putting the kilos of cocaine in their cars
and it's the biggest drug bust ever and—"

Annie broke in. "Where's Pete gone now?"

Mavis was abruptly quiet.

"I have to talk to him, Mavis. We've learned something important about Meredith Muir."

"Well"—her voice dropped—"there was something
else on the tape. I guess you know the Crawford house
isn't far from where Kay Nevis lived. Pete's got a lead.
He's gone out to the high school. You can catch him
there."

A cheer erupted as the center fielder made an over-the-
shoulder catch on the warning track. The wooden
stands near the baseball diamond reverberated as a
group of boys stomped and shouted. About fifteen cars
were clustered in the high school parking lot at the
point nearest the ball field. A police cruiser sat at the
other end of the lot, a short walk from the pier that jutted into the water. Annie parked next to the cruiser.

As they started up the dusty path, Annie shaded her

eyes. "The door to the boathouse is open. What do you suppose they're doing in there?" She shot Max a startled look. "Mavis said something about the Crawford place not being far from the Nevis house. Laurel must have got a shot of that motorboat Wednesday night. Oh, Max, maybe everything's going to be okay for Diane, after all. You know, they can enhance tapes. Maybe they even know who was in the boat." They reached the pier and their shoes clattered on the wooden planks.

Billy Cameron poked his head out of the boathouse. He called over his shoulder, "Chief, the Darlings are here."

In a moment, a slump-shouldered Pete Garrett stepped out into the sunlight. He blinked bloodshot eyes. In one hand, he held an oversized flashlight. He clicked it off.

Annie stopped in front of him. She craned to look past him and saw a motorboat in the shadowy interior.

Garrett jerked his head at Billy. "Lock the boathouse and put up no-entry tape." He yawned hugely. "Folks, if you'll excuse me, I'm going home for a while."

"Pete, we've been looking everywhere for you. We know who killed Kay Nevis and Meredith Muir." Annie ignored Max's waving hands.

The police chief blinked. He managed a dour smile. "You got a confession from somebody? Annie, I haven't had any sleep since Wednesday. Whatever you've got will keep."

Annie clapped her hands on her hips. "Did you know Meredith Muir was having an affair with a teacher? Well, anyway . . ." She couldn't ignore Max's strangled "Annie!" She avoided meeting his glare. "Chief, we're almost sure about that. Kay Nevis was worried about a student and she was upset with one of the teachers at her lunch table. We've found out why. Ben Bradford, he used to date—"

Garrett yawned again, began to walk toward the shore. "I know. He was the girl's old boyfriend."

Annie was impressed. Garrett was apparently on top of the murder investigations. Somehow, between the stakeout for Jud Hamilton and the drug bust, Garrett had kept apprised of the details in the murder investigations. She relaxed a little, but she wished Garrett would stop and listen. She kept pace with him. "That's right. But get this! Meredith dropped Ben"—Annie paused—"for an older man."

They reached the end of the pier. Garrett rubbed his face. "So that's the boy's story, huh? Maybe. Maybe not. Look, Annie, we have a lot more investigating to do, but so far there's no trace of the Muir girl being involved with anybody. That's the first thing we look for in a murder investigation"—his tone was faintly patronizing—"the sex angle. Sure, Ben Bradford wants there to be another guy. Otherwise, he's hanging out there by himself because she got tired of him. Maybe he was one big bore. Anyway, it's pretty obvious what happened. The girl knew something about the teacher's murder. Either she looked across the inlet Wednesday night—"

"Chief"—they were at the black-and-white cruiser now—"that's what I'm trying to tell you. Look at it another way. What if Kay Nevis looked across the inlet one night recently and saw someone she knew at the Muir cabana? What if she saw a man and he was coming or going late at night? What if she recognized him?"

Garrett rubbed his blotchy face. "So is Nevis going to keep quiet about it if one of the teacher's scr— fooling around with a student? Get real, Annie." He pulled open the passenger door, slumped wearily on the seat.

Annie clenched her hands. "That's the point! Kay Nevis warned him. Maybe she insisted he resign, quit teaching. Maybe she said she'd tell Dr. Allensworth and that would mean he'd never ever get another job in a school. Don't you see?"

Garrett slammed the door.

Annie opened it, leaned into the car. "What was he going to do? Quit his job? And what was he going to tell his wife? Both of the men—the ones who sat at her lunch table, Jack Quinn and George Wilson—are married. So Quinn or Wilson, one of them, decided Kay had to die. The murderer was clever as hell. He saw one of my WHODUNIT flyers and realized he could come up with accusations that had some basis in fact and would be sure to upset the people mentioned. And look what happened—the whole island started talking about old crimes. But it was just a smoke screen, like Emma said."

If he hadn't been tired to the bone, Garrett might not have responded. He pushed his fists against his eyes, then glared at her. "That red Jeep's no smoke screen, Annie. And Diane Littlefield was at the Muir house Wednesday night, and she and Meredith quarreled at the assembly."

Annie flung her arm toward the boathouse. "You came here to check out that boat, didn't you? Diane Littlefield has a motorboat. Why would she use that one? And surely you got some kind of picture of who was driving it? Was it a man or a woman?"

Garrett looked toward the boathouse, frowned. "We got enough of the registration number to trace the boat here. But who knows? Nothing's ever a complete fit in any case. Diane goes to school here. Maybe she didn't want to use her own boat. Maybe this boat had nothing to do with anything. There's no way to tell who was driving it. Dark clothes, hunched over the wheel. Could have been anybody. But we know where we found those damn flyers. They were in the Nevis house. Henny Brawley's on my case, says her friend wouldn't do anything like that. Well, Nevis taught here, she knew the background on Jud Hamilton, and she lived across from the Muir girl. Maybe she saw that Jeep the morning Bob Tower was killed and didn't put it all together until later. I'll tell you something else, Annie: You can come up with all the fancy theories you want, but we got to have proof. Can you prove one of those men ever saw Muir outside of class? Can you prove one of them was ever in that cabana? Oh, I'll check 'em out, but there's not a shred of evidence that either one of them was involved with Meredith Muir."

∴ *Eighteen* ∾

MAX GLANCED toward the clock. Almost three. Confidential Commissions was, of course, closed on a Saturday afternoon, but he'd been able to round up quite a bit of information about Jack Quinn and George Wilson. Would it do any good? Annie was convinced that she was on the right track, but Max had a hollow feeling that Garrett's insistence was correct. Theories were fine, but proof was essential.

Max picked up a sheaf of papers. There were, for sure, some suggestive points.

JOHN EDWARD (JACK) QUINN

The most successful track coach in the history of Broward's Rock High School. Under his leadership, the boys' track and field team has captured either first or second in at least four events over the past ten years at the state championships. His girls' team has done even better, taking five firsts four years in a row. One of his graduates, Samantha Jenkins, is considered a top prospect for the next Olympics.

Quinn is a native of Bluffton and a graduate of the University of South Carolina. He was a varsity runner, excelling in the mile. He is married to a Bluffton native, Louise Compton, who practices law in the Broward's Rock firm of Hoolaby, Harris and Grant. They have two children, John Jr., 6, and Janice, 4. Land transactions four years ago recorded the purchase of a house on the perimeter of the golf course for $440,000, deed in the name of Louise Compton Quinn. In April of this year, Louise Compton Quinn filed for divorce. The petition was later dropped. A feature story in *The Island Gazette* sports section two years ago included this comment:

> Quinn and his wife, marine law expert Louise Compton, typify today's modern marriages, with both spouses involved in demanding careers and sharing equally the pleasures and burdens of home and family. You are as likely to find Quinn in the kitchen as his wife. In fact, he is the main provider of meals for the children, as Ms. Compton is often off island on business. . . .

Quinn received the Outstanding Teacher of the Year Award last year. A story in the school newspaper quoted a senior girl, who declined to be identified: "Mr. Quinn is a hotty! All the girls think he's simply the coolest."

"In your dreams," Max muttered. He flipped to the next sheet, which contained a confidential assessment by Mrs. Riley, provided only after many promises of utter discretion on Max's part.

". . . girls simply hang around him. But that's natural. I mean, you know, sex is very natural, and handsome teachers are always fascinating to the girls. Jack reminds me so much of Alan Alda when he was on *M*A*S*H*, not now when he's old and he emcees those TV programs. Jack is so appealing, that black hair and bony face. But Jack's kind of different. There's something a little dark about him. I don't know what it is, a kind of dissatisfied look sometimes, and he usually comes to faculty parties by himself. I mean, she's gone so much. To tell the truth, she seems a little disdainful of us. Of course, teachers don't make the kind of money lawyers do, but if that mattered to her, why didn't she marry another lawyer? And Jack loves what he does. He's so good with the kids."

But maybe not so good at maintaining his marriage. Max put those sheets aside. And then there was . . .

GEORGE HENRY WILSON

Senior counselor at Broward's Rock High School. A native of Kansas, B.A. in psychology, University of Kansas; M.A., University of Oklahoma; Ph.D., University of California at Los Angeles. Counselor in private practice in Los Angeles for three years, joined faculty on Broward's Rock ten years ago. Specializes in gifted and talented students. Also a winner of Outstanding Teacher of the Year Award.

Married to the former Elena Richardson, a pharmaceutical rep. No children. Wife travels . . .

Max picked up a highlighter, turned the words bright orange.

. . . on the West Coast, owns a condo in La Jolla. The Wilsons maintain a long-distance marriage. He travels twice a month on weekends to California; she flies to Atlanta twice a month on weekends.

Wilson enjoys backpacking, scuba diving, and kayaking. He is an amateur historian and collects Early Greek coins. He presents numismatic shows describing a day in the life of the ancient Greeks, using the coins to illustrate likely financial activities.

Max returned to Mrs. Riley's comments:

Mrs. Riley, shaking her head but laughing: "That George! He's more fun than a comedy club. But always quite clean, you know. Not disgusting like so many of them. I always think of the *Our Gang* movies and that little guy with the tight curly hair and freckles. That must be what George looked like as a little boy. He keeps everybody laughing. Maybe that's why he's such a good counselor. Not that he can't be serious. I remember when the Murray boy died. Leukemia, you know. Such a heartbreak for all of us. The nicest boy. The kids took it so hard. George really helped them. Attractive to the girls? . . . There was one girl but she had so many problems. She came after George and he finally had to insist she talk with Mrs. Heaston. Of course, that didn't satisfy her. The girl just didn't come to the counselors' office then. She dropped out of school not long after that."

Max stacked the sheets, slipped them into a folder. His face was thoughtful as he clicked off the desk light. On his way out of the office, he stopped to look once again at the photographs spread on the worktable. They were printed through his computer, primarily from newspaper archives.

Five photos in the top row:

Jack Quinn, angular face solemn, looking down at his radiant bride.

Jack Quinn lifting high a huge silver trophy, eyes gleaming, lips spread in a triumphant grin.

Jack Quinn, unsmiling, dark brows drawn in a tight frown, gesturing emphatically as he leaned toward a bench filled with boys in running tops and shorts.

Jack Quinn laughing as the platform on which he stood plunked into a tank as a student hit the bull's-eye at the school carnival.

Jack Quinn grinning as he handed the Sportsman of the Year Award to a graduating senior boy.

Five photos in the bottom row:

George Wilson, red hair gleaming, nose peeling on his sunburned face, balanced on the side of a boat, ready to dive.

George Wilson, his round face ebullient, heaving his mortarboard into the air as he received his doctorate.

George Wilson beaming as he shakes hands with the president of the senior class.

George Wilson, muscular and stocky, pounding

toward the finish line of the annual Broward's Rock Marathon.

George Wilson shouting as he pounded a big drum at a fall football game.

Max hesitated, then swept the pictures into a pile, added them to his folder. He'd show them to Annie. Would she see the face of a murderer?

Annie edged along the pittosporum hedge. The sweet bananalike fragrance attracted bumblebees. Annie ducked, hoped she wouldn't be stung. Damn, she didn't like the huge, awkward, dramatically striped bees, but if she kept close to the hedge she was out of sight of the Muir house.

Her heart thudded. So okay, she wasn't cut out to be a cat burglar. It sounded so damn glamorous. Maybe if she could handle stress better, like they do in the movies. Cary Grant and Pierce Brosnan were always cool.

A bumblebee zoomed within inches of her face. Annie bolted away from the hedge, thudded up the steps onto the veranda and lunged toward the door. She stopped, looked toward the Muir house. There were some cars, but the blinds were drawn at the windows. Quickly, she checked the Nevis house. Still lots of cars but no one was on the porch that overlooked both the inlet and the entrance to the cabana where Annie stood, trying to look a part of the weathered gray wood.

Okay, okay. She reached for the doorknob, froze. Fingerprints. Annie took a deep breath, pulled out her blouse, used it to clutch the knob. The door opened.

Was it usually kept locked, or had Meredith walked out of the cabana Thursday night, leaving it open?

Annie slipped inside the shadowy room. She glanced toward the windows. The shutters were closed. She turned on the light, using her elbow to nudge up the switch. The cabana was long and narrow. A wooden plaque inscribed GUYS hung on the bright blue door opposite her. GALS adorned a plaque on the pink door to the right. A curved sofa faced the near end of the room and a giant-screen TV. Small sofas sat on either side of a big low coffee table in the middle of the room opposite a wet bar. A half-dozen small vials of fingernail polish were scattered atop the coffee table. Annie came closer, noted various shades of pink. There was a mound of used cotton balls. A bottle of polish remover was open. Annie wrinkled her nose at the cloying scent. A copy of *Cosmopolitan* lay atop a stack of magazines. At the end of the room, next to a closed door, was a CD player on a stand. Brightly colored CDs were carelessly flung next to the player. Annie didn't even recognize the names of most of the groups.

She looked at the closed door. The GUYS and GALS doors at the other end of the room likely indicated bathrooms with space to change and shower. This door wouldn't open to a kitchen. All of those appliances—a microwave, small refrigerator, sink—were in the wet bar.

Annie hurried to the door, gripped the knob through the fabric of her blouse, pushed. She looked at an unmade bed, the spread flung carelessly to the floor, the pillows rumpled. Annie studied the bedroom. If she was right about Meredith and a man, this would be where they had met. Not in her house, not even when her parents were absent. The cabana was Meredith's preserve. How recently had that bed been slept in? Last week, perhaps? Was that when Kay Nevis looked across the inlet and recognized a visitor who should never have been there? But how could Annie—or the police—ever link that shadowy figure to this room, to Meredith?

There might be a way.

Max shoved his hand through thick blond curls. "Annie, that smacks of entrapment." He glanced down at his array of photos spread atop the Death on Demand coffee bar: the confident track coach, the laugh-a-minute counselor. Two men . . . Which one?

"We . . ." Her hand hesitated above the sugar bowl. Was a splash of brown sugar sheer indulgence atop the whipped cream on the caffe latte? The lid clinked as she removed it, scooped a huge golden heap of sugar and deposited it on the mound of cream. ". . . are not the police. Look at it, Max, if my plan works we can at the very least get a picture of the murderer. At the best, Pete captures the killer."

She poked her tongue into the whipped cream with the dissolving crystals of sugar. "Hmm."

"You have a whipped-cream mustache." Max raised an eyebrow. "I don't think that's what the national milk council had in mind."

"The more fools they." Annie picked out two of the pictures, Quinn on the platform above the tank of water, Wilson diving from the side of the boat. "Good-looking men." Her tone was admiring.

Max leaned against the coffee bar, his expression skeptical. "Do you think so?"

Annie grinned. "Not, of course, to me personally." The smile slipped away. "But to a teenage girl? She'd be impressed, Max." Annie shuffled the pictures into a pile, turned them facedown, her mouth in a tight line. "Damn him. Whichever one it is. Listen, we have to give it a try. It can't do any harm. We know Pete pays attention to tips about crimes. For all he knows, this tip will come from the person who took the videos of the cocaine arriving at the Crawford house. He won't dare ignore a message." She reached for the phone.

"That's a hell of a good point." Max's brows drew into a straight line. "But what if the guy comes after you—"

She reached out, placed a finger on his lips. "That would be killing the messenger, wouldn't it?" She glanced at the two numbers written on a pad and punched in the first. "Hello. Mr. Quinn? Annie Darling here." Her gray eyes glinted with determination. "Yes, I just wanted to let you know that we've learned a great deal since I last spoke with you and I knew you'd want to know . . . Your information about Meredith scratching Mrs. Nevis's car was very helpful. Anyway, my sister heard all about this from one of the senior girls who told the police that Meredith was having an affair with an older man and the police have arranged for the state crime lab to send over some technicians Monday to take some DNA samples from the Muir cabana. . . . As you well know, there have been extraordinary strides in the use of DNA in criminal investigations. Anyway, the details don't matter, but I was sure you'd be pleased to know the police are making great progress. . . . No, the girls didn't seem to know who the man might be. I don't suppose you've heard anything about this?" Annie poked at the pile of photos. "Yes, of course, I'll call you if we learn anything else. Thanks." She hung up.

Annie gulped down some coffee. "Funny thing is, he kind of wondered who the man might be."

Max shook his head. "A natural question, Annie."

She flicked on the phone. "Now for Mr. Wilson. Hey, I wonder if he's—" She broke off, gave a quick sigh of relief. "Hello, Mr. Wilson, I'm glad I caught you. This is Annie Darling. I understand you're often out of town. . . . Oh, of course, I know you feel you should be available in case any students need you this weekend." Annie made yakety-yak motions with her fingers, moved restively, finally broke in. "Right. I understand. Truly awful. I know you are sorry you didn't have a chance to talk to Meredith that last day. . . . Anyway, I thought it might make you feel better if you knew the police are getting close to a solution. Yes, they are. Apparently, Meredith was involved with some man and they're going to test the Muir cabana for DNA and they think they'll get a good lead. . . . Right. So it should all be over pretty soon. Right. I'll keep in touch." She clicked off the phone. She took a deep breath. "Okay, Max, the ball's in your court."

In late March, the beach attracts more walkers and volleyball players than swimmers, but on a cloudless Saturday afternoon there were plenty of sunbathers, surfers, joggers and hot-dog hounds. Boom boxes boomed, a golden retriever bounded into the surf, girls in bikinis the size of postage stamps smiled winsomely as boys helped them apply coconut oil on hard-to-reach spots. Max nodded approvingly. Those boys must be Eagle Scouts, always prepared, ready to assist any damsel in distress. "Oh, yeah," he huzzahed softly. Sea oats rippled in the breeze. A lifeguard used a megaphone to warn beachgoers about an influx of sea wasps, the rectangular jellyfish with dangling tentacles.

Wearing a Braves ball cap, aviator sunglasses, boxer swim trunks and huaraches, Max strolled casually on the boardwalk. A huge beach towel was slung casually over one shoulder. He stopped at an outdoor phone. He used a corner of the towel to pick up the receiver. He dropped in the coins, punched the number written on the palm of his hand. The phone rang twice. A tinny recorded voice announced:

"You have reached the Broward's Rock Police Department Crime Stoppers. If you have information about a crime or criminal activity, your identity will be protected. If you wish to arrange for an officer to meet you or if you wish to leave information, please do so after the long beep."

Max bent close to the receiver, whispered:

"You got the video." Sometimes, he had to admit, Annie was inspired. "Listen up. Meredith Muir's murderer will be at the Muir cabana tonight. If you stake it out, you'll catch him."

Annie stopped breathing while she sprayed bug repellent. She paused and looked inquiringly at Max. "Do you suppose police on stakeouts wear Off?"

Max held out his hand for the can. "Around here I bet they do." He jiggled the can, lifted his cap to squirt the back of his neck and his hair. He dropped the can into a canvas carryall. He shaded his eyes against the early-evening sky. The setting sun stained the horizon a rich rosy red. The motorboat rocked in a gentle swell. The rowboat to the stern dipped and swayed.

Max craned to see around a saw palmetto. They were anchored on the lee side of a six-foot-long hummock. The small clump of heavily vegetated land was near enough the inlet for them to watch the Muir cabana, but their motorboat and attached rowboat were hidden from view on the shore. They had arrived and taken their position behind the hummock well before dusk. "After all," Annie pointed out reasonably, "we have to get there before the police do." They'd finished their picnic supper, a carryout from Parotti's—an oyster sandwich and fries for Annie and grilled chicken sandwich with chutney for Max, and sipped iced tea.

"So far, so good," Max muttered. "I thought I saw the crape myrtle move a minute ago. Actually"—his face was worried—"if they're coming, they should be here."

Annie patted the waterproof camera on the seat beside her. "If the police don't come, we'll get a picture of him. And if the police are any good, we shouldn't see them." She leaned back contentedly against the red leather seat, admiring the last iridescent spill of light across the darkening water.

The motorboat rocked in a swell. Crows cawed. Something rustled on the hummock, perhaps a raccoon. The night was very dark, only a sliver of moon and the faraway stars glittering cold and distant. Max leaned over the stern, pulled the line hand over hand, drawing the rowboat close. "Come on. It's dark enough now that no one will see us. I'll hold it steady."

Annie stepped carefully over the stern and into the rowboat, balancing until she settled in the front. Max climbed aboard, handed her the oversize waterproof flashlight. She rested the rubber-sheathed light and the camera in her lap.

In only a moment, he was sculling the boat easily through the water, the dip of the oars a whisper of sound lost in the rustle of the spartina grass and the gurgle as the tide flooded ashore. When the boat drew up on the far side of the Muir pier, Max tied the rope to a piling, bent close to Annie to whisper, "Let's go up on the pier. We can get behind the boathouse. No one will see us."

Max eased up the ladder first, crouched on the pier, ran lightly to the shadow of the boathouse. Annie followed, dropped down beside him. They took turns watching the cabana. The low-slung structure lay dark and silent. Across the inlet, the Nevis house blazed with lights. Once Annie pointed toward the Muir house. "There's nobody there."

His breath was warm against her ear. "Shh. They're probably staying with friends."

Annie nodded. She understood. The Muirs might never wish to come back to the house that overlooked the place where their daughter died.

At eleven, Annie tugged on Max's arm. His turn to watch. She yawned and snuggled against him, wishing she'd worn a heavier jacket. The night was dank and chilly. If nobody came, tomorrow might see Diane's arrest. That shouldn't happen. Annie wished— She came awake with a jerk, Max's hand tight on her arm, his lips against her cheek. "Somebody's coming. Look!"

Annie bent forward. Was that a shadow near the front steps of the cabana? A dark form reached the porch, slipped to the door.

Suddenly lights blazed. Huge swaths of light pinned a dark figure in a circle of brightness. A gloved hand rose to hide a white face. A black knitted cap was pulled low on the forehead. Black sweater, black slacks. One hand held a metal tin of gasoline.

Harsh shouts came from every direction. "Hands up. Police. Hands up!"

The figure dropped the heavy tin and darted to the side of the porch. He jumped to the uneven ground, stumbled and ran toward the water, pausing once to reach into a pocket and pull free a gun. The gloved hand rose and a flash of light came from the barrel of the gun.

A gun answered in return and the running figure tilted to one side, slowly slumped to the ground.

Annie held tight to Max's arm. "Oh, Max, oh, Max!"

Max pulled her close. "He shot first."

Heavy running feet thudded across the ground. More shouts. "Watch him, watch him!"

But the figure lay unmoving, the gun beside him on the dusty ground. A light illuminated the slack muscles of the blanched face. A hand reached down and pulled away the knitted cap to reveal bright red hair.

"George Wilson." Annie nodded with sad finality. "Meredith tried to talk to him Thursday afternoon. I saw her in the corridor by the counselors' offices. Oh, Max, she was scared. Meredith didn't talk to him that afternoon, but she must have called him, and when he came that night she accused him of killing Mrs. Nevis—so he killed her."

∾ *Nineteen* ∾

ANNIE WORMED her way through the crowd. Death on Demand was packed. This was starting April with a bang, all right. The gathering might be the store's most successful book signing ever. She'd better get a bunch more books out. Annie was almost to the storeroom when a hand touched her lightly on the shoulder.

"Hi, Annie." Frank Saulter bent close so she could hear over the cocktail-party roar. "Can I help you carry some stuff?"

"Frank, that would be great." Annie smiled up at his dear familiar face, his brown eyes somber above a subdued smile. "You're wonderful to come. I know Emma's not one of your favorite—" Remembering tact at the last instant, Annie regrouped. "Hey, I've got the new Bob Crais saved for you. On the house."

His eyes lighted. "That's great. But"—a shrug—"I couldn't miss a signing at my favorite mystery bookstore."

They reached the storeroom door and stepped inside. Annie closed it and the hubbub of Emma Clyde's signing receded to a roar on a level with a college football game in the next block, distant but still awesome.

Annie found two more boxes of books, handed one to Frank.

She was reaching for the knob when he said. "Annie, thanks."

She stopped. Frank wasn't thanking her for the new book. She looked at his lined face.

He crooked one arm to hold the box, lifted his hand to rub at his cheek. "That day you came to see me. You had those flyers." His eyes brightened. "You did good work there, Annie, catching that guy. But the deal is, if you hadn't taken the time to come and tell me you didn't have anything to do with that stuff about Jud—" He broke off, pressed his lips together. "You're a lot like Colleen, Annie. You're a sweet girl. And that got me to thinking about what was going to happen."

Annie blinked back tears. "You would have done the right thing, Frank, whether or not I'd come."

His head shake was slow but definite.

They stared at each other wordlessly for a moment. Annie stood on tiptoe, leaned forward, kissed his weathered cheek. "You're a good man, Frank."

He ducked his head, pulled open the door, stepped aside for her. Annie struggled against the crowd. Her arms ached from lugging books. It was a bookseller's dream, but honestly, how could Emma's books sell this well? Weren't people ever going to tire of Marigold Rembrandt, who was always odiously right? Apparently not.

Emma lifted a flute of champagne. "*Salud*, Annie!" Emma's broad face was flushed. Today her hair was an improbable metallic blue in swooping waves reminiscent of the 1930s. Her vertically striped caftan, alternating bands of silver and emerald-green, rippled as she rose to her feet. *"Salud!"*

The jammed bookstore, after a moment's pause, erupted with applause, though the customers looked puzzled.

Emma hoisted herself atop the wooden chair, peered gaily around the coffee area of Death on Demand.

Annie drew her breath in sharply. Oh damn. How much champagne had the woman downed?

Emma leaned forward, wavering precariously, and snatched up a bottle, refilled her glass. "We are gathered here—" She gave a snort of laughter. "Another time. But I wish to honor our hostess. Not only has she provided us with the grandest book event in the history of our island—"

Annie shot a desperate glance at Max behind the coffee bar, handing out cookies with "Whodunit" written in icing. He lifted his shoulders, let them fall. His message was clear: *Que sera sera.* Annie edged nearer Emma's table.

Emma gestured dramatically with the glass, champagne sloshing perilously near the rim. "Oh, I say. Desperate moments require desperate measures"— Emma eyed the flute—"and I'm just the lady to meet the challenge." She upended the glass, downed the wine. "I always meet challenges. I have to compliment Annie because she created a superb contest to attract readers to the store for the signing of my latest book, *Whodunit.* And"—Emma pulled a sheet from her pocket—"I wish to announce the answers."

Annie stood on tiptoe. "Emma," she shouted, "the

contest is for everybody attending your signing. The winner gets—"

Emma's gravelly voice rose, drowning out Annie:

"Book 1—A country doctor knows there is more behind the murder of his old friend than anyone realizes. Answer: *The Murder of Roger Ackroyd,* by Agatha Christie.

"Book 2—A messenger dies in a mysterious plane crash, leaving behind a list of ten names. Answer: *The List of Adrian Messenger,* by Philip MacDonald.

"Book 3—Two strangers travel on a train and talk about murder. Answer: *Strangers on a Train,* by Patricia Highsmith.

"Book 4—A smart-mouth reporter investigates the drug scene on a California beach and meets a man who wants to die. Answer: *Fletch,* by Gregory Mcdonald.

"Book 5—A half-English, half-Egyptian con man, who never quite succeeds at anything, drives a car to Istanbul and finds himself in the middle of a daring robbery. Answer: *The Light of Day,* by Eric Ambler.

"Book 6—A very conventional English lawyer defends an attractive dark-haired woman and her eccentric mother against a charge of kidnapping. Answer: *The Franchise Affair,* by Josephine Tey.

"Book 7—A middle-aged spinster takes a house in the country for the summer, a man is shot to death in the clubroom, and her niece and nephew seem to know more than they admit. Answer: *The Circular Staircase,* by Mary Roberts Rinehart.

"Book 8—Three children try to solve a neighborhood murder while their mystery writer mom races to meet a deadline. Answer: *Home Sweet Homicide,* by Craig Rice.

"Book 9—Can the new mistress of Manderly ever escape the shadow of her husband's first wife? Answer: *Rebecca,* by Daphne du Maurier."

Max moved out from behind the coffee bar, reached up to grip Emma's elbow. "That's very good, Emma. And now some of the customers have some more books for you to sign." He helped her step down.

Annie plunked down the box of books next to Emma's chair. She didn't slam them down. Of course not.

The author settled into the chair, waggled her pen. "Annie, I got them right. Didn't I?"

Annie bent forward, tried to smile. "But Emma, the winner gets an autographed book from you."

Emma blinked. "Oh, well, we can always make an adjustment. And besides, I know the books in the watercolors, too—"

A light voice sang out, "I'm just back from Atlanta. I had such a wonderful time, exploring all different sorts of photography, always a fascinating study. It is simply fascinating to know about some of the technical advances in the field and their ramifications for the good of society." Dark blue eyes gleaming with good humor, Laurel burbled, "It's so sweet of you, Annie, to make it easier for your devoted readers to identify these wonderful Southern mysteries by giving us the letters in the alphabet of the authors' initials and naming the state bird where the books are set."

Laurel pointed at each painting in turn:

"*To Live and Die in Dixie,* by Kathy Hogan Trocheck. *K* is the eleventh letter in the alphabet, *H* the eighth and *T* the twentieth. The book is set in Atlanta and the brown thrasher is the state bird of Georgia.

"*Killer Market,* by Margaret Maron. Her initials are the thirteenth letter and the cardinal is the state bird of North Carolina.

"*Mama Stalks the Past,* by Nora DeLoach. Her initials are the fourteenth and fourth letters and the Carolina wren is the South Carolina state bird.

"*Murder Shoots the Bull,* by Anne George. Her initials are the first and seventh letters and the yellowhammer is the state bird of Alabama.

"*Angel at Troublesome Creek,* by Mignon F. Ballard. Her initials are the thirteenth, sixth and second letters and the cardinal is the state bird of North Carolina."

Laurel wafted near the table. "Dear Emma, of course I will take *Whodunit* as my prize."

"*Whodunit.*" Emma grinned. She picked up a pen, signed her name in bold strokes. "It's a ripping good title, if I say so myself."

Laurel beamed. "It will probably sell enough copies to afford you a new Rolls-Royce. But until then, have you given Annie the keys yet? After all, it was Annie who figured out whodunit."

Annie felt as exposed as John Mortimer's dodgy barrister Rumpole confronting She Who Must Be Obeyed.

"And of course," Laurel trilled, "everyone on the island knows you are a truly generous spirit, Emma, and will be delighted to provide Annie with free use of your Rolls-Royce for a week in honor of Annie's success in unmasking a particularly devious miscreant."

If Emma's yacht was her pride, her pink Rolls was her joy. Emma's eyes glittered for an instant, then, with a shrug, she poked her hand in her pocket, pulled out a key chain hanging from a miniature silver dagger. She thrust the keys at Annie.

Annie's fingers closed around the little dagger. A Rolls-Royce. And there was that track in Florida where anybody could race. . . . "Emma, I scarcely know what to say, but—"

Before she could finish, Emma's lips curved in a lopsided Cheshire-cat grin of delight and she yanked the keys away. "April fool, Annie!"

Enjoy this exciting look at the next
Death on Demand Mystery from
Carolyn Hart

ENGAGED TO DIE

Available Now Wherever Books Are Sold

Annie juggled the folder under her arm as she unlocked the front door of Death on Demand. She reached out, flicked on the lights, welcomed the cheery bright colors of book jackets, heard Agatha's irritated yowl.

"Okay, okay. Coming." She moved down the center aisle, heading for the coffee bar. Where was Chloe? She should have opened the store an hour ago. She certainly couldn't have picked a worse morning to be late. Annie plopped the green folder on the coffee bar. Agatha jumped up, spat out a series of querulous meows.

"Sweetheart, I'm sorry." Damn Chloe. Annie shook her head. To be fair, she hadn't called the store to report she was running late. Annie filled Agatha's bowl, and the imperious black cat, still meowing, leaped to the floor, hunched over the food, and began to eat in a fury of impatience.

"Chloe?" Annie didn't try to keep the irritation from her voice. There was no answer. Annie grabbed the phone, hesitated, loosened her hold. Max would be glad to take over, but he was busy. For her. She touched the folder. It was amazing how much information about Snug Harbor, its owners, employees, and residents he'd retrieved on the Internet from government records and articles that had appeared in *The Island Gazette*. If Chloe didn't show up, Annie would simply hang out the Closed sign. She had no intention of being late for her appointment at Snug Harbor.

The phone rang.

Annie snatched up the receiver. Chloe better have a good excuse. "Death on—"

"He was known to have written a novel over the weekend." Henny sounded as satisfied as if she were sipping a Singapore sling created especially for her by Madeline Bean, Jerrilyn Farmer's sleuth in *Dim Sum Dead,* a catering mystery featuring a Chinese New Year banquet.

Annie's reply was equally smooth. "Oh, sure. Edgar Wallace."

"Oh. Yes. Right—" Call waiting clicked.

"Talk to you later." Annie ended Henny's call, took the incoming call. "Death on Demand, the best—"

"Annie." Chloe's husky voice dragged. "I'm sorry. I'll be there as soon as I can. I overslept."

Annie frowned. "Can you hurry? I've got an important appointment at eleven." Annie glanced at her watch. A quarter after ten.

"Yes." Chloe's voice sounded as if she were at the far end of a cellar. "I'll be right there." The connection ended.

Annie glared at the phone. Up to now, Chloe had been utterly dependable. Of course, anyone could oversleep. . . .

As Annie brewed her favorite smooth Kona, she opened Max's folder and began to read the information Max had gathered:

Snug Harbor

Opened three years ago, the Broward's Rock retirement home is a franchise granted by Warman Corporation of Atlanta, Miami, and Chicago, a holding company for retirement, assisted living, and nursing homes, which operates in eleven states. The local franchise is held by Crispus Markham of Charleston. Markham visited the island when the community opened. The local manager is Stephanie Hammond. Snug Harbor has twenty-four employees, including a cook, kitchen help, custodians, and aides.

Annie highlighted the name of the manager. She scanned the text impatiently. Ahh. Here's what she wanted:

Joseph J. Brown, 62, is a resident assistant in charge of the premises after hours.

Brown was the big moon-faced jerk. Annie was impressed. Max had certainly found out buckets about the retirement home's bad apple, proving once again that the Internet, assiduously searched, could provide more than most people would want revealed about their lives.

Brown, 62, is a native of Butte, Montana. Married three times. Each marriage ended in divorce. No children. Has lived in Washington, Texas, California, Alaska, Illinois, Michigan, and Florida. Work history includes stints as a stevedore, night watchman, photographer, radio ad salesman, nurseryman, trucker, and bartender. Has lived on Broward's Rock for two years. Was employed by Morgan's Diner until accepting the position as night manager of Snug Harbor. Free room and meals and a small salary in exchange for overnight supervision of the facility. Snug Harbor brochures emphasize that guests are assured of security because assistance is available twenty-four hours a day.

In the margin, Max had written, "Got a call out to the owner of Morgan's Diner, but he's down in Cozumel scuba diving. I'll see what else I can dig up."

Annie's gaze moved to the paragraph on Stephanie Hammond. In the margin, Max's red pencil had noted, "See photo on next page." Annie lifted the sheet. Stephanie Hammond beamed from the color photograph, blue eyes bright, lips curved in a cheerful smile. Tawny hair in stylish tangles bushed to a crest. She looked wholesome and forthright, energetic and eager. In a postscript, Max had added, "Got this from their web site. Full color. Fancy. Everybody looked happy."

Annie sipped her coffee, turned back to the manager's bio.

Stephanie Hammond, 24, a native of Charleston. Master's degree in sociology. Single. Worked for the state in nursing home inspections division until accepting the assistant to the manager position at Snug Harbor.

Was named interim manager when Leah Carew, an army reservist, was called to active duty. . . .

The dangling bells at the front door jangled.

"Annie, I'm here." Chloe came down the central aisle, moving as if every muscle ached. Her auburn hair was unevenly brushed. She wore no makeup. Freckles stood out against pale skin. Her eyes were tired and mournful. A violet turtleneck clashed with orange slacks.

Annie took a last gulp of coffee, closed the file. She was on her feet, heading for the door, car keys in hand. It wouldn't hurt to get to Snug Harbor a little before her appointment. "Chloe, I'm not sure when I'll be back. I doubt we'll have many customers today unless there's a business conference at the Buccaneer." The resort hotel offered guests a map of the island that included a thumbnail description of the businesses on the boardwalk by the marina.

She was almost to the door when Chloe called out. "Annie . . ."

Annie wanted to dash out the door, but she couldn't ignore the appeal in Chloe's voice. Annie paused, looked back.

Chloe's mournful face drooped like an iris beaten down by heavy rain. "I can't work the whole day." Chloe squeezed her hands into fists, pressed them against her cheeks. Her lips quivered.

Annie moved toward her. "What's wrong?" There was no doubt that Chloe was upset. But of all mornings . . .

"I stayed on the pier all night." She choked back a

sob. "He didn't come." Her hands dropped. Her fists opened.

Annie's first instinct was to ask what Chloe had expected. After all, if the guy wouldn't even give his name . . . The pain in Chloe's face stilled the words. Annie remembered her so clearly as a bouncy happy teenager talking about Harrison Ford and how someday she'd find a man like him. Maybe Chloe's hunger for romance had begun so long ago, was so deep that nothing Annie said would help. "I'm sorry, honey. Maybe . . ." Car trouble? Not on an island. No matter where he lived, it wouldn't take long to walk to the pier. Sick? Oh, sure. Struck down by a mysterious pox known as cold feet. The fact was that Chloe's mystery romance had ended in a whimper, not a bang. Annie looked at the grandfather clock near the fireplace. Fifteen to eleven. Okay, she could be at Snug Harbor in five minutes. But she wanted time to look around during visiting hours.

Chloe burst into frantic speech. "Annie, I didn't tell you before. He said he loved me, that he knew we would always be together, that we were perfect for each other. We made love there on the pier"—her gaze was defiant—"and it wasn't just any old one-night stand. I know it wasn't. It didn't matter that it was cold and damp. Nothing mattered but being together. I have to find him." Her breathing was quick and shallow. "I've been thinking. He has to work somewhere. It can't be here on the boardwalk or I would have seen him. I'm going to make a list of all the businesses on the island and go to each one. Annie, will you help me?"

Annie gripped her car keys. "Chloe, give it up. If he wants to find you—"

"He doesn't know my name." It was a stricken wail. "Annie, I have to find him. I've never met anyone like him. Never. If you'd ever seen him, you'd remember him. His face is kind of uneven. High cheekbones and a long jaw and sharp chin. He looks like one of those courtiers you see in fifteenth-century French paintings. I told him he should wear a ruffled shirt and brandish a sword and he laughed. But he was pleased. Annie, he was different." His voice quivered with eagerness. "I've got to find him."

A sword? Annie wasn't impressed. "Chloe, I've got to go." She dashed toward the front door, paused only long enough to call, "I'll keep on the lookout."

Chloe touched the top of her dark red head. "He always wears a cap, one of those round tweedy kind that are soft. Like golfers wear. And an argyle sweater."

The door closed and Annie broke into a run. How could Chloe be such a passionate idiot? Annie had a sudden cold thought of how she would have felt if Max had walked out of her life without a word. Funny, when she thought about it. She'd tried to run away from Max, but Max had come to the island, looking for her. That was different. He darn sure knew her name and she his. Well, she didn't have time to worry about Chloe. She had to do something about Denise's grandmother.

Get cozy with

CAROLYN HART's
award-winning
DEATH ON DEMAND mysteries

dead days of summer

978-0-06-072404-7 • $6.99 US • $9.99 Can

Annie Darling is understandably upset when her p.i. husband Max disappears and his car is found with a brutally slain woman nearby.

death of the party

978-0-06-000477-4 • $6.99 US • $9.99 Can

Annie and Max Darling are left stranded on an island with a handful of invited guests—including a murderer.

murder walks the plank

978-0-06-000475-0 • $6.99 US • $9.99 Can

Annie Darling's murder mystery cruise is going swimmingly—until one of the revelers plunges overboard and faux murder turns all too quickly into real-life death.

engaged to die

978-0-06-000470-5 • $6.99 US • $9.99 Can

When wealthy Virginia Neville officially announces her engagement to Jake O'Neill, her handsome, charming and *much* younger fiancé at a gala art gallery opening, not everyone is pleased. And before the last champagne bubble pops, murder disrupts the grand celebration.